True Believer

The Adventures of W. W. Ronin
Book Four

By Gregg Edwards Townsley
Two Bears Books Saint Helens, Oregon

Cover design by Olivia Passieux
Video book trailer(s) by Bill Fogle

Published by Two Bears Books
245 N. Vernonia Road
Saint Helens, Oregon 97051 U.S.A.
www.greggtownsley.com

International Standard Book Number:
Library of Congress Number:

Ordering Information:

Quantity sales: Special discounts are available on quantity purchases by corporations, associations, and others. For details, contact the publisher at the address above.Orders by U.S. trade bookstores and wholesalers. Please contact the publisher or visit www.twobearsbooks. com.

Printed in the United States of America

ISBN: 0615995314
ISBN 13: 9780615995311

Also by Gregg Edwards Townsley:

East Jesus, Nevada
Lady of the Lake
The Pinkerton Years

CONTENTS

To my children, Rachel and Joshua, and to Nancy's, Lindsey, Kelly and Tim, who busy themselves living successful lives. Dear ones, it's taken me too long to realize — not all that is green is money.

December 1881

ELKO, NEVADA

Chapter 1
HOW LONG, O LORD?

It didn't take more than a couple of hours before Dustsucker — an Ormsby County deputy when he wasn't out adventuring and Ronin's best friend — whined the too-often-heard question of travelers throughout history. "Are we there yet?" he asked, a little too militantly to be taken seriously by Storey County Sheriff Tom Kelly, or by W. W. Ronin, who was singularly focused on collecting his due.

A bounty hunter by trade and a former Episcopal priest by training, William Washington Ronin had been nearly killed by a Virginia City fortune teller, who, for whatever reason — the unfortunate death of her sister or the poor opinion formed when Ronin attempted to evict them from their Virginia City home — had pushed an old Paterson revolver to the side of his head, having already shot him in the chest. Their mutual interest — a short little man named Toro Latigo — had stirred decidedly different passions within them. Ronin was intent on bringing his to its most obvious conclusion: a dead midget, though the phrase didn't seem appropriate, but then neither did the small man's assault or attempted murder. The fortune teller hoped only to find a new source or friend in life that could take her to where she wanted to go, or anywhere for that matter, as where she was wasn't going to be safe or happy.

Dustsucker was looking out the window of the train when he uttered the question. The simple mention of it raised feelings Tom Kelly was hoping to keep quiet.

"I'm going to say this once, Slade. You ask how long it's going to take us, or complain about the seats or the food, and I'm going to reach across the aisle and treat you like the child you're pretending to be. Am I being clear?" he asked.

Marcus T. Slade, alias "Dustsucker," was a good 300 pounds heavier than any of Kelly's children, but the pain of Kelly's wife's death a couple of months prior to their meeting made the otherwise dangerous remark understandable. "Sorry, Tom," he said, apologizing. "Happy that you're here," he added. "We'll try to behave."

W. W. Ronin, Slade and Kelly were headed to Wells, Nevada — a tiny town of little more than 200 residents along the Central Pacific Railroad. Humboldt Wells, as it had originally been named for a dependable spring along the California Trail, had become a city when the Central Pacific Railroad moved on, leaving a boxcar for a railroad office and the Bulls Head Saloon — the town's first business, christened on Christmas Eve, 1869 — open for anyone who needed courage or refreshment. Before too many people noticed, a general store, hotel, livery, post office and school followed. When a fire struck in 1877, destroying many of the town's business structures, too few people cared, as the soldiers, shippers and railroad workers who built the town had already moved on. As bad as it sounds, things hadn't been the same since.

"*You'll* try to behave or *we'll* try to behave?" Kelly asked the deputy, not leaving things alone.

"Jesus, Tom. Let it go, would you?" Ronin asked.

Slade looked at Ronin, who had his eyes fixed on Kelly, who had spent a good many years as police chief in Virginia City before "graduating to sheriff," he liked to say, though the election wasn't much to be proud of given that his primary responsibility was to keep the county's prisoners behind bars, including those he'd befriended in the business of being police chief or sheriff.

"There's no reason to rail against Dusty, Tom," Ronin said. "No one wants to go to Wells. It just happens to be where the sorry sack of shit we're trailing is, his having family there and all."

"He *used* to have family there," Dustsucker corrected.

It took a while for the county law dogs to catch up in their investigation of the Latigo deaths. But in time, everyone figured it was the tiny deranged man who had murdered his parents a good many years ago — faithful Latter-day Saints church goers and owners of a freight business in Wells when business was good, which it wasn't anymore, not since the Central and Union Pacific Railroads completed their transcontinental railway.

The freight business was yesterday, everyone said, after trains from the east and west coasts met at Promontory Point, Utah. In time, the family economic crisis likely wore on Latigo's nerves, with their reminiscences of better times visiting folks along the Humboldt River or the system of trails that branched off north, south, west, and everywhere.

Ronin wondered how Alvira would fare, though neither Ronin nor Dustsucker personally cared after proof of the woman's collusion in attempting to harm the two of them surfaced. "You're right, Dusty. Used to," he said, looking back toward the passing landscape. "I keep thinking he's the General Tom Thumb of saloon opera stars — President Lincoln's best friend, his having a wedding in the White House and all that. But he's not. He's the murdering son of a bitch that shot that woman's sister and tried to kill the two of us. He needs to..."

"... die or end up in a circus, you said."

"I was kidding when I said that, Dusty."

"Maybe."

Ronin folded his arms across his chest and sat back in the rich, leather-appointed coach car traveling just a couple of hours out of Reno. Given that the railroad offered an eight-day trip from west coast to east coast, he hadn't asked how long it would take to get to Wells, Nevada, a fact that hadn't escaped Dustsucker's notice. Ash had deferred when Ronin offered him a fare, arguing that a Utah marshal was more appropriate to Latigo's pursuit and certainly closer. "One day is long enough," he'd said, "and two days is two too many." The time it took, whatever it was, would help his chest heal, having left the American Gospel Mission a month or so earlier than either his host or doctor wanted.

"You'll die out there," Emma had said, while shuffling papers in the mission director's office, a responsibility she had only recently become comfortable living with.

"Not likely, Emma," he'd argued. "No one wants to live eternally in Wells." He thought the response was clever given its religious tone, but Emma had frowned.

"Holy things ought to remain holy," she'd said, having regularly made clear that Ronin's carelessness with things he'd once considered sacred was both bothersome and annoying. "A preacher, an ex-preacher — whatever it is you think you are — ought not to express himself that way," she'd said, not that it made a difference, though it had become something of a major irritation to Ronin, who was used to having things his own way.

"How many miles is it?" Dustsucker whispered, not wanting to set Kelly off again.

"Jesus, Dusty! Look, Truckee to Salt Lake is something like 600 miles. So it's less than that, okay?" Ronin closed his eyes.

"I wish you had asked," Dustsucker said quietly, looking back out the window to the quickly passing dry, flat, desert terrain.

"If I had asked," Ronin responded, "I wouldn't have gotten on the train."

Chapter 2
ELKO, NEVADA

A little less than 300 miles east of Reno, the town that started with four canvas tents on a site selected by two railroad men began to come into view. "Is that Elko?" Kelly asked, waking the other two, their sock-bound feet propped high on each other's benches. A December snow had recently sprinkled itself across nearby hills and mountains. Smoke from hundreds of homes and businesses waved a generous hello from a good twenty miles away as the train began to slow.

Ronin woke first.

"Jesus. As much as I hate trains, soon as I hear that 'clicke-ty-clack, clickety-clack' it sends me right to sleep, you know?" He rubbed the crud from his eyes and kicked at Dustsucker, who was seated across from him and was still snoring.

"Yeah, well ... is that Elko up ahead?" Kelly asked again. Kelly had agreed to accompany the two as Ash's deputy — a now-and-then occurrence for the Storey County sheriff — though there was some question whether a deputy U.S. marshal from Nevada would be recognized that close to Utah, not that Kelly cared all that much given Ronin's explanation. "We'll simply catch 'em and kill 'em." Ash would probably have been the better man, Kelly thought to himself while waiting for Ronin or Slade to answer. At least there would be people in Elko County who would recognize him that far east.

In 1869, just three months after the Nevada legislature carved Elko County out of neighboring Lander County, the town named after one of the largest land mammals in North America had 2,000 people living in it. With twenty-two stores, seventeen restaurants, ten blacksmiths, eight doctors and an equal number of attorneys, Elko was considered a boom town. But ten years later — like so many other western cities ravaged by the economies of railroads, mining and fire — Elko was struggling to stay half as alive.

"Hell if I know, Tom. It's been a long time since I've been here. I visited a Presbyterian church there once on my way out west, not that it impressed me much. And I spent an afternoon in a hot springs out toward the Lamoille canyon. That was nice."

"Not if it's the one I'm thinking," Kelly said. "It was always a little too hot for me."

"Just saying," Ronin responded, kicking at his friend again.

"No whorehouses, then?" Kelly asked. Ronin looked at him. Truth be told, the only time he'd been in a whorehouse was to drag men out of them. He'd never had personal business there.

Dustsucker turned over onto his right side, his sock unintentionally inching toward Ronin's sidearm, his head facing the windows backward, the past in front of him, the future behind. Ronin slapped his foot to the floor as he leaned forward, protecting the 4-inch Colt single action revolver the Saint John's Episcopal Church had given him as a fond reminder of better times. "Wake up!" he yelled, "Tom's asking you something!"

The big man woke with a start, growling. "Don't know why the two of you are disrespecting me so," he said, pushing himself into an upright position. He tilted a well-worn butternut-colored cavalry hat forward so that it sat squarely on his head, a gift from his friend in recent months after Ronin took to a sharper hat and image investigating the Spiritualist twins in Virginia City. The hat's brim was folded straight up "so that I can see," he'd explained to Ronin, a veteran of several southern cavalry campaigns with Biffle's 13th Tennessee Cavalry when Dustsucker was just beginning a career in western law enforcement. "What is it the two of you want?" he rumbled before pulling his duster up off the floor and placing it in the seat beside him.

"Tom wants to know if this is the town of Elko ahead?"

Dustsucker turned in his seat so that he could see. A little girl's glance caught his — her blond locks and twinkling blue eyes caused him to smile. The mother frowned as Dustsucker touched the front of his hat. Two things you couldn't criticize about an otherwise easily disapproved-of man. Dirty, maybe — Dusty didn't like to bathe and cleaning up was always a hassle — but the man was courteous and punctual.

"Looks like it, from what I can see," he answered, shouting above the train's whistle. "Last time I was here it was a shanty town, a couple of thousand people with maybe 500 tents. They were talking about a university, though."

"We're not asking for a travelogue, Dusty, just whether we should get off here."

"I thought we were headed to Wells, Ronin?"

"We were, Dusty. But Tom thinks it might serve us to off load our horses here and pick-up some supplies before heading over the Rubies. He's says there's a lot of towns between here and the Salt Lake border."

"Ain't no towns to speak of, Tom, unless you want to look a little ways south toward some of the mining communities. There's the fort, too."

"Fort?" Tom asked.

"Yup, not much of one anymore, save a few ranches and some stragglers who haven't quite yet decided to move on. The railroad closed it down, that and the trails. You're thinking of looking there?"

"I am now."

"Why's that?" Slade said, pulling his blanket from the seat and unfolding it across his legs.

"If it's a place that Latigo's family would have run to when they were in business, then it's interesting to me. Sort of want to check the spaces that were most familiar to him, prior to his parents' death, that is."

"Well then, that's a good place to start."

"I'm sorry?" Kelly said.

"It's not only a good place to start, it may also be a good place to end."

"The fort?" Ronin asked.

"Yup," Dustsucker said. "The fort is where he killed his mother and father."

Chapter 3
FORT RUBY

Antonio Latigo pulled a shirt from one of the trunks and shimmied into it, big hole over his head and small holes for each of his arms he reminded himself, not that he needed to. He was well into his twenties and didn't need a woman anymore to tell him what to do, but it felt good to remember his mother that way, and his father sometimes, too. "The Latigo Family Trust and Mining Company" had pulled freight from Salt Lake City to distant parts west and some parts south for a good twenty years before seeing the bulk of their business driven away by the Central Pacific Railroad, which was now running daily trains between Salt Lake City and San Francisco like it was anybody's business.

When it was the Latigo family's business, business was good. The Emigrant Trail, a northern network of wagon roads throughout the West, was good business for freighters, which is essentially the commerce The Latigo Family Trust and Mining Company offered. Rufus Latigo, Anthony's father and founder of the company as he liked to be called, believed that an extraordinarily expansive name might someday lead to separate but similarly expansive endeavors: a healthy bank (thus the word "Trust") wealthy real estate holdings (thus the word "Mining") as well as a perpetual spring of committed employees (thus the word "Company").

Rufus Latigo's reach extended way past his grasp — like a lot of western men, but not all — and the family, at one time enamored with the old man's entrepreneurial vision, had to in time make do with what the railroad didn't do, which is to say, the family business ended up servicing the tiny towns ignored by the rail route, which laid considerably north of them.

The Ruby Valley offered a few such towns, all of them small, as did other similar valleys, plains, "all deserts and holes in the ground," Tony used to say in protest to his father's continually hopeful hand. The occasional trips to Virginia City to the west and Salt Lake City to the east were history, he'd told his father, who believed the railroad to be an insensitive piece of Americana "that would prove unable to adapt to the certainty of other homes and cities springing up someday."

Antonio didn't much understand his father, being so much different from him. Rufus had been a significant contributor to Elko's first schoolhouse in 1870, and a big-time supporter of "Broadhorns" Bradley's effort to see a university in Elko County as well. "The unfortunate dwarf" never saw the inside of a schoolhouse, despite his mother's insistence that he be treated the same as his brother, an Elko educator of all things who liked to argue that someday there would be colleges in Reno and Carson City, as well.

When Bradley signed the bill establishing the university at Elko, Tony thought things might turn around, particularly when the family's freight company was chosen to deliver stone for local building contractors James McBurney and J. B. Fitch. But the boost to business didn't last long. He could have told him so had his father asked, but of course he didn't. So when the men turned in a different direction to haul additional materials for the $15,000 school, Tony did what he knew he'd someday have to do if the business was to grow and flourish. He killed his dad.

It seemed like the right idea at the time.

He tried to explain it to his mom and brother, but after tempers flared, both his parents laid dead. The brother wasn't far behind, as three murders didn't feel any worse than the first two and "one testifying university ninny," he said to his brother prior to pushing him into a hot spring just outside of town, wouldn't be a good business move either.

The father's death had been quite maddening, using his whip and gun as a flail and cudgel until he discovered he could do both with the opposite end of the tool he'd driven the family's wagon train with all those years. A couple of hits upside the head, and the badly torn man — the leather fall and popper having made a mess of the big man's skin when he hit it, and it didn't need to hit his father all that hard to do damage — was pushed over the edge literally onto a cottonwood snag a few feet in front of their last business asset, a reasonably-sized "two-horse" farm wagon.

His mother, who had spent a good deal of time hoping to rebuild the family's business and to keep the two of them from fighting — they fought nearly all the time despite the disparity in size, his father being so much taller and stronger — immediately began to wail when she saw the ragged end of a tree protruding out of her husband's huge belly. Latigo couldn't tolerate the emotional back and forth any more than his mother could, so in one thoughtless movement — he might have considered differently had he considered it longer — he took advantage of her head sagging forward. Looping the whip around his mother's neck, he pulled her up and over his back and choked her to death. His mother's last words? "Oh, Tony ..."

He'd gone by the name "Toro" ever since then, though intimate friendships like the one he was enjoying with Alvira Fae Livestock usually wheedled his real name from him.

"Oh, Tony, I hate to be leaving here," Alvira said when the two of them began moving things from the cabin into the wagon so as to continue on toward Wells.

"I've liked it, too, honey," he said.

He'd not enjoyed a relationship of any real length before with a normal woman. There'd been a few entertainers along the way, of course, working women who had found his unusual talents or size something to explore. The fact that he could sing like a church lady caused some women to pause, or even to discount their services if he offered or tune or two. And the novelty that he was a small man — a really small man, as in a "dwarf or a midget," his father used to say — allowed some women a certain curiosity that other women would never have thought or asked about. It had been three months so far with Alvira. He didn't think it could get any better.

"Do you really think Wells will be wonderful, Tony?"

"Sure, I do, dear. It's been four years since I've been there, but you'll love the place. If Bob Hamill is still there, he'll show us a good time. He used to run the Wells Fargo depot and helped out on the railroad as well. And there's a school there too, if you want to go. A big old locomotive bell used to ring there every morning."

"It sounds like a wonderful place, Tony."

"You bet. There's a saloon, and a store, a hotel, and I don't know what else it's been so long since I've been back. But it will be a nice place to stop, baby. And if we don't like Wells, we can go to Salt Lake. The Mormons aren't all that bad," he said, smiling. "Being with you is all I care about, my love."

"And I you," Alvira said, picking up one of the carpets they'd found sitting rolled up in one of Fort Ruby's painted log structures. "As much as I've enjoyed being here dear, I've got to say, this house has seen better days."

"Alvira, you should have seen this place before they abandoned it. Some people thought it was the worst place you could end up in Nevada, anywhere in the west for that matter. But my folks and me, well, we sorta liked it. A few people stayed around and we serviced them best we could, despite my dad always wanting something better and bigger." He wiped the moisture from one of his eyes.

"You crying, baby?"

"Nah, just thinking about the good days. When folks moved on from here, we moved on, too."

Alvira looked at her man. Sure, he was short, maybe a whole foot shorter than she was. He wasn't the brightest star in the sky either, but then neither was she. Still, he protected her and kept her warm at night and occasionally sang to her. She liked that, especially now that her sister was gone. It wasn't his fault that she was dead. The gun had simply gone off, Tony had said.

"Honey, I bet these buildings have a lot of stories to tell."

"They do, dear, but none that I'm telling tonight, Alvira. Let's get everything loaded. I want to be on the road before sunset."

Chapter 4

THE DEPOT HOTEL

Fred Wilson's ice business meant that the railroad would have what it needed and that Elko residents would have what they needed. But an ice-cold beer was not in W. W. Ronin's future when he stepped off the train at the Depot Hotel in Elko. Jumping down from the train and bounding up the steps that led into the hotel's dining room, the ex-preacher didn't stop until he plowed right into James Clark's office. "Hello you old coot!" he exclaimed.

"Well, I'll be damned," Clark said, coming around the front of his desk. "I wasn't expecting you, Ronin! If I had known I'd had a beer ready."

"Cold and frosty?"

"Just like you like 'em, though the habit hasn't caught on here yet." Ronin frowned. It hadn't caught on anywhere to his knowledge, except for Philadelphia, and Philly was 2500 miles away. "How the hell are you?" the old man asked.

"Not bad," Ronin said. "Got a little hole in my side from an angry female, but except for that I'm doing right fine, Jim." The men smiled at each other, in the way that men sometimes do, meaning so much more while saying so much less. "Golly, you look good," he said, thinking about the last time he'd seen Clark. In Virginia City he suspected, but maybe Reno.

"Just turned eighty, William. Had a big party here at the hotel. Where the hell were you?"

Ronin laughed. Clark had taken what money he'd made on his 650-acre spread in the Washoe Valley just south of Reno and plowed a good piece of it into a half interest in the Depot Hotel. A few years later, he bought the whole thing. Not bad for an honest to God Nevada pioneer, even if he was a Presbyterian.

"Me? The usual places, Jimmy — Carson City, Virginia City, Reno, Lake Tahoe. Northern Nevada keeps me real busy, my friend. And as long as I'm busy I don't get into trouble, not much anyway."

"Hell, I've never seen you on the wrong side of the track, William. Too much reverend left in you is my guess." Clark touched Ronin's left shoulder. "This trouble you're talking about, son, is it a woman?"

"Nah," he laughed, "well, not really anyway. I'll look you up as soon as we get checked in."

"We?"

"Yup, I've brought a couple of guests with me, if you can handle them."

Jim Clark gestured toward the dining room. "Holds 112 people Ronin, and there's 80 some rooms upstairs give or take, above a billiard hall of all things. Even got a barbershop — looks like you might need one!" he laughed. "Who do you have with you?" He sat back behind the desk, a good deal older than Ronin remembered him but genuinely happy. He tapped on a leather blotter next to an engraved silver pen and ink well.

"Tom Kelly from Virginia City..."

"Know him."

"...and Deputy Slade from Carson City."

"Don't know him."

"You sure? Big man — goes by the name of Dustsucker."

"Well, hell yes! Who doesn't? You should've brought him in here with you."

"It's a small office, Jim."

"That it is," he said, standing up and coming around the front of the desk again to place his hand on Ronin's shoulder. "It's been a long time we've seen each other, my friend. Three or four years, I imagine."

"A lot of things happen in three or four years," Ronin said.

"Indeed they do. Town has slowed down a great deal. Maybe only half the people you remember still live here, William. And business... well, business will always be good if you know what you're doing. But it's been a good deal slower."

"It's been slow all over the state, Jim."

"Yes it has. Let's go get your luggage, son. I can't wait to catch up."

"Mister Clark?" Dustsucker peaked around the partially closed door, not wanting to interrupt. "Is that you? I wasn't sure you'd still be here."

"As in defunct, Mister Slade? As in dead?"

Dustsucker lowered his head. While it'd been a half-dozen years or so since he'd seen the eastern Nevada pioneer — he'd met him last pushing hay and potatoes in Virginia City — he was pleased to be remembered. "As in moved on, sir," Dustsucker said. "I'd heard you were looking at a dinner house up the track aways."

"I'm always looking to make money, son. And I'm not getting any younger."

"None of us are, Jim." Ronin looked over at Dustsucker. "Frankly I thought I'd be dead if I was headed back through Wells again."

"Son, this is Elko."

"We're hoping to get some provisions Jim, and then head that way over the Rubies."

"Don't want to take the train to Wells? It'd be a hell of a lot easier than riding over the Rubies."

"Nope," Ronin said, looking over at a pile of newspapers. "Kelly says there's a good number of towns between here and there where a felon might hide. He says he wants to check each and every one of them."

"Hell Ronin, that sounds like a real bad idea if you ask me. Nothing but gold and silver camps and places that used to be."

"Maybe."

"Well, let's get your bags then, I'll have a man take care of your horses. Then you can tell me what all of this is about, and how it is that a man of your caliber Reverend is out looking for bad guys."

Chapter 5
ALVIRA FAE LIVESTOCK

An otherwise happy girl when she wasn't thinking about the loss of her only sister, Alivra Fae Livestock was pleased that she finally had found a man.

Virginia City had meant the good life for the twins — living as "middle class girls" on D Street, doing what they could for food and money. Though it hadn't led to the life she had hoped for when the girls left Iowa, it had led to a more intimate life though it wasn't always easy.

The occasional man, "or men" her sister occasionally suggested, meant that the girls would sometimes entertain an evening guest or two, not that she was against that though it was hard to understand given Ellie's other talents as a seer and fortune-teller. "The mornings are for sleeping," Ellie said. "The afternoons and evenings are for entertaining other people," she'd instructed when they moved into their small single-story D Street home, a little ways down from the Catholic Church in Virginia City. "It's all the Lord's business," she often said, not discriminating between the more spiritual moments the sisters shared with men and women on the Comstock — northern Nevada's gold and silver mines — or the more physical moments they shared with men alone.

"It's all God," her sister once told her while smoothing the pants of an older man who was making up his mind as to whether he was staying the night or not. "It's not like God discriminates between the good and the bad, the heart-felt or the holy. This is how God made us," she said, speaking to the sexual urges Alvira sometimes felt when watching her sister pleasure a Comstock man. "Whether we're working with a man physically or spiritually, it helps them get to where they're going."

The work was never crude, though others thought of it that way, church women in particular who had their keep already by caring for miners or businessmen. Given that they'd brought no other skills with them from the Midwest — neither girl liked to wash or iron, and only Ellie May had any business sense — it didn't make any sense at all for them to be seamstresses or servers when what they were really cut out for was pleasing other people.

When they were just building a home — not literally, but figuratively speaking as there were plenty of homes to live in when they first arrived — Ellie tried nursing at the St. Mary Louise Hospital in Virginia City, but the Daughters of Charity who operated the hospital preferred a spiritual commitment when working out their faiths, which both of the girls understood being Methodists and all. But neither of the twins had much of a fondness for church beyond the occasional church dinner. The pageantry — the traditional garb of the sisters being blue and white, whether they worked in the asylum, school or hospital, not to speak of the sacraments with which the sisters were sometimes asked to assist — offered even less appeal.

The Daughters of Charity work wasn't bad, caring for the broken-hearted and broken-down in a brand new building that boasted thirty-six patient rooms, five patient wards and a dozen private rooms as well. But when the sisters made it clear that they could find a place for Ellie at the hospital but there'd be no space for Alvira —"there's something wrong with that women," they'd said, not stopping to consider that she might simply be slower or different — the twins figured they'd be better suited for something more home-grown, something they could invest their lives in, something they could nurture on their own and control.

A local newspaperman pointed the way the way forward, which was really backwards not that it mattered as long as they were achieving something one way or another. "There's a bunch of men on the Comstock," Alfred Doten said, remembering they'd come from spiritually-talented parents. "They need what your family has to offer," he said, "and you won't find as many critical people outside of the traditional churches as you do inside."

Doten seemed like "a really nice man," Ellie May said, and Alvira agreed. She couldn't help but notice that Doten was taking a personal interest in them. "Listen," he'd said one night after a large meeting of the Virginia City Spiritualist Society underneath the dentist's office on B Street between Taylor and Union Streets. "The Comstock is coarse, but it's also very cosmopolitan. It can easily host another fortuneteller, particularly an attractive one like you." Doten, the owner of the *Gold Hill Daily News,* had a way of making women smile. As much as Ellie May enjoyed the comment, Alvira Fae did too. After all, the sisters seemed and sounded the same in practically every way except that Ellie was a bit quicker with everything, not just with the men.

Alvira Fae sat up tall in the wagon as she and Anthony pulled away from Fort Ruby a few minutes before sundown. The creak of the old two-horse farm wagon was strangely comforting as she let go of the past — filled for the most part with pleasant memories of men and women her sister and she had lived with on the Comstock: a neighbor boy who first introduced her to the joys of physical intimacy, certain members of the Washoe Club that had purchased their services while living there, and a congregation full of men and women they'd worshipped and practiced with.

When they'd arrived at Fort Ruby a couple of weeks ago, Anthony had recalled for her similar memories, of growing up in

the family business and of occasions when he'd played with soldiers at the fort, the fort's structures having been sold, moved or
dismantled by valley ranchers nearly twenty years ago. It'd been
fun for the two of them to visit the ruins, sharing their memories,
talking out their future together and what they might do next.

Tony was everything she'd hoped a man would ever be,
save his being a little small but not in the ways that mattered.
Sometimes angry, sometimes violent, but deep down inside of this
man God had given her there was a courage that was big enough
to face the mountains ahead.

"Are we headed there?" she asked, pointing toward the
Rubies, toward peaks that seemed as large as anything she'd seen
in Carson City or Reno.

"We are not, dear. We're headed home, honey, to Wells
where I was born. And where I hope we'll build a life together,
you and me."

Could it get any better?

Chapter 6

SUPPER

Ronin sat back in the chair, tipping it so that his head rested against the wall. He placed his hat on the table thinking he'd remove it when supper was set. A man's hat ought not sit on one's knee too long, or God forbid on the floor, unless there was good reason for it to do so. But given the surroundings, it didn't look like it belonged on his head, either. He began looking around for a hat peg.

"This is a pretty impressive place, Jim," he said. "Confession time, if you don't mind me saying."

"Of course not, William."

"I didn't think you had this in you."

"The hotel?" Clark asked. "Hell, this is nothing compared to running a 650-acre ranch!" Clark looked every bit like a Protestant clergyman, all trussed up with a starched collar, frock coat and tie. Ronin smiled. Seeing him dressed that way brought back memories both good and bad.

"I'm just saying, Jim, you've had an adventuresome life thus far, what with the ranch in Washoe Valley ..."

"You never saw it, Ronin," he chided.

"I know ... then there was Washoe County politics ..."

"That never did amount to much."

"Well sure, but still." Ronin touched the top of his beer glass and looked toward the server. *If it isn't cold, at least it's wet.* "Then meeting you here on my way west, well ..."

"Been here since '74, Ronin," Clark interrupted. "What's that make it?"

The ex-preacher laughed. "Shoot, like you can't add? Seven years, I imagine, give or take. I just figured when we met, you being single and all, that you were a rolling stone. I didn't think you'd be running this place, that's for sure." Jimmy Clark smiled, though his otherwise stern appearance didn't give regular warning of his having an informal name or being all that friendly.

The two men had met at the Presbyterian Church when Ronin had passed through Elko on his way west. Ronin had figured him a businessman and social climber, typical of most Presbyterians, he thought, though his personality and finances would have made him a better Episcopalian had the choice been available. Seven years later, there was a Master Mason's emblem pinned to his left lapel and talk in the hotel of his someday entering Elko County politics. It was clear that he had found his niche. "I'm just saying ..." Ronin said, hoping he hadn't offended his friend.

"Truth be told, Ronin, I'm remarried. I tumble one way nowadays, and only with my wife." The two men laughed, though neither was sure that the other understood what was being said or laughed at. "Hell, I've even got a seven-year old daughter."

"No kidding, seriously? Well, my apologies then, Mister Clark. You're quite the established citizen. I misjudged you."

"None needed, my friend. Someday I suspect she'll return the favor. You might, too." The two men smiled at each other, clinking beer glasses as Ronin waited for an explanation.

"Help, Jim? You don't look like you need anything at all. You own the best hotel in town. It sits here in the *center* of town. Hell, the railroad and the stage line empty into your front door. What would a man like you need from a rolling piece of brush like me?"

"Well, I thought maybe we'd wait for the others to come to supper before I said anything. But since I brought it up, let me ask you a couple of personal questions if you don't mind."

"Shoot." The server looked nervously Ronin's way. Ronin winked at him.

"Dustsucker says you're something of a lawman, is that true?"

"I don't wear a badge, Jim. That's for better men than you and me. We see things a bit too clearly at times, don't we?" He was thinking of Clark's considerable reputation as a decisive businessman and entrepreneur.

"We do," Clark nodded.

"Let me just say. Slade, Kelly, Ash and others, they're good men to be sure. But they have to tolerate a much slower pace than I'm willing to."

"I understand that," Clark said.

"What is it you're asking?" Ronin pulled his beer closer to the edge of the table and leaned forward so that all four chair legs now rested comfortably on the dining room's wooden floor.

"I don't mean to drag things out, Ronin, but this is important to me. Seven years ago, when I was just starting here at the hotel, they called it the Chamberlain then ..."

"I remember."

"Used to be called the Cosmopolitan."

"Is that right?"

"... well, the first time I met you I sensed you were a good man, and that you had strong feelings about right and wrong."

"I do."

"... and that I could trust you ..."

"You can." He took a sip of beer, swished it around in his mouth and swallowed it after some consideration. He hadn't remembered Clark being so methodical. "What are you asking me, Jim?"

"I hear you're the kind of man that makes things right."

Ronin smiled. The same thought had occurred to him many times. It is what he did, and what he had always done, as a former pastor and priest and more recently as a bounty hunter. Whether he was picking up a criminal wanted by a lawman who was too busy or too scared to round him up on his own or running down a couple of murders or some lost kids, what he did was to make things right. That's why he was sitting in Elko. There was at least one loose end from the business he'd conducted in Virginia City, and maybe two if he could bring himself to deal harshly with a woman who was a good deal worse than what he wanted her to be.

Clark was looking at him, waiting.

"Jim, what's wrong?"

"I'm trying to care for my daughter, Mattie."

Ronin fidgeted. "Listen, Jim. I'm not real good with kids." He thought of the children at Emma Nauman's mission, just south of Carson City. He'd done well enough with some of them — Sophia, Grace, Creighton, Sammy and Bekah. But he never had any children of his own, having never been married. And he hadn't spent enough time at the mission to think of any of Emma's other children as close, which was fine with him though at times he wondered if his life wouldn't be better off if he had. *Such is the kingdom of heaven, Jesus said.* "I've been around a few," he said.

Clark began laughing as Dustsucker and Tom Kelly entered the room and approached the table. Ronin moved to a chair closer to the window so as to make room.

"What's so funny?" Dustsucker asked.

"Oh nothing," Clark roared, "except that Ronin thinks I'm going to ask him to babysit!"

"What?" Kelly exclaimed, raising his eyebrows.

"No, I don't!" Ronin said, though he wasn't exactly sure what Clark was going to ask him to do, not that babysitting was beneath him and maybe it would do him some good given how angry and tense he'd been. A couple of days watching someone else's kid would certainly improve his mood ... or not.

"Yeah, you do," the hotel owner said, continuing to laugh as he pushed away from the table and stood to greet Kelly and Dustsucker. "It sure is good to see you, old friend," Clark said, giving Dustsucker a huge hug. The big man blushed.

"It is that, Jim," Dustsucker stuttered.

"Calling me Jim now, are you?" he said as he held onto the Ormsby County deputy's arms, squeezing him like an accordion.

"Well, I thought ..."

"Just kidding, Dusty," he said. "Kelly, good to see you again. Sit down, would you? He pulled a chair away from the table and patted Kelly's shoulders as he sat down. "Let me tell you what I need." The group crowded around a small table in a quiet corner of the Depot Hotel's dining room. The dining room was nearly empty. "You men are headed toward Wells?" Everyone nodded. "And I hear, and if you don't mind me saying, I find this funny given that it would take you no time at all to go by rail, that you're making a few stops along the way?" They nodded again, impatient but smiling. "So I'm wondering," he said, picking up the pace. "Would you mind dropping my little girl off at a ranch in the Lamoille Canyon? I mean if you're going that way."

Ronin looked at Dustsucker who looked at Kelly who looked back at both of them, each uncertain as to how to respond. It was a kid, for Christ's sake. And the trip, at some points, would be dangerous. Sensing their hesitation, Clark, always the business-man — "Hell, someday he'll make a fine county commissioner," people used to say in Washoe County and now in Elko County, too — blurted out, "I'd be happy to comp you your rooms, if you would."

Ronin, never real happy to sleep inside if sleeping outside was just as comfortable, and Dustsucker — who didn't much cotton to spending money on things he didn't have money for, and who knew when the U.S. marshal would reimburse him for monies spent in the arrest of these suspects? — looked over at Kelly, who didn't care where he slept after the death of his wife except that he constantly worried about his children — and said almost simultaneously, "If you'll throw in the cost of our supper, we'd be happy to."

James Clark smiled. "At two bucks a room and a dollar for dinner, it's a deal," he said. He signaled to a waiter. "Henry, would you cut us a couple of steaks?"

Chapter 7

TOUGH TIMES

"Look, I figured we'd lean on the locals for this sort of business. But given how busy we are and how stretched out Elko County has become, this little thing seems like a big thing. To be frank, it's keeping me up at night."

Clark leaned back in his office chair as Kelly, Slade and Ronin stood in front of him, having just enjoyed ranch-size steaks in the Depot Hotel dining room. An old oak railroad desk — cluttered with newspapers, legal documents, hotel hand towels and kitchen pans — sat between them. The contrast was staggering. "Jim, I'm trying to make sense of all of this," Ronin said, wondering if the chaotic condition of Clark's office suggested a state of mind or something worse. "You want your daughter out of town. We're happy to do that. But there's a situation in town that you think you need help with?"

"I'm just wondering," he said, moving a stack of legal papers to a table behind him. "I don't want to abuse our friendship, gentlemen, or your time."

"It's not our friendship that you need to be thinking about, Jim," Kelly said. "We're duly deputized by the U.S. marshal to conduct his business in eastern Nevada. There's no reason we can't help you with something he didn't anticipate. It's your safety I'm beginning to be concerned about."

Tom Kelly stood tall when speaking about the law. While Ronin never thought seriously about becoming a lawman — his mother and father, now both gone, would have been pleased to see him select a second "calling" when he abandoned his first

— it was the singular courage of men like Sheriff Tom Kelly and Marshal Augustus Ash that occasionally made Ronin wonder if he wouldn't have been a better fit for police work than the priesthood. Nerve came easy. The piddling pastoral tasks he'd had to suffer as a priest seemed so much harder. He was glad they were over and done with.

"Is it your safety, Jim? Is that what we're talking about?" Ronin asked. Clark swallowed hard. If Ronin didn't know the man, he'd easily mistake him for Wyatt Earp, who was a policeman in Wichita when he was pastor of the Saint John's parish. Earp had gone on to bigger things. Clark was, perhaps, at the top rung of his ladder and maybe barely hanging on.

"It is."

"And your daughter's also?"

"Exactly." It was all beginning to make sense.

The town of Elko was born between two long-legged rails laid by the Central Pacific Railroad, building west from California. Racing to meet the construction crews of the east-bound Union Pacific Railroad, the Central Pacific tent town quickly became the center of a major stage and freight system. When the land agents began selling lots — $300 for an inside lot, $500 if you wanted something on the corner — the town, crisscrossed by numerous stage and rail road lines, was not too softly caressed into a modern Nevada city, complete with stores, schools, restaurants and hotels. With progress came the miscreants, and neither mining nor fire could control the crime. Admittedly, the rough and tumble days of early Elko didn't last long, but a piece of that past was causing "Uncle Jimmy Clark," as he was sometimes called, to stutter.

"Jimmy, how can we help?"

"You can wait here a couple of days and then take Mattie with you."

"We'll do that."

"Listen, we've had a history of citizen committees cleaning up this old tent city. It used to be quite fashionable for folks hereabouts to blow the tops off each other's heads. But the word's out. Behaving that way is no longer considered a virtue."

"Don't imagine that it is," Ronin said.

"The building of a nice courthouse helped as well. Maybe you want to see it before you leave town? It's on Idaho and Sixth Streets."

"Ever work out the issue with keys?" Dustsucker asked. Clark winced.

"Keys?" Kelly asked.

"Yeah, twelve years ago," Dustsucker said, "when the city built the courthouse, there was a significant cost overrun. The county commissioners didn't have the money and were, as you might imagine, real irritated. The contractor, apparently not a very thoughtful man, compounded things by asking for an additional $240 for locks he'd installed. When they refused payment, the contractor had duplicate keys made of everything including the jail and gave them out all over town."

"Wow."

"Yeah, Dusty, they worked it out. Moved the goddamned privies out of the courthouse, too, okay — which is something I think everyone is beginning to regret! But back to my point. The courthouse, the jail, the citizen committees, the sheriff, it's all quieted things down a bit, and I'm grateful. It's not easy being an old man."

"You're not old, Jim," Ronin said.

"Yeah, I am," Clark said. "I've had a pack full of kids, a couple of wives and one new one."

"Maybe you're just tired."

"Old, tired, it doesn't make any difference, Ronin. Listen, there's a man we need to find. Elko County authorities haven't had any luck, and it's got me all upset. Mind keeping an eye out for him as you head south?"

"Of course not. We're already looking for a couple of people, so it won't hurt us to look for another. But maybe you should tell us the story, first."

"Alright, why don't you sit down?" he said, taking a deep breath. "A few days back, a man named Sam Mills shot and killed his best friend at Halleck Station. Halleck is about 20 miles from here, has maybe a hundred people, twenty-some buildings and some cattle ranches. It ships beef to a fort nearby. Well, Sam Mills used to work as a cook at the Halleck Hotel, and in an argument with his employer — a nice lady named Deering — Mills pulled a knife on a man who jumped in to protect the woman. Being unsuccessful with that, he went looking for a gun."

"Okay." Ronin shifted in his chair.

"Now, here's the sad piece. His friend, a man named James Finnerty, felt like he could talk to Mills. But when he went and found him, he made the mistake of opening the door and was killed instead."

"Jesus, you mean the shooting might have been an accident?"

"Exactly."

"So what's your connection to all of this?" Ronin asked, looking at his companions. "Why is it bothering you?"

"That's a good question, Ronin. So let me give you a good answer. Fact is, I'm supposed to sit on that jury."

"Huh."

"It's a bit unusual to select a jury before a man's been caught, Jim," Kelly said. "I don't quite understand."

"You're right, Tom. But it's a big county, and given that everyone pretty much knows everyone else, the judge thinks it's going to be hard to find a fair-minded group of people to sit in judgment of the man."

"Who's that?"

"Judge Flack. Know him?"

"I do, though I wouldn't want it heard that I called him a drunk and a cheapskate," Dustsucker said.

"What are you talking about, Marcus?"

"The man turns every two-bit bar into a one-bit bar, whether the bar wants to be that or not. When he's done, he staggers drunk through maybe a dozen saloons and not spent more than a dollar."

"Is that true?" Ronin asked. Clark nodded.

"Okay, tell me something about the man," Ronin replied.

"Well, he's got a some history of violence, though I can't say it's always been his fault. And he's spent a little bit of time in a Carson City prison, I'm told. But James Finnerty was Sam Mills' best friend, so I'm guessing when he's found he's going to tell a different story."

"You think he's innocent?" Kelly asked.

"I have no idea, Tom, but I know Halleck. I know the people who live there. I've been to the brewery, sat in the saloon, talked to the soldiers, and have some sense how to keep cattle out of a hotel living room." The men laughed.

"So this guy Mills is threatening you then?" Dustsucker asked.

"No, gentlemen," Clark said. "Halleck is upset, the whole town, from the people at the post office to the ranch foreman at Dan Murphy's cattle company. If you want to see me smile again, I need the pressure to go away."

"And that's why you need Mattie out of town." Ronin looked at his friends and was silent. The list of things they were trying to do was growing. But it would build character to handle an old man's requests. And patience — something he'd never had a lot of, but could practice if given the chance — might be well served to help Jim Clark out. He raised his eyebrows, so as to ask their opinions. Dustsucker and Kelly nodded. "We'll find him," Ronin said, "and we'll bring him back alive to face trial."

"I'd appreciate it, Ronin. Anybody else finds him and he's a dead man."

Chapter 8

PROMISED LAND

Truth be told, W. W. Ronin was the rolling stone, not James Clark. A *former* pastor now gunfighter and detective, he hadn't quite found his "sea legs yet, to mix the metaphor" he said to his best friend who was sitting opposite him in an Elko, Nevada hotel room. "I just don't get it," he said to Dustsucker, who had his eyes closed, his hands folded neatly on his chest and was beginning to make the sounds of a pleasant night's sleep even though he was still sitting up.

"You don't get what?" he mumbled.

"I don't get how a man like Jim Clark can make so much of his life in just a couple of years and I find myself still struggling to understand what I want to do with mine. You know what I mean?" A tall, good-looking man at about 185 pounds, seminary educated and in anybody's mind still quite young, Ronin could do pretty much anything he wanted to do. His Pennsylvania friends had told him the same thing eleven years prior when he set out to minister to a small Wichita, Iowa congregation, soon to be a railroad town just north of the Seven Mile Prairie.

"You don't like railroads. You don't like cattle. And you sure as hell hate horses. Why are you heading west?" his mother said in an uncharacteristically critical voice, weeks before he left to take the Saint John's parish and make it into something an Episcopal bishop could be proud of.

"I want to see the West, mother," he'd replied, though he wasn't sure that was the attraction.

There were a lot of personal miles he needed to get rid of, he told himself privately, and the memories that went with them, he figured — having served as a southern cavalry man in the War Between the States. He didn't have rank or the authority that sometimes went with it, but he'd seen a lot of killing, even as a cook and livery man. The occasional "pot shot," the colonel called it — oblivious to the cooking reference of killing another creature for the cook pot — earned him a reputation that was difficult to live with. He'd long ago lost count of the number of men he'd killed with his Henry — "a twenty-four inch octagonal-barreled death machine," he called it — because what he aimed at never got a chance to write home again. It was a battlefield trophy taken off of a Union soldier, all sixteen rounds of it spent killing men, fallen by his side. When he slammed a pot upside a Union soldier's head, catching the spent rifle in mid-air, a company corporal remarked that killing other Union soldiers would be the only way he'd be able to keep it fed, which is what he did.

"I mean, think about it," Ronin continued. "The guy travels to California by boat from Pennsylvania, that took some money, I guess. It doesn't take him long to find out that he doesn't want to be a prospector, no big surprise there. He retreats to Sacramento in time for a spring flood, invests in a ranch and some rental properties on the other side of the Sierra. Somewhere along the way he gets robbed and the next thing you know, everybody in Elko County wants this guy on a jury or involved in his or her business. What's wrong with me, Dusty? Why haven't I done as well?"

"There's nothing wrong with you Ronin that putting your feet down won't fix. How 'bout you turn down the light and go to sleep?" Dustsucker rolled over toward the wall as Ronin considered the twists and turns of his life that had brought to the place where he was sharing a room with a deputy sheriff in the middle of the nowhere cattle town of Elko. It wasn't like he had lost his way. He'd been conscious about the decisions he was making from the very beginning, leaving his family on the East Coast and moving to the Midwest to explore a new ministry — a "calling" he hoped would heal some of the hurt he had caused himself by fighting alongside his father in a Tennessee Calvary unit. But the hurt didn't go away, and the calling wasn't at all healing.

The eighteen people who banded together to begin the congregation in September of 1870, three years later were wondering why their pastor — a Pennsylvania-bred southern-sympathizer, except on the issue of slavery — wasn't able to relax or forget the harm that had come to Americans in the south and the north. Six years later, they built a small frame church and consecrated it, moving from the small log church he had built between two rivers to the corner of Third and Main Streets: Sabbath School every Sunday at 2 o'clock, a Wednesday lecture at 7 and musical practice at 8. But by then the former Reverend W. W. Ronin was gone, no longer interested in their personal hopes and dreams. He was pursuing his own with the Pinkerton National Detective Agency, and didn't care at all if he was at peace with himself.

He'd hadn't left his religion behind, though it took a couple of years for him to notice that it had changed somewhere along the dirty rails and trails the Pinkertons had led him on. It was an easy way to see the West, in someone else's employ guarding gold shipments, investigating fraud, murders and other crimes while still looking for the central myth he thought the West would provide his life — good guys, bad guys and a large promise-filled space in-between.

When he washed out of the detective agency by getting involved with a client, a well-known clairvoyant and psychic whose actual name he was never able to determine, he told himself he'd never go back. Forward took him to Carson City, where a very similar calling caught his attention. He'd been a man-hunter ever since, and neither dough nor dames had kept him from the passion of setting things straight when situations needed fixing. Still, at times it didn't seem to be enough.

"Dusty, are you asleep?"

The big man wheezed, rubbing his nose with his right hand and pulling his sheet up over his head. "Sort of," he said.

"Do you think we can do this?"

"Do what, Ronin?"

"Find this guy, protect him and the little girl we're protecting while looking for that son of a bitch Toro Latigo and his not-so-little girl, Alvira? Do you think we can handle this?"

Dustsucker turned over so that he could face his friend. It was rare day or evening when he needed to talk heart-to-heart with him. The man didn't need much, having seen practically everything, having suffered through it and come out on the other side. "Ronin, this isn't like you. You sound timid. What's going on?"

W. W. Ronin took a deep breath. "I feel like we're more in danger this time than ever before, and I don't want to get either of us killed before both of us find what we're looking for."

"Looking for? You mean Emma? What are you talking about?"

"I'm talking about the Promised Land, Dusty, whatever that is. I want to see it before I die."

"Hell, you're not going to die, Ronin. Not here in Elko. And not likely in Wells, either. Nobody dies out here, don't you know? They simply move away."

Chapter 9
FORTY MILE DESERT

"If you're given to flat, this is something you're going to want to see," Latigo said as their wagon — a couple of horses, a small skid (except for wheels) and a pile of everything the small man owned, which wasn't much — pulled out of Reno so as to find the Humboldt River some forty miles away. Alvira had kept her eyes closed for the first few hours expecting a wonderful surprise, but when the heat got so high that the chickens began to wilt like garden lettuce in a hot summer sun, she couldn't stand it any longer. What she saw wasn't what she expected.

The high desert — barely nurturing the rabbit weed, scrub pine, sage brush and occasional cottonwood tree that she had come to know and appreciate in her northern Nevada home — had given way to dry-cracked earth, capable of growing only dark and troubling thoughts. No wonder people in Reno had remarked, "Going to see the elephant, aren't you?" when Toro had stopped for feed and water.

Latigo had taken the reference personally, thinking they were talking about the circus and maybe his belonging there, but Alvira convinced him they meant only a new sort of excitement, an adventure that she or he had never imagined. The expanse before her was so dry and unimaginative, she didn't know what they meant now. It was a page from an illustrated Dante's *Inferno*.

"You like this?" she asked.

"Sure," he said, "though it gets a little hot. We'll stop up ahead a bit and shelter ourselves until it gets dark. It's even more beautiful then, with all the stars shining and the silence and all."

She'd come to appreciate the desert during her and her sister's journey west some years before. The drier, more desolate parts of Utah and Nevada weren't as busy or populated, and no one judged her there like they did in Iowa, where townspeople sometimes pointed and asked if she was "okay." Her parents had raised her not to point like that and had never suggested she was "slow" or "dim-witted," words she hadn't heard until they'd settled in Nevada amidst the tonier citizens of Virginia City. Not that the people around her were much smarter, she figured, though they dressed nice and belonged to clubs and had dreams and goals.

She and her sister often sat around at night on their small porch on D Street, when they didn't have guests over or were attending meetings. They talked about what *their* future might look like, and Alvira hung on every word — imagining cool streams, green grass and a house built with bricks or stone. "Someday we'll be rich and maybe famous," Ellie used to say when they sat talking about her prophetic gifts, gifts that God had given her to help people find things, communicate with their loved ones, or interpret "the signs and portents," her sister said, that often determined people's futures. The money they collected wasn't much different than "the usual missionary offerings," her sister explained, though Alvira wondered if that held true when some men stayed overnight and paid more for other services usually more intimate and embarrassing.

"I don't think I've ever seen anything like this," she said to her friend, who was now the source of everything that was good and true in her life, including a new understanding of what the future might bring. *But not like this.* "Toro, do they have grass in Wells, Nevada? Will there be trees there? Can we someday have a house?" she asked, hoping that the end of their journey wouldn't look like the beginning, and that the meaning of it — the death of her sister, her meeting so small but so sensitive a man and the journey they were taking together — would someday become clear. It was getting hot. It was getting hard to breathe.

"Sure, honey," he said. "I just wanted you to see this part of the world. Some folks never see all of this. This is the California Trail, from Missouri river towns all the way to the Pacific Ocean in California. It's maybe the worst part of it," he said, "as some people died here just a few miles short of their goal. The air was often thick and powdery, so much so that sometimes the drivers couldn't see maybe eight to ten feet in front of them. The dust was so bad baby that everyone coughed, even the horses and cattle."

"And the chickens, too?" she asked.

"Maybe the chickens, dear," he laughed. He didn't know shit about chickens, but he did remember the dust.

"Did your parents make it, Tony?" She moved closer to her man, putting her hand on his leg.

"Well, sure," he said. "For years, we guided folks through the 40 mile deserts. One 40-mile trail went south to the Carson River. The other road went north to the Truckee River. Once the Humboldt disappeared — that's called 'the Sink,' baby, the river just drops right down into the desert, no lake, no nothing — the worst was on everyone. 'Source to Sink,' they used to say up until a dozen years ago when people started preferring the train to the terror of the trail."

Alvira groaned thinking about it.

"When I was a kid, honey, I used to say 'source to stink.'" Latigo laughed. She loved when he laughed. "Oh hell, it wasn't that bad. It just wasn't the river or lake anyone was expecting."

"Did your folks die out here, sweetie?" He winced, but her hand felt good on his pants. He liked her touching him that way.

"My brother did," he said. "My parents more or less. We'll talk more about that when we get to Wells dear, where the Humboldt River begins as a little rivulet. That's a funny word." They both laughed. "Enough to say that you'll be glad we've got all this water and feed. There's nothing out here for a very long time."

A long time, she thought, wondering what that would feel like, she and him alone under the stars. He wondered the same, their relationship so new, the first real connection with a woman he could think of.

The 40-mile desert wasn't the easiest of trips for anyone. It hadn't been for his family, or anyone whoever traveled with them, though taking the lead from some Mexicans who knew about such things, they'd learned to let the animals graze and drink as much as wanted to before starting out. A certain rhythm needed to be maintained, even when traveling at night. Ten minutes' rest every two hours, a two hour graze when daylight came, paying some attention to how the beasts were acting as it got late into the afternoon and all. *Journada del Muerto,* they called it. There were lots of them in the West. People needed to pay attention to such things as putting hay in their boots and filling every goddamned canteen and coffee mug with water so that they could survive.

It caused him some pause to bring Alvira this way, but he imagined that railroad detectives, local sheriffs and such were probably looking for them. The trail was safer than the train, at least for a while.

"Do people live out here?" she asked, looking around.

"Well sort of. Some people do. You'll find a spring here or there, though not many have good water and some only at the edge of things. We're going to rest in an abandoned mine up ahead. There likely wasn't enough water to keep it going or feed for cattle. What water there is, baby, is pretty bad, so don't be wandering off."

It was a simple thing to go crazy in these parts, he remembered. People and animals had a hard time holding it together. That's why folks had started traveling at night. You couldn't see the death and dying that way, or the discarded trunks and other treasures. If folks could see what they were walking on or past, they might not keep going. And of course the heat was easier that way, too.

"Just a few minutes longer," he said, happy that the yammering had stopped. *Tony, don't you want this? Tony, don't you ever think about that? Tony, wouldn't it be great if we did this?* God, when would it stop?

He saw the glint of metal just a few hundred feet off to his right. The roof hadn't rusted as much as he thought it might, though the mine's entrance had since collapsed. The past would soon be behind them — all that stuff in Virginia City, before that Reno and before that Big Meadows, now the railroad town of Lovelock. He wondered if they should board the train there, as Alvira's chattering was tiring. If they got far enough away, all the negative memories would be gone too, maybe even dropping his brother in a hot water drink at a hot spring just outside of Elko. He was a good man.

"Tony?"

"Yes dear?"

"Do you ever think about having children?"

Damn.

Chapter 10
THE CALIFORNIA TRAIL

He was thinking about it all a month later, having taken the train to Elko, and then driving the wagon through the Hastings Cutoff so as to see a little bit of the Ruby Mountains before they settled in Wells, or parts further east ... he wasn't sure.

She'd done alright, given that it was her first time traveling without her sister. And the unforgiving starkness of the Nevada desert hadn't proven to be much of an obstacle either, though she did talk a lot — and if he had to answer one more question as to what their life would look like together he'd have buried her underneath a pile of rocks like so many other emigrants along the California Trail. The rail ride, commencing a hundred or so miles out of Reno, had been a good idea, in that it took most of the tension out of the trip. And the gentle rocking of the coach, save for the occasional stop and whistle, seemed to relax the woman he'd come to like and sort of respect, if admiring a woman was possible.

Truth be told, the thought of being with a woman was kind of inspiring. Maybe there could be an end to his "sinful ways," as his mother put it prior to his looping a wagon lash around her neck and choking her to death. He was still smarting over that one. Was it possible there was some hope for his sorry soul after all?

He looked at Alvira as they headed north, away from the fort, up the eastern side of the Ruby Mountains via a road that used to be part of the Hastings Cutoff. The Donner party had traveled that way — though going in the opposite direction — in an effort to cut a couple hundred miles off the main trail just a few miles north. There had been others of course who had followed the self-serving advice of Lansford Hastings, an ambitious lawyer who hoped to one day lead Californians in a fight for independence against Mexico. A lot had happened in 30 years, including the Donner group getting caught in the wintry snows west of Reno and pretty much freezing to death prior to eating their friends and families. That was something he'd never do.

The whole California Trail had had been a big disappointment to some people, the Humboldt River anyway, hoping to see water just like home. What wasn't alkali and dusty in the Nevada section of the trail was largely sandy and unpalatable for any man or beast. The Humboldt wasn't the cascading mountain stream people were hoping for. In some places it wasn't more than a couple of inches deep. It was never more than a stone's toss across. He hadn't ever heard of fish living in it. And as for trees, well, there wasn't timber enough along its 350-mile trek from Illinois to California to make a damned cartridge box.

Latigo heard an early traveler of the trail complain there wasn't "adequate anything along the river bank to shade a rabbit," though he'd found plenty of jack rabbits along its winding way. It took a man five or more months to make the trip from Missouri to Hangtown, which made for some truly hungry and thirsty people. And while it wasn't his family's first wish to sell such necessities as flour, salt and coffee at such an extravagant rate, it did put food on the table once their freight and livery business began to fail.

"Tony, do you think we could stop soon? I'm so tired," Alvira said just a few miles past Ruby Lake. They hadn't been at it for more than a couple of hours, but they were in no hurry.

"Sure, baby. We can stop for the night," he said, though he couldn't remember if there was a hospitable place nearby.

The first travelers on the trail were similarly ignorant of the best route along the Rubies, or west of there for that matter. The early maps — drawn by previous emigrants in the 1840s, some before that — showed non-existent lakes and rivers and a country thought to be so rough that it might only be passable by skiff or canoe. Others said the trip west would be like a walk in paradise, that food and water was plentiful, and that the Indians were friendly, which it turned out wasn't true, their having to compete with a whole new bunch of emigrants scrounging for resources that were already too scarce to support those who lived there.

The trip began in Iowa or a little ways south in Missouri, where rolling hills gave way to rivers and toll bridges and enormous herds of buffalo and windy fields of grass. Forts along the way provided supplies — some more than others — and encouraged a gentle bliss about things ahead, though powerful Wyoming winds gave ample warning as to what was still ahead. For some, cholera and scurvy became intimate companions. Then Utah and Idaho brought a first-hand inspection of mountains that tried everyone's abilities and patience. Finally, the Humboldt — three hundred and some miles of choking dust and alkali-tainted water which meant diarrhea and disease, not to mention offering an early death to those who were unprepared to make a final forty-mile sprint toward the Truckee or Carson Rivers. It was no walk in the park.

"Can we stop, baby?" she repeated. He had probably pushed her far enough already. There was no hurry. They could take their time.

"Love, there's a town up ahead called Cave Creek. We can stop there." There used to be a distillery there, back when Fort Ruby was open and a couple of soldiers discovered a cave entrance at the head of a creek bed. While the town grew to include a restaurant and saloon, story of the discovery wasn't a particularly happy one given that all of the soldiers except one died when they rowed into the cave in order to explore. Silver was discovered a couple of years later, though Latigo couldn't remember if the mines had since played out. It'd been a long time since he'd been up that way.

"A drink would be a nice thing about now," he said to Alvira, who was struggling to stay awake, "maybe two." Alvira smiled. She had been thinking instead about breakfast.

Chapter 11
GUT SHRUNK

Breakfast the next day was an easy one. Ronin had stayed up all night, wondering about the journey ahead. It wasn't typical for the man he thought he had become. Worry was something he saw in others. Anxiety, appreciated or not, was an attitude he brushed off in the same fashion as cleaning the new Sunday-go-to-meeting suit he'd bought last fall in Carson City. It had been frustrating standing there in Koppel and Platt's clothing store, a few doors down from the Ormsby House, with Emma getting all apprehensive as to why he was buying it and what woman was he seeing and so on, not that she voiced it. Still, this thing with Latigo and Latigo's apparent paramour, the sister of the late Ellie May Livestock — a woman he liked despite her being a psychic of sorts — had him feeling just the same, like he'd just finished plowing an ungrateful neighbor's corn field or been yelled at by someone else's wife. His muscles were tense. His mind was unfocused. And there was an anger building in him such that he didn't think he could move, even for a prairie fire. He didn't know what to do, though he darn well knew he'd have to do something.

"You getting up or are you just going to lie there?" he said to Dustsucker, who was reclining there in all of his morning glory on a modern mattress, appreciating an Elko sunrise and wondering why he hadn't insisted on a room all alone as well, given that Tom had gotten one and the owner of the hotel was paying for it all.

"Mind keeping some of those feelings to yourself?" Dustsucker said. "I've been up all night with you, Ronin. I mean really. I feel like I'm sleeping with a needy woman."

"Excuse me?" Ronin said, kicking at Dustsucker's bed with one leg while still pulling a boot on to his other. "Like you'd know what a needy woman feels like, Dusty!" He began laughing.

"I'd know," he said, realizing he didn't know and had only imagined what it would feel like to sleep with someone who wouldn't leave him alone all night and had pretty much admitted so by saying "I'd know," the conditional tense, instead of the present tense, "I know."

"Geesh buddy. Stop kicking, would you? At least let me go find a privy. That was a hell of a lot of supper we had last night."

"That may be. But I'm just feeling a little gut-shrunk, Dusty. I'll meet you downstairs."

He grabbed his gun belt and firearms — a long-barreled Colt .45 he liked to keep in a cross draw holster so that his faster gun, a 4-inch Colt, cut just a little bit shorter than what was usual, sat on his strong side. He could dump draw and fire the 4-inch gun in less time than it took for a man to blink his eyes, which he had done many times, spewing a lead breakfast toward men who would never again see the light of day and damn well deserved it.

Some Utah, New Mexico and Nevada lawmen had told him to his face that he liked "too much to dabble in gore." But Ronin thought otherwise, having a profound respect for men and women who didn't need to die and who sometimes needed to be protected so that they could go on living. There was a category of men — dangerous men, reprobate and repulsive men — "who needed to die sooner than later," he often said to those who were critical of his trigger finger occasionally losing its conscience. And Latigo — the son of a bitch who had attempted to kill him and who he now suspected left a miscreant trail of killings across Nevada — was certainly one of those men. He didn't know what he'd do with the woman who was accompanying him, despite her appearing to deserve pretty much the same fate. But it all made him nervous for some reason, more this time than any other time.

"Did you get out of Clark how we were going to find his man?" Dustsucker asked, sliding from the covers and pulling a coat over his red long johns which had seen better days, but then both of them had, the man and the underwear. Ronin smiled.

"I'm sorry, Dusty. Are you planning on going outside?" he asked, amused.

"I was."

"The privy is inside. This is a real nice hotel."

"Fine, then I'll use the inside privy," Dustsucker said, pulling off his jacket and wondering how far down the hallway he'd have to walk to secure an indoor sink and toilet. He tugged at his shirt, draped over the bottom of the bed and caught on its footboard. "Did you stay up long enough for Clark to give you a description of this Mills character he wants us to find?"

"I did."

"And?"

"Well," he said, turning the door handle to go downstairs to the dining room, "he's got one eye."

"Jesus, Ronin. No wonder you've been up all night. What kind of man has one eye and shoots his own best friend?"

"I don't know, Dusty. But more importantly, Clark says he's got a very disagreeable attitude."

"Why not?" he replied, standing and looking around for his pants. "He's got one eye. Hey, mind handing me those?" he said, pointing to a pile of pants at the end of his bed. "He's probably scared as hell and isn't looking forward to seeing a Nevada marshal, a deputy sheriff and one sleepless, screwed-up ex-preacher hoping to find the Promised Land out here in no man's land."

"Hell, Dusty, Elko is kind of beautiful. You see the Rubies this morning?"

"No."

"Well, when you do you'll see why a couple thousand people like this place. They're tall mountains, my friend, lovely mountains.

"Yeah, with plenty of places to hide."

"Hell, it won't be hard to find Clark's man."

"Why do you say that?"

"Cause if he's as hungry as I am — and everyone eats my friend, even bad guys — he's going to be where there's water and food. He won't be anywhere else."

Chapter 12
EMMA NAUMAN

"So tell me about the hole in your side, son," Clark said, motioning for one of his staff to bring coffee.

"There's not much to tell," Ronin replied, "save that I was working in Virginia City for a couple of members of the Washoe Club, when a woman I was investigating rolled her gun into my side. I was laying in one of the newer cemeteries at the time, 'handsomely fenced, lovingly cared for,' the brochure said. The Masonic section was actually irrigated."

"Good to hear about that."

"I naturally figured she had pretty well killed me."

"Naturally," Clark said, laughing.

"I mean I'm out of it — life review, angels singing, the whole kit and caboodle on my way to meeting the man upstairs — when the next thing I know Dustsucker is standing over me, shouting."

Clark sat there, unmoving. His eyebrows were raised. He was stunned. "Wow, I'm sorry I made light of it."

"No, no. That's fine. It's good to talk about it." Ronin turned his cup over so that it sat upright and pointed to it. While he generally didn't like coffee — "most coffee tastes like dirt," he liked to say — the Depot was offering several custom blends, so why not? *When in Rome...*

"So what, then?" Clark said, shifting in his chair to accommodate the server, who was moving additional chairs to the table. "There will be three of us I think, Francis, or will it be four?"

Ronin shrugged. "I haven't talked to Tom yet. I don't think he's up. Let's set it for four." The server nodded, and Ronin continued. "So they took me to the hospital up there — Saint Mary Louise something or other, has space for maybe 60 or 70 people and is operated by Catholic nuns — you know, the Daughters of Charity. They figured out that I was okay. Then they moved me to a friend's house in the Carson Valley. Emma Nauman, you probably don't know her. She owns a mission just south of Carson City that teaches Indian kids. I'd stayed there the year prior when my leg got all busted up during that jail explosion."

"I remember reading about that. So it worked out?"

"The leg? Sure, I was back to normal in two or three months."

"Your wound, Ronin... the chest wound."

"Oh, right, that too. So then I got involved with a couple of murders at the lake, and when that was over, I took up with the Washoe Club at the suggestion of a businessman in Virginia City, Versal McBride. Do you know him?"

"I do."

"Well, I made some good money and was closing the operation down when I got shot."

"She's a good woman?"

"The woman who shot me?"

"No, Ronin, the woman you stayed with."

"Of course, Emma Nauman. Yes, but why do you ask?"

"Because you ought to be settling down, my friend. Make some money. Find someone you like and can live with, maybe marry her, that sort of thing."

The ex-preacher smiled. He hadn't expected this from Clark, who was a man he couldn't keep track of, not that he was trying. *Washoe County, Storey County and now Elko County? Who knows where he'll end up next.* "Where's this coming from, Jim?"

"Hell, I don't know. I was thinking. It was good visiting with you boys last night ... kinda felt like a piece of civilization landed in my lap. So I got to wondering this morning what would it be like if Ronin came east a bit and worked for us here at the hotel, a sort of private policeman and such. We'd help you get settled and pay you well. And the work would be meaningful, to be sure. There's a lot of mining going on in these parts, Ronin. In your off times you could go dig gold or silver."

Ronin smiled. It had never occurred to him to move to Elko, a town you'd have to take a train to find. Nor had he thought of slowing down. "Jim, that's very kind," he said. "But I don't know what I'd do out here. It's a long way to somewhere. And to be frank, I don't do that kind of work anymore. The Pinkerton years are way behind me."

"Not that far behind you, Ronin. You were talking about them last night, even."

"Well, that's true. But three years is three years. And while I learned a lot in their employ, my time with the Agency was too similar to my time with the church — too many bosses, too many things to do, and the constant press of people hoping you'll do and be something other than what you've set your mind to be and do."

"I understand."

"Listen, I really appreciate the offer, but I work for myself now and it's a good fit." He lifted a creamer from the table with his left hand, and grabbing a spoon with his right happened to look up. Clark shook his head. He put the spoon down. "What stirred those thoughts?" he asked, curious if Clark was as unsettled as he appeared.

"I'm getting up there I guess," he responded. "And I've weathered the train station phase of our business here — fifty people for supper, fifty people for breakfast, fifty people for lunch — it gets real old, real quick." Ronin laughed. The press of people wanting something other than what he wanted to give seemed familiar. Clark had hung in there.

"You've got a good deal more going on here than that, Jimmy."

"I do, and that's why I've been thinking of something smaller, Ronin. A road house maybe — a couple of rooms, a small dining room and some trees out back I can sit under as I grow old." He smiled, stirring his coffee even though there was nothing in it.

"You always liked people, Jim, even the troubled ones."

"Truth there, son. And you, Ronin, what are you looking for?"

"Hell Jim, I don't know. I'm a rolling stone, I guess. I have a sense that something's up ahead of me, but I don't know what it is. And I don't mind telling you, I'm beginning to be afraid that my time will run out before I find it."

Clark nodded. He'd felt the same way for years. *Hell, everybody feels that way.*

"This I know," Ronin said, "this woman's a keeper, and I hope I'm the one who's keeping her. But who knows? I've got a hole in my pocket as big as my pant leg, and there isn't a woman in all of God's creation who likes any of that."

"And this gal you're hoping to hold on to? What's her name again?"

"Emma. Emma Nauman."

"East coast gal? West coast? Tell me about her."

"She's a missionary ..."

"Oh, God ..."

"Now, hold on, it's not that bad," he said. "She's got some growing up to do. A lot of Bible talk and she prays as many hours as the day is long. But she's got a heart as big as the house she lives in. And the kids she serves — I don't know all of them, but I can see it in some of their eyes — they love her, Jim. She came to the Carson Valley maybe a dozen years ago, from Zanesville, Ohio. Used to be the capital of the state, she told me though I'd never heard of it. She married a man from Pittsburgh, who's now gone, dead maybe. No one knows. And while I don't follow such things, I'm hearing from others in town that she may well run for state office someday."

"In Nevada?"

"Yup."

"I find that hard to believe Ronin, given that women can't vote." The two men laughed.

"That may be. Like I said, I don't pay attention to such things, but I've heard people talk and they say she's got something the rest of the state needs."

"What's that?"

"You're putting me on the spot, Jim. But I'll tell you what I think it is — a conscience. Folks have got to start thinking about the future of this state. It may be that it will be the women who will best help them do it."

"Good morning gentlemen," Dustsucker said, pulling a chair from underneath the table and sitting down. "It's sure a nice Elko morning."

"It is that, Mister Slade," Clark said, motioning to a server. "Say, we're sitting here talking about Missus Emma Nauman running for a state office. You have an opinion on that?" Clark said, laughing.

Dusty shook his head. "I imagine Emma could do just about anything she set her mind to."

"How's that, Mister Slade?"

"She's a true believer, Jim."

"Hell, boys. We're all true believers, of one sort or another. Even the bad boys believe."

Chapter 13
HALLECK, NEVADA

Tom Kelly tied his horse onto a column outside the Halleck Hotel as the sun came up about 20 miles from Elko. Something sounded familiar about the man Clark had described. It took him half the night to remember, and when he did he couldn't get back to sleep again. Mills had been previously arrested — outside a saloon in Eureka a couple of years back. He'd lost an eye in the fracas.

"Don't tie that horse there," an old man yelled from the hotel porch. "Wasn't that long ago a damn horse pulled the whole hotel down!"

Kelly smiled, brushed the weather off his jacket before removing the leather strap from one of the uprights supporting the hotel's second story porch. He re-secured it to a hitching post nearby.

"The whole hotel?" he quipped as he skipped up the steps to the hotel's entrance. "I find that real hard to believe," he said, winking.

"It was a big horse," the old man said seriously, before breaking out in laughter.

"Or a badly built hotel, right?" Kelly said.

In 1870, Halleck had a population of thirty-five. A railroad town, like everything else between Reno and Salt Lake, a brewery, a saloon and a two-story hotel soon followed. Soldiers from Fort Halleck, about 12 miles away, soon wore a path to the saloon doorway as had the old man who was sipping from a brown bottle before the sun had hit mid-sky. "The owner here?" Kelly asked, before opening the hotel door.

"Mrs. Deering? Doubt it, but Sheriff Deering is back there."

"Sheriff Deering?"

"Yeah, the town constable and postmaster," he said. "He owns the hotel too, with the missus that is." The old man pulled a crumpled brown hat down over his forehead so that it covered his eyes. "Don't be telling him I'm out here. He kind of frowns on my having breakfast on his porch." Kelly laughed as he opened the door.

"How can I help you?" a grouchy man said from behind the counter.

"Sheriff Tom Kelly, Virginia City," Kelly said, extending his hand.

"Sheriff John Deering, at your service," the man said, putting a smile where his frown had just been.

"Postmaster, sheriff and bartender? Sir, you've got your hands full."

"I do at that. My wife's headed up to the fort with some supplies and asked me to tend to things for a while."

"Asked you or told you?" Kelly laughed.

"Sounds like you know how things work, sheriff. How can I help you?"

He took off his gloves and put both hands on the counter. "I'm staying over in Elko, at the Depot Hotel with some friends."

"Nice hotel. Had dinner there last weekend."

"Well, Jim Clark asked if we'd look around a bit for a young man who killed his best friend in Halleck a couple of days ago."

"Wasn't that recent," Deering said, "but thereabouts, I imagine. You deputized or something, Mister Kelly?"

"Yeah, there's a couple of us out this way, looking for another man and working for Marshal Ash. Jim thought we might come across your guy as well."

"Well, he isn't our guy any longer. Worthless son of a bitch, if you ask me, from day one. But I don't hire 'em — the wife does. I never liked the man. He always seemed sorta shifty to me. She wouldn't allow him to carry a gun on the property, given that he'd spent some time in prison. That seemed to bother him some..."

"So you knew about his time in Carson City."

"We did, and the fist-fight in Eureka. Fact is, Mills had a chip on his shoulder. But he could be helpful and he was a good cook. The missus liked that. She wanted to give him a chance, thinking he'd someday turn into a Bible thumper, though I didn't know or care until the day came that he drew down on her. That really fried my omelet."

"Your omelet?"

"It's an egg dish, son. You have some sort of identification?" Kelly showed him a silver badge. "That's real nice. We don't see much silver out here, not badges anyway. So here's the deal. He got all up in her face. So we fired him, paid him what we owed him and figured everything was good until we heard he was heading for Griffin's."

"Griffin's?"

"The saloon."

"Okay."

"Somehow he gets hold of a shotgun, heads to the saloon and is sitting there drinking when his friend walks in. Gonna save us from having to arrest him."

"Right. Jim Finnerty."

"That's right, William James Finnerty. Sounds like you've heard this story before. So Jimmy opens the door of the saloon and Mills is sitting there about six feet away, drinking himself stupid, and Mills pulls the trigger. Like wham! He blows a hole in Finnerty's chest. Jimmy cries out, 'Pray for me,' or something like that, 'I'm gone,' and dies without saying another word.

"Wow, that's awful."

"Goddamn right it is. The one-eyed Negro..."

"He's black?"

"Yup, a former slave, says his parents were slaves, too. Well, the fool shoots his friend, steals a horse — neither of which is okay out here, but the horse really sealed it — rides out of town and hasn't been seen since."

"You mount a posse?"

"Sure thing. A couple of cowboys went after him, and some men from Fort Halleck. But he was gone. Are you going looking for him?"

"Hell, sheriff, we've got our hands full already looking for someone out of Virginia City. But Clark is friends with my friend, so Ronin says we're going to look for him. You know how it is."

"W. W. Ronin?"

"That's right, you've heard of him?"

"Hell son, everyone's heard of W. W. Ronin. Don't imagine that Mills has much of a chance if Ronin's looking for him." Kelly smiled. It took a village, not that Deering would understand that. "Odd thing about Sam Mills, Tom."

"What's that?"

"Well, I don't mind telling you, I'm not much of a Jesus man, though I try to keep my bills paid and my eyes straight ahead, if you know what I'm saying. The wife would kill me if I didn't, I suppose. Well, that damn fool used to sing a lot of hymns while working in the kitchen here."

"So?"

"Well, I sort of miss it."

Chapter 14

BREAKFAST

Kelly walked into the dining room just as Dustsucker was sitting down. He paused long enough to remove his canvas riding coat and hang it by the doorway, stomping his feet. His spurs jingled. Even with the stove fully ablaze, Kelly was cold. The early morning ride to Halleck and back had put frost in his beard. The breakfast crowd was gone and an early lunch bunch was sitting around a few tables waiting for the hour to turn to order their lunches. Clark ran a tight ship.

"Jesus, it's cold outside!" he said, pulling an oak chair from underneath the table. He rubbed his hands together and sat down. Everyone turned and looked at him, silently. It was as if he'd interrupted a Lutheran grace. "What?" he said, smiling.

"You know what," Ronin said.

"No, I don't."

"Why are you saying it's cold out? You just got up, you knucklehead."

"Hell I have! I've been up since 3 o'clock. I couldn't sleep, so I rode over to the Halleck Hotel and talked to the sheriff there.

"You've been back and forth to Halleck?"

"Yeah, it's only 20 miles."

"It's only 20 miles?"

"Well, twenty over and twenty back."

"Okay. And it didn't take long?"

"Long enough," Kelly said.

"So how's John Deering this morning?" Clark interrupted, as a plate of pancakes was set in front of him and a couple of eggs

alongside. Bacon followed. Dustsucker's breakfast came next —
eggs, bacon, potatoes, pancakes and coffee. Kelly reached for the
coffee.

"May I?" he asked.

"Of course," Dustsucker said, before sliding his eggs and
bacon onto his pancakes and setting the empty plate on the floor.
Ronin sat there with a glass of fresh-squeezed orange juice and
some toast.

"You eating, Ronin?"

"Don't think I can, Tom. Jimmy here just told us that Toro
Latigo had a room here about a month ago. They're pulling his
signature card now. He had a woman with him."

"Wow, that's quite a break. Any sense where they were
headed, Jim?"

Clark put his utensils down and folded his hands. "Well,
that's sort of the interesting thing, boys. It turns out your man
used to live in these parts, or at least travel through them. He
was quite the entertaining little man the night he stayed here.
Jumped up on a piano bench and sang opera songs like a full-
grown soprano."

"Yeah," Ronin said, "I suppose you kept your mouth shut?"

"I did," Clark replied. "But why?"

"Well, he gets pretty riled up when you criticize."
Dustsucker offered as he pushed a piece of bacon into his mouth.

"Real riled up, Jim. That was our first run-in with the
man."

"Well, it's been a while since we heard any real music.
We didn't grow up with anything so interesting in Greenville,
Pennsylvania as a midget singing opera. So we just hooted and
hollered our way along with the man. When he was finished we
threw some coins at him and invited him back the following
night. But he was headed out with his girlfriend."

"A tiny brunette-looking woman, right?"

"That's right, with a gold tooth in the front of an otherwise normal looking mouth."

"Yup, that would be her. Get to talk to them?" Kelly asked, making a snowball with his hands, rubbing and blowing into them to get them warm.

"He did," Ronin responded, cutting Clark off, who was just as happy to put a piece of egg into his mouth as to answer another question. He took a long sip of coffee before lifting his napkin to his mouth.

"What did he say?" Kelly asked, putting his hands around his coffee cup and lifting it to his lips.

"He said he was headed to Lamoille."

"Isn't that on our way?" Kelly asked. Dustsucker nodded as he shoveled a forkful of potatoes into his mouth with his right hand while holding a couple of pieces of bacon in his left.

"I'm sorry," he mumbled, bacon pieces falling onto his plate.

"It is," Ronin said, "though we're a few weeks behind him. And then there's the question of snow."

"I'm not following, the passage ought to be clear, right?"

"It is," Clark responded.

"So the issue is?"

"The issue is it's almost Christmas. Latigo said he was hoping to camp at what's left of Fort Ruby."

"Okay, so …"

"So, it's too cold to be camping out there right now. And it was getting cold three or four weeks ago." The server handed him a signature card. "Three weeks ago, it looks like. So they will have moved on by now."

"Too bad," Ronin said, putting a Hangtown strawberry onto his toast and casting a wary eye toward his friend, who was already gesturing that he wanted the jam. "But I imagine there will be somebody out that way who might have seen them." Kelly pointed to Clark's plate and gave a thumb up to the server as he swallowed some coffee.

"Here's what we know about the man, Jim. He hangs around too long after he's done something that would make a normal man scoot."

"You mean a taller man," Dustsucker said as he stuffed half a pancake into his mouth while laughing. "I'm sorry."

"Taller, smaller, it doesn't matter, Dusty. He doesn't have a normal sense of what he's done, or any understanding of when he should hide or explain himself. Something is missing inside him," Ronin said, drawing circles around his ear with his right hand. "It's like he thinks he owns a place, jumping up on a piano bench to sing and such. You know what I mean?"

"Like he's *entitled* to be there," Clark nodded. "He totally acted that way."

"Exactly, so he leaves a big footprint," Ronin said. "What he's done in one place, he does in another, because he thinks he can get away with it." Dustsucker and Kelly nodded. He took a moment, grabbing the jam and stirring it to find another strawberry. "We'll find him. He'll be living right out in the open, if we give him enough time. What did you find out, Tom?"

"I'm glad I went out there. I guess I didn't get that Jim's man, Sam Mills, has some history."

"I told you what I knew."

"That's true, but I didn't hear you say that the man has an anger problem and is generally regarded as pretty unpredictable."

"Did the sheriff say that he drinks, Tom?"

"Hell, Ronin, everyone drinks out here except you," Clark said, laughing.

"He did. And while he was drinking, he apparently took a borrowed shotgun to his best friend and blew a real nice hole in his chest."

"Jesus."

"Boys," Clark said, lifting a glass. "Not to be concerned. Jesus didn't promise any of us a rose garden. He told us there would be a lot of suffering in the world and that we could suffer with him through it."

"Jim," Ronin said, "I respect you being Presbyterian and all. So pardon me for saying, but I don't think that Jesus has a whole hell of a lot to do with any of this."

Chapter 15
SHANTY TOWN, NEVADA

The town of Cave Creek looked so bad people were calling it "Shanty Town" a long time before the silver mines closed. The broken-down buildings hid underneath a pile of lumber and nails. A ranch house — the likely recipient of whatever materials were scavenged after the town's economy collapsed — could be seen off in the distance. Latigo was hopeful they hadn't attracted anyone's attention.

"We've gone dozens of miles so far," Alvira complained, though it couldn't have been more than eight or so. Still, her tone said it all. It was time to stop and set up camp for the night.

"Alvira," Latigo said sweetly while pulling tight on the reins. "If we don't make better time, we'll run out of food." It was an overstatement of course, but he wanted to make a point. The more time spent in transit — stopping here, looking there — the more likely it was the two of them would sooner or later be seen. It wasn't easy for a midget to hide out. A small man needs to keep moving if he doesn't want people to stare.

Tears welled up in Alvira's eyes. "Not that we're going that far," he rushed to add. "We can probably take it easier than I had planned."

Growing up in a family where everyone else was "normal height," Latigo had learned that it was important to act confident, even when one didn't have a plan. So when one did, or sort of did

— like when he kicked Ronin's ass at the Bucket of Blood Saloon in Virginia City, or took pot shots at him and his friend in the International Hotel there — Latigo believed in pretending to be doing exactly what he was doing even if it included doing what he hadn't planned on doing.

"Sweetie," he said as he lashed the horses to a post, "let's stay in the wagon tonight. We'll be safer that way." He didn't want her wandering off talking to people — she could be so friendly. "You don't know what creatures are lurking in these old wooden buildings." And as soon as he said the words, as quickly as they popped from his brain and escaped from his mouth, he wished he hadn't said anything.

"Creatures?" she inquired.

Great.

What was left of Shanty Town — a not-quite-ever-thriving enterprise begun by a couple of men who owned a distillery and later built a saw mill, restaurant and saloon — had kept the soldiers at Fort Ruby entertained for lack of anything else to do. When the Cave Creek Mining District was organized a few years later, the hope was that the two men's little dream would soon turn into a bigger dream, a sort of metropolis in the middle of the eastern Nevada sun. But it wasn't long before the silver was played out — if ever there was any — and the liquor most men were looking for on their way to Wells was just as scarce or disappointing.

"You said 'creatures,' Tony. What kind of creatures are you talking about?"

The little man swallowed. *Should have kept my mouth shut. I shouldn't have said anything at all.*

In 1863, the United States government built a fort at the south end of the Ruby Valley to protect the California Trail. It was perhaps the worst fort for a soldier to wish for, and not all that helpful a fort — say like Halleck or Bridger — for an California or Oregon-bound emigrant to resupply. Save for a couple of bored soldiers, the extraordinary cave might never have been discovered by white men.

The way Tony heard it, after Fort Ruby had been constructed, about a half dozen men from the fort visited the cave. Hearing the sound of water churning nearby, they found a small hole in the earth that led to a much larger cavern underground. They built a boat — in pieces of course, having to put it together once they were inside — and found a certain happiness to their adventure until one of their them died trying to swim past an underwater wall. The soldier who died was said to haunt the stalactites and stalagmites that sparkled nearby.

While Latigo had never heard or seen the man's ghost, he'd suffered through his family's stories about Cave Creek and been continuously haunted by their attempts to lower him down into the hole to see the cavern which was said to lay beneath. It was probably a personal thing — his family hoping to fit him into so tiny a hole, no small man ever wanted to be caught with so little a place to go — but the thought of going anywhere near the hole again gave him the shivers.

"You said 'creatures,' Tony," she said, again. "What kind of creatures are we talking about?"

"Dear one," he said, getting back in the wagon, wondering how to tell the tale so as to not make it worse, "there was once a man who loved a woman in these parts. He was a soldier from Fort Ruby, who was kept from seeking the affections of a woman he cared for..."

"The fort we just left?"

"That very one," he said. "Well, as I heard the story, a colonel there prevented him from seeing her. So there came a time when her feelings ran cold..."

"My feelings will never run cold for you, Tony."

"That's good, Alvira. That's real good. One day she just moved away ..."

"To where, Tony? Where did she move?"

"I don't know where, Alvira," he said, his blood beginning to boil because of the interruptions. "I'm trying to tell you something, Alvira."

"I'm sorry."

"So, in the course of his frustrations, he drank a good amount of alcohol and died swimming in a nearby cave."

"Oh, dear," Alvira said, wistfully. "Can we see the cave, Tony?"

Latigo was silent. There wasn't a part of him that was at peace with seeing that hole again, or remember the times his family had taunted him to "climb down in there," his father used to demand, "tell us what's in there," his brother used to say. He'd kill them over again to keep from looking in that hole again. But of course they were already dead.

"Alvira," he said, trying to be more thoughtful in his response, "there are people," he said, "silly people who say that the soldier still haunts that cave, dear." He grabbed his suspenders with both of his thumbs, and pushed his hips out to make a point, even if it wasn't true. A small man needs to do what a small man needs to do. "I don't believe in such things," he said. "Do you?"

And she sat there — she really did, ass up in the wagon like the little woman that she was, listening to her man but still wondering. Her eyes were real open, just sitting there thinking. Could it be that this man didn't understand anything about her? I mean, if he didn't understand this one point — that she and her sister lived for such times as these, that the Spirit world was within each of us, just a whisper or a sideways glance away — could it be that he understood anything about her at all? "Tony," she said, "just because you think one thing, doesn't mean that I don't think another."

He balled up his fists and began to cry.

Chapter 16
COWBOY HAS A FUTURE

Ronin was lashing his bedroll to the back of his saddle outside the hotel, when Jackson shivered nervously. A little girl was standing too close to the horse's hind quarters. He hadn't been paying attention. "Young lady," he said, "you need to step back. Anyone ever tell you about standing too close to the back end of a horse?" he asked, before breaking into laughter.

"Something strike you as funny, mister?" Mattie Clark asked, unclear as to why the man in front of her was laughing.

"Mattie. I thought your father told me he was coming downstairs with you. I never intended a little girl like you to have to heft so big a bag all by yourself." Ronin covered his mouth, so as to stifle his grin.

"So it's the bag that has you amused then," Mattie Clark said, shifting the red and black cut velvet valise from her left hand to her right, easily acting Ronin's equal. It was still early yet and the cheeky ten-year old's tone hadn't even begun to bloom when a younger man — someone Ronin didn't recognize — came tumbling ass forward out of the hotel doors with Jimmy Clark's right leg following close behind.

"Don't let me catch you in here again," Clark yelled, as a grizzled cowboy in his twenties or thirties fell into the middle of the street. He immediately stood up and began brushing himself off.

"Who are you calling a son of a bitch?" the cowboy asked, his best yellow go to meeting shirt torn and now dirty.

"I'm calling *you* that, you son of a bitch!" Before the words were half out of Jimmy Clark's mouth the cowboy went from grooming his trousers to grabbing his gun.

"Mattie, get down!" Ronin yelled, punching at the horse's rear flank with his left hand while cross-drawing his 7 ½ inch Colt from its holster. Clark's eyes were wide. He wasn't heeled. He hadn't seen the need to, having left the Washoe Valley where snakes, coyotes and the occasional bear sometimes needed a speedy dispatch. Ronin pushed Jackson's back end out of the way. The cowboy with the gun was now hesitating, the hammer on his hog leg ratcheted back while standing at the half ready, his gun still pointing at the ground. "Let's think this through, partner," Ronin said, half expecting to drop the man with a head shot but hoping for something different, something more.

A bevy of sage hens ran across the street having hid all morning between the railroad tracks. Mattie crouched down to the left of the steps, her father standing with his mouth open in the middle. "James, back away from the door, would you?" Ronin asked. "Not that direction," he interjected, "the other," he said, motioning the hotel owner to stand farther away from his daughter instead of closer.

"Mister, this isn't any of your business," the cowboy said.

"Son, what's your name?" Ronin asked.

"My ...my ...my name's none of your business, either," the cowboy stuttered.

"Listen to me," Ronin said. "I'm just trying to help. This man's my friend, and you'll be a dead man standing there should you try to make him my *late* friend." He paused and waited. "There's no need for you to do that, son."

The boy stood still in the middle of the street, about ten feet away from Clark and his daughter. He looked at Ronin and then glanced back at the hotel owner, who had taken to leaning up against a door jamb with one hand on his chest.

"Jimmy, are you okay?"

"I'll live," he squeaked.

"Son," he said, redirecting his attention to the cowboy in the middle of the street. Do we understand each other?" Nothing. He tried again. "What do you say you put that iron back in your holster and head down the street?"

The cowboy nodded, but didn't move.

"Son, put the gun down."

He nodded again. Ronin took a couple of steps toward the boy, and seeing no movement, reached out and gently put his hand on the man's right arm. He pushed the revolver down until it was pointed at his feet. The cowboy wore no shoes. "Son, just put it away," he said quietly. The boy nodded. Still not moving, Ronin lifted the gun from his hand and tucked it into his own gun belt instead. "What's your name, boy?"

"His name is Slaven," Clark growled. "He's a silver miner, and he's down on his luck."

"I can see that," Ronin said, glancing over at Clark's daughter, who was now sitting on the steps with her bag open, rooting around inside. "Son, where are your boots?" he asked.

"I don't know," the boy said, shaking.

"What's going on here, Jim?"

"Mister Slaven here lost his boots in a card game last night. We were treating him to some breakfast, on the house of course," he snarled, "when the boy started begging from folks in the dining room. I'll not have that in my hotel."

"I was not begging," the boy said. "Some people offered to buy me some shoes. I was just answering them."

"I'm sure," Clark said. "Well, he got a little testy with me when I asked him to leave."

"Father, can I give him some of my socks?" Mattie Clark interrupted, pulling two balls of grey wool from her satchel.

"How many times have I told you not to roll your socks that way?" Clark barked.

"Jesus, Jim. Let's all calm down a little." The cowboy was now crying. Clark looked at the young man and then at Ronin. He put his arms up, palms extended, and frowned.

"You both do what you want to do with this man," he said, "I'm done with him. But this is the kind of thing I was talking about last night, Ronin. I want the craziness to go away."

"Go take a seat inside," he said. "Mattie, go with your father. I'll be inside in a minute." Mattie tossed a pair of socks to the cowboy and then took her father's hand and walked into the lobby. "Mister Slaven. What do you say you and I sit down for a few moments then I'll give you your gun back?"

"All right, mister."

The two of them slid onto the second step of the Depot Hotel as Tom Kelly and Dustsucker came out the front door. "Everything okay?" Dustsucker asked.

"Everything is fine, Dusty. How about you guys get your horses, and Mattie's too, and bring them around front? I'll meet you here in just a few minutes." Kelly nodded.

"Saving the world?" Dustsucker asked.

"One man at a time," Ronin laughed, pointing the way toward the livery with his head.

"He's a lucky man then."

"Both of us are. Get out of here, would you?" Kelly and Dustsucker shrugged, turned around and headed toward the horses. Ronin paused and then asked, "Son, what the hell is going on?"

"You already heard the old man. I lost my boots in a card game. That's all there is to it."

"That's all there is to it then," Ronin repeated his words. He'd learned a long time ago when doing ministry that everybody liked to hear themselves talk, even those who were less than honest. The church was full of less than honest folks. "A house of sinners," he often said on Sunday mornings just prior to mass. Saying so didn't generally go too well

"Well, I guess I got a little riled up," the boy said.

"A little riled up?" he asked, not that it mattered. Most of what people did and said didn't matter. It was the damn drama people attached to such things that was so painful. "Just a little riled up?" he repeated, looking at the boy. The boy was clear-eyed and strong, despite being up all night playing cards. The cowboy had a future.

"I called him an old man."

Ronin laughed. "You called him that at least twice, son. I don't think I would have gotten away with that either." He smiled at the boy and pulled a couple of silver dollars from his vest pocket. "Take these, would you, and get some boots. You're going to need them."

"Need them, sir?"

"Son, you've got a long life ahead of you. It's important you face it with shoes on."

Chapter 17
SEND OFF

Ian Slavin hung his head down between his legs — or so it seemed anyway — and scooted down the street toward a dry goods and tailor shop just east of the post office, swinging his arms as if he had somewhere to go which he did given that he was clutching a couple of Carson City dollars in his right fist. A man doesn't shoot if he's got new found money in his hands, not without blinking anyways. That's what Ronin figured. Even the baby Jesus would be distracted with silver in his hands. The kindness had saved him from having to kill someone a couple of times in his violent career.

"What the hell was that?" Dustsucker said as the four of them piled back out onto the steps of the Depot Hotel and looked up the street past a steam engine and some passenger cars.

"That," Ronin emphasized, "was a young man looking for his future." He took the cowboy's gun from his belt and tossed it toward Clark, who was still fuming over the shoeless man's insolence. "Anyway, I thought I told you to stay inside," he continued, keeping an eye on his new friend who moments before showed some propensity for shooting at old friends. He hadn't asked if the man had a second gun, nor did he know if he'd go in search of one. But with Slavin a good fifty yards down the street, the ex-preacher visibly relaxed. Kelly was staring at him when he looked back.

"You looked finished, so we came outside," he said.

Tom Kelly had been a good hand the previous spring, when U.S. Marshal Augustus Ash, Dustsucker and he were dealing with kidnappers in Reno. The Virginia City sheriff was a better rifle shot than he was, though he wasn't one to easily take direction. Ronin had never gotten used to the attitude. "Expect so," he said, briefly meeting Kelly's eyes to make a point, then looking away to see if Mattie was okay. She was unshaken. *Amazing.*

"Jim, you make friends with that man," he said, putting his hand on Clark's shoulder. "With a little coaching, he might be the answer to all your troubles."

"I doubt it," Clark said, brushing at Mattie's hair and turning to pick- up her satchel to attach to one of the horses. "I've got better things to do than raise disappointed little boys into grown men. Which one is hers?" he asked, looking at the horses someone had brought around to the front of the hotel.

"The gray sorrel," Dustsucker said. "The livery said that's what she preferred."

"I didn't know that," he frowned.

"Papa, you've been real busy lately. How could you?" Mattie asked. The truth of what she said hurt more than the grace she was extending. He had been busy, and hadn't been as focused on his wife and daughter as he wanted to be. Business had been too erratic, and the recent boom in railroad riff raff hadn't made things any easier. There wasn't enough work in the mines and the town could only absorb so much.

"Look Ronin, I'm sorry for getting all worked up. I'll try to pull it together. And I'm sure I'll calm down when I know Mattie's at the ranch in Lamoille and you're on your way to Wells.

"You might," Ronin said, "and you might not, Jim. You've always been a little bit driven."

"I'm slowing down."

"We all are, my friend.

It wasn't Clark's fault that things were so taut in Elko. Jim Finnerty's death at Halleck Station had shaken more than a few people. The fact that he'd been killed by his best friend — a scarred-up, one-eyed man with a shotgun — hadn't been missed, or that he'd been working in the Halleck Hotel kitchen before taking after the owner with a knife.

The incident "had put decent people on edge," Clark had said, before professing the belief that Mills, if caught and tried in Elko County, wouldn't get a fair trial for what was possibly an accidental discharge. "He'll be lucky to get manslaughter," Clark told them. "Given his appearance, he'll be hanged no matter what. It was clear that Clark thought he'd be chosen for the jury — if a jury was even called — and he'd be caught in the middle. "There will be good people on both sides," he'd said the night before. "You think my business is hurting now."

Ronin helped Mattie with a stirrup and pushed her up into the saddle. She sat like a man, gripping the horse with her knees — a Paiute Indian wouldn't be any more comfortable. "Just get her there, safely, Ronin. No more Mister Nice Guy takes a chance next to a crazy shoeless man with a gun, okay?" Ronin laughed, but nodded. Talking about it further wasn't going to help anyone, and Clark was clearly upset enough already.

"Well, Mattie?" Ronin said, strapping the velvet valise to the saddle so that it hung tightly to the side. "You ready to go?"

"I am, Mister Ronin." *What a bright little girl.* "Goodbye Papa," she called, as the others mounted.

"Be safe, Mattie," her father replied. And Ronin, who wasn't one to see the unexpected synchronicities in life — who didn't always catch the unusual glance between two people, or the singularly strange appearance of a beast or a bird flying overhead — took silent note of this one. If Mattie had been his daughter, he'd likely have said, "I'll miss you."

Chapter 18

SAM MILLS

Sam Mills didn't intend to kill his best friend. Hell, Jim Finnerty was his only friend, in a small town that guaranteed a handful of acquaintances at best, despite soldiers from the nearby fort and cattlemen occasionally stopping by the hotel to find a midday meal.

Had he known that the gun was loaded, or that his best friend was coming to talk to him, he might have thought differently about placing it on the table with the barrel-end pointed toward the front door, but how could he? He was drunk and barely functioning, given the loss of his job at the hotel, the measly amount of cash he'd been tendered for his services and the unlikely possibility of being offered a job ever again from Salt Lake to San Francisco. A one-eyed Negro with a prison sentence wasn't going to find work any more than a hungry Nevada jackrabbit might find a shade tree and underneath it a fresh patch of lettuce.

The odd thing was that he hadn't seen any of this coming, given his talents as a "fortune-teller," his mother used to say. When Sam Mills could, he would break from the kitchen at the back of the hotel to read cards at tables out front, or at Camp Halleck 10 miles away. It took a special sort of gentleman or lady to tolerate Mills' appearance and tone, but he made a few coins telling people what they didn't know about cattle costs, the price of love or the generally bumpy roads ahead of them. Pretty much everyone had something going on, though it wasn't always easy to pick 'em. But if he could get someone to sit down at a table and buy him a beer, he was halfway into their wallet or purse and pretty much on his way to living the dream, not that he understood what the dream was or whether he'd ever be able to live it.

He did know white people however, better than most people his color. He'd been born in the south. While his parents were freedmen — he wasn't at all certain how or when — his father one day contributed a princely sum of money to buy his son's liberty. He learned a lesson from that. Some people worked hard, while others needed *to be* worked over so that they got the black man's point of view. He was happy to contribute what he could, as ignorant people were everywhere.

One time in Eureka, a white man got right up into his face, and didn't pay attention to the years of scars and bruises that said "fuck off, you might lose your life if you push things too far." The man had insulted him with slurs a black man, hell any man, should never have to hear. So he pounded him, until that piece of abusive white shit was turned into white man soup — red and creamy and ready to be served up to the next son of a bitch who spoke to a black man that way. Well, a nearby marshal took umbrage with the event, as did one of his eyes which branded him a very bad character though deep down inside all he ever wanted was a solid and generous break.

When his friend William James Finnerty, or "Jimmy" for short, came through the door some hours later — maybe the only man he ever trusted, inside of prison or out — he just didn't think of what he was supposed to be doing or what came next. He just did what he did. It wasn't as if he meant to pull the trigger, it's just that the gun went off before he even had his hand on it. "Pray for me," his friend had cried and Sam really tried to before a tumble of men and emotion forced him out the door and onto a neighbor's horse. He'd barely gotten out of town before they were after him.

The desert was the place to go, Sam figured, though he understood there wasn't much to support him there. So he headed to the Lamoille Canyon, where he'd heard there were ranches and water but barely any people to run into. He found a place he could hide and feed himself, though it was important that he didn't take too much or be seen outside during the daylight hours. He'd been successful at it for a couple of days, stealing from a local dirt farmer who ran some cattle but not so many that he hired other white men to work with him, and the saloon, there though he stayed away from the Cottonwood Hotel where he was afraid people would ask questions. It was unlikely that any man or woman in Lamoille would go out at night — and there were 207 of them, if he'd heard correctly — because some folks believed he was hiding in those parts. And he was, of course.

Ralph Streeter, who ran the Lamoille, Pleasant Valley and Elko stage line, sometimes left food outside for his drivers, which offered a nice break from the fish he caught and the left over saloon meals he was able to forage. But there was no Post Office, and no real sheriff or constable to be afraid of, no government buildings for people to come by day and night, and no camp or fort — there were 120 soldiers ten miles north of Halleck always looking for something to do given that Indians even attended church services there. So things looked as if they'd be fine and dandy for some time — maybe even through the winter months if he could build shelter — until a little girl one night caught sight of his legs hanging outside of haystack because it had turned warm, goddamnit. And then everything went to hell and there wasn't anything he could do about it. Not anything at all.

Chapter 19

THE JOURNEY

Ronin wasn't even a mile out of town before Mattie Clark opened her mouth. "I see that these men wear badges, Mister Ronin. What is it that you do?" she asked, with a smile that suggested if he answered that question there were more coming. Ronin looked at her and thought for a moment.

It had taken the ex-preacher a long time to conclude that he was anything now that he was no longer an Episcopal priest, not that he was thinking of going back. In fact, he had come to the conclusion that people weren't what they did, or how many children they had, or who they were married to or what they were hoping for. "Personhood," he figured, was a pretty big mystery, even in the bad guys he'd encountered. Who could say what a person does or was? He smiled just thinking about it.

"Mattie, I'm a bounty hunter," he said, glancing over at the grandness which was the Ruby Mountains and thinking the answer very inadequate. Jimmy had suggested they keep the mountains on their left as they headed south out of town. "You'll hit Lamoille dead on," he said, a poor selection of words to be sure though Ronin didn't say anything in front of the youngster. He didn't want her any more alarmed that she might already be, given the drama they'd just been through in Elko. "Most of the time, I look for people the law sometimes can't find, or maybe people the law doesn't want to find because there aren't enough deputies to do the work, or the folks they're looking for are too dangerous or mean."

"Oh," she said, her eyes looking straight forward. He glanced at the snow accumulating at the top of some the peaks. He had never seen Yosemite, though he'd known people who had. Nor had he ever met a ten-year old girl as pretty or smart as she. *Neither could be any more remarkable.*

"My father said that you sometimes kill people, Mister Ronin. Is that true?"

W. W. Ronin turned away and watched as Dustsucker and Kelly smiled. It was always the gun play that interested people, particularly the children. "How many people have you killed? Are you a really good shot? How fast are you? I hear that Wild Bill Hickock is faster than you." Whatever. Few folks knew how boring his otherwise interesting life could sometimes be. When he wasn't reading reports, he was talking to people who had nothing to say because they'd already talked to a local sheriff or police chief. "And what is it that you do, anyway?" And then there was the travel. Most of it was by horse. God, he hated riding horses, but he hated railroads more.

"Yup, I guess I do," he replied. "But I try to make it a point to only kill those that need killing. I don't like killing people who might otherwise turn their lives around."

The little girl was silent, like little children ought to be, he thought — taking in the world, asking questions of it, sure. But not judging it. Hell, he didn't have anything worthwhile to say until he was in his thirties. And he was sure he'd feel the same when he was forty, even fifty years of age or more.

"Do you think there's much chance that Mister Slaven will turn his life around?" Mattie asked.

"Is that what's bothering you?" he asked.

"Well, it's not so much as bothering me as the fact that he's following us."

All three men turned their heads. Sure enough, a little bit of dust was kicking up behind them. And that damn yellow shirt, it was a sure give away.

"Stir up a cloud," he said to Dustsucker and Kelly, "and then circle back behind us. We'll slow down a bit."

"You can't be going any slower than you already are," Kelly said, looking at Slade who had already taken off at a fast gallop.

"We'll pick it up then, and then pull into those trees ahead. You can meet us there." Ronin said, realizing that if they merely stopped, or slowed down and then stopped, Slade and Kelly would never be able to take up their rear.

Kelly was gone and was gaining on Dustsucker when Mattie said, "You don't think he's the kind of man who will turn his life around then." Ronin shrugged.

"Look, Mattie. There's not a whole lot in life that I don't find interesting. I love a mystery. I'm interested in a man or woman who says one thing and does another. Fast gun play pleases me, oddly enough, and I'm good at it. But I'd much rather take a hand or a foot to man who needs a beating, because it gives him an opportunity to pull himself up out of the gutter I just put him in, apologize and determine to be a better man afterwards."

He looked back at Slavin, who had slowed, perhaps to consider what the faster riders were doing. They paused for a moment by a tree. Ronin smiled. "And I like long walks on the beach, good books and a cold beer, but that doesn't mean that you're ever get to know me, or understand me or become the woman you're meant to be by trying to figure out what all the adults around you are doing. The important journey is inside you, little girl. Everybody has their own journey. You shouldn't ignore yours."

"I'm not sure I understand," Mattie said, looking back at Slavin, who had begun to pick up his pace.

"Maybe not. Hopefully we'll return to our conversation, Mattie. But right now, we're going to figure out what this man wants, and whether it's his intent to cause further trouble. Let's go," he said, kicking his horse into a fast trot.

A mile or so later, Slaven was calling to them from behind. "Mister Ronin!" he said. Ronin pulled up on his reins, putting himself between the two of them. Mattie was closest to the mountains, and to Dustsucker and Kelly who were now less than a hundred yards away, hidden behind some trees but well within range with their rifles. Kelly had dismounted so as to take a supported shooting position.

"Mister Slaven, I have to say I'm a little surprised to see you shopping out here."

"Shopping?"

"You were looking for shoes last I saw you, boots perhaps."

"Oh, right," he said, pulling his feet out of the stirrups long enough to show Ronin the bottom of his soles. "Sorry to slip up on you like this, Miss," he nodded to Mattie, who immediately looked away.

"State your business, Mister Slaven. I'm a nervous man stopping in the middle of the desert to talk to someone I do not know."

"Tell your men that I mean you no harm," he said.

"My men, Mister Slaven?"

"In the trees there," he said, gesturing to Dustsucker and Kelly, who were only partially obscured. Ronin raised his hand and motioned. Dustsucker's horse began loping toward them. Kelly stayed behind cover, his 1873 Winchester resting in the crotch of an olive tree pointing in their direction. "And please, call me Ian."

"I'll call you a dead man in a minute Mister Slaven, if I don't hear why you've stopped me."

"Fair enough," he said, tugging at a tear in his shirt so as to keep warm. A cool breeze suggested a cold night in the Rubies if they didn't get a move on. The cowboy was shorter than he remembered, maybe 5'8", a hundred and fifty pounds which was enough to flesh him out. He was well muscled, sported a mustache, had very large hands, and was maybe on the far end of his twenties.

"Mister Slaven, I'm waiting," Ronin said as Dustsucker pulled up to them, framing Mattie in-between them should trouble arise. "Ian?" he asked.

"I'm about to say it. Give me a chance."

"Okay."

"I don't have anywhere to go, Mister Ronin. Mister Clark has made it clear that there's no work in town, and I'm afraid I got onto his bad side anyway."

"That's too bad, son…" Ronin started to say.

"Wait a minute sir, if you would. Fact is I'd like to go with you. I've got my own food and I hear you've got a lot to teach a young man like me."

"Son, I'm no school teacher. I'm sorry."

"No sir, but you were a preacher, I hear. So I'm hoping you've got a good heart."

Dustsucker smiled. If anyone had a good heart, his friend William Washington Ronin did. Raised a Yankee, but choosing to fight alongside of his father in a Confederate Cavalry regiment because his father "needed him too," Ronin had said, before telling him he was an abolitionist at heart, but hated the Federal Government telling everyone what to do. He'd gone home to his mother after the war, and to divinity school after that. A church and a stint with the Pinkertons followed, all of it adding up to an incredibly gracious heart, when a heart is what one needed.

"Son?"

"I need a second chance, sir. And I'm afraid I won't get one if I go back to where I came from."

"There is no back, son. There's only forward." Dustsucker smiled. He had heard that before.

"That's why I came out to talk to you, sir. I think I know where your midget friend is, sir. I'd be happy to accompany you along the way if I can be useful. And to be frank, I need to."

Ronin looked at Dustsucker, who was still smiling and then motioned to Kelly who lowered his rifle. It looked like they were taking on a new partner. But it was important to get Clark's little girl to safety before nightfall. "You say you think you know where he is?" he asked, looking at the boy in a new way.

"He told me he was headed to Fort Ruby, sir, maybe a month or so ago. What he didn't know I didn't say."

"What's that?" Dustsucker asked.

"Fort Ruby is pretty much gone, sir. A pile of sticks and stones, maybe a shack or two. If he's intending to live there, he'll have quite a surprise coming when winter sets in. I expect he's moved on by now."

"Well let's go find him, son. Ian, meet Deputy Sheriff Marcus T. Slade, from Carson City." Dustsucker nodded. "And Sheriff Tom Kelly, from Virginia City." Kelly nodded, too.

"Never been to your counties, gentlemen," Slaven said. "Always been a Salt Lake boy until I moved to Fort Ruby a few years ago."

"Didn't think we'd seen you before, Mister Slaven," Dustsucker said. "Not many people in these parts we don't know."

"Ian, sir. I've never been in trouble before, until the other night that is. Always been a soldier, sirs, at Fort Ruby actually. I'm afraid I'm also not much for card playing or drinking, 'Word of Wisdom,' you know."

"Oh, God! You're not just from Salt Lake City," Ronin said, "You're Mormon."

"Second generation, sir, a true believer."

"Let's ride," Ronin said, shaking his head and missing the fact that neither Kelly nor Slade knew anything about what he was saying. But the precocious Miss Clark — all ten years of her, thank you and all grown up — was all lit up and laughing.

Chapter 20

RANCH TIME

Myron Pixley opened the door to his Lamoille Valley home and greeted his guests. "Jim said you were coming. I kind of expected you earlier in the afternoon. Is everything okay?"

Ronin looked back at Dustsucker, who looked at Kelly who was already untying Mattie Clark's satchel from her horse and appeared to be in a hurry. Since no one said anything, Ronin offered his hand. "W. W. Ronin," he said, "at your service, and with what appears to be the not-so-quick delivery of Jim's daughter, Mattie."

"Yup, we know each other," Pixley said, smiling.

"We certainly do," Mattie chimed in. She curtsied and then gave Pixley a hug. A few seconds later, Kelly dropped her oversize valise at her feet. "I imagine they're pretty anxious to get rid of me, Mister Pixley. I've been chattering all the way from Elko!"

The man laughed. "You never were the quiet sort," he responded. "But the missus and me will appreciate having you here, Mattie. We're about ready to sit down for supper. Wanna take your bag back to your room?"

"Yes sir," she said, running down the hallway dragging the red and black cut velvet suitcase behind her.

"The damned thing needs wheels," Kelly said, shaking his head.

"I imagine you're happy to see her go, fellas. She can be quite the rattle box. Funny thing, don't you think? Jim isn't all that talkative. Maybe it's his wife?"

"Can't tell you, Mister Pixley, never met her," Ronin replied. "We'll be going now." Kelly and Slade stood by the doorway, patting at their pants to stir some warmth before heading out into the evening cold.

"You sure as hell will not! Dinner's practically on the table and a friend of mine is stopping by. Says he's got some information for you. Are you looking for a little man, about circus size?"

Kelly and Dustsucker nodded.

"Well, apparently he's seen 'em. Had a bit of a run in with him, actually."

Ronin's ears perked up, but not before Dustsucker's lips uttered, "I imagine we *can* stay a while," he said, tapping his stomach now as well. We'd only be setting up camp an hour or so from here. Might as well warm the middle parts, I always say!" Ronin smiled. He'd never heard Dustsucker use the phrase before, but it was descriptive. Everything the deputy cared about was within a foot of his waist, up or down — it didn't matter.

"Hell, you boys can stay all night if you like," Pixley guffawed. "Get a fresh run for the mountains in the morning. No need to be out there shivering when you can lay your blankets here by the fire. After dinner, we'll paint our tonsils and make some noise!"

Pixley put his arm around Slade, who was a good hundred pounds heavier than him, and not much less given that both of them couldn't get through the archway into the house dining room, despite trying. A long, dark pine table was set for eight. Ronin reached for the water immediately.

"You're only a dozen or so miles from Elko, Myron, right? Sure as hell felt like more."

"We're about 20 miles away," he answered. "We're close enough to appreciate the big city amenities, but far enough away not to be invited to choir practice." The men laughed. "It works out," Pixley said. "I'm not much of a Presbyterian anyway."

Mattie approached the table with Pixley's wife. They were carrying steaming bowlfuls of food. "Look's like John's is coming up the porch now, Mister Ronin."

"Good morning, friends!" Pixley's friend said when he opened the door.

"It's evening, John," Pixley said, laughing. "John Maverick meet W. W. Ronin." Ronin got up from the table and extended his hand.

"Pleased to meet you, John."

"This here is Marcus T. Slade, from Ormsby County, and Tom Kelly, from Storey County. Don't let the badges put you off, John. They're here about the midget."

"Now Myron, I'm not sure we should be calling the man a 'midget,' dear," Pixley's wife said.

"She's the Presbyterian, Mister Ronin. I worship under a quilt most Sunday mornings. Don't need me a church. Hell, the day they build a church in this valley I'll be packing up and moving on."

"Oh, pa! I was just trying to help," she said. Mattie snickered.

"John Maverick, gentlemen. And if you don't mind me saying, you can call him a midget or a son of a bitch for all I care, as long as you don't call me late for fried chicken!" Laughter filled the room as Pixley lifted a chair off of the wall for his friend. "We've been in and around this valley for years, Mister Ronin. So we pretty much see everything here or in Elko, Halleck and so on. Myron and me don't miss much. So when a goddamned midget rolls one of my horses with a whip..."

"He took a whip to one of your horses?" Ronin asked.

"Sure did, a couple of days back. Caught his leg as sure as I have your attention," Maverick insisted. "So I jumped off my wagon to see what the hell was going on, when the son of a bitch — no light headed man, if you know what I'm saying

— cracked his goddamned whip at me! Bad enough he injured my horse, but at me? Well, that wasn't going to do. So I look at my horse, she's fine, and I grab my rifle and I've cocked the damn thing when his woman — an otherwise pretty little lady save for a gold tooth in the middle of her mouth — raises an old Patterson revolver my way and tells me to go on about my business. 'My business,' I say? 'This is my business,' I said. But she just kept that rusty old piece of iron pointed at my head until he got down from his wagon hell bent for trouble, walks on over to and pulls my rifle from my hands. I never was so mad!"

Pixley looked over at Ronin. "He was pretty angry, all right — plumb cactus over the whole thing."

"You saw this, Mister Pixley?"

"Call me Myron, son. You're sitting at my supper table."

"Of course, sir. So you saw this?"

"I did not. But I sure as sin have heard about it, all day yesterday and now today again!" Pixley and Maverick broke into laughter, pounding the table and slapping each other's backs.

"He hurt that horse real bad, Mister Ronin," Maverick continued, "and nearly hurt me."

"Enough of this sorry talk, Myron. Would someone say grace?" his wife asked. The laughter stopped with a snort. Pixley was clearly not pleased. Mattie laughed.

"Mattie," Ronin said.

"I'm sorry, sir."

"Mister Pixley, I'd be happy to offer a prayer," Ronin continued. Dustsucker looked over at Kelly who just shrugged. In the three years he'd known the man, Dusty had yet to see the bounty hunter anything other than a benediction to a bad man prior to killing him.

"Sure thing, Mister Ronin," Pixley said. "We'd be right happy to have you do so, wouldn't we mother?" Missus Pixley nodded.

"Let's fold our hands, then," Ronin said. He waited until every head was bowed and every hand was folded. "Almighty God," he began, "come and bless this meal tonight. And do not tolerate any fright. Keep us safe, as we eat and pray. For someday soon, we'll kill and not say. A simple reason for this man to live. A simple prayer, his life please give. And for the task before us now, grace for the meal and journey, allow." He took a breath. "Amen!" he said, unfolding his hands and picking up a knife and fork.

"Mister Ronin, I don't know that I've ever heard a prayer like that," Pixley said. "Course as I told you, I don't get to church much. Ma, do they pray like that in Elko?"

"They don't pray like that in Elko, Myron."

"Well there you have it, Mister Ronin. They don't pray like that at the Presbyterian Church in Elko."

"I don't know that I've ever heard you pray," Dustsucker said.

"Are you some kind of Mormon?" Pixley asked.

"Not hardly, Myron. I'm just a man who's determined to see another man die."

Chapter 21
CHICKEN LEGS

"I brought a Mormon with me though," Ronin said, lifting a platter of chicken from the table and offering it to his host.

"Pardon?" Pixley said, taking a hold of a couple of crispy-fried chicken legs. He passed the plate to his left.

"A Mormon," Ronin repeated. "I brought a Mormon with me. He's out by your barn with the horses. I'm thinking we should invite him in."

"Well, hell yes!" he said. "It's cold out. What's he doing out there?"

"Tending the horses, I imagine." Ronin slid a thigh off of the plate with his fork, counted the pieces of chicken and wondered if he should take another. "He's probably guessed by now that we're staying the night. Pass the gravy Mister Maverick?" Pixley's friend nodded, as Missus Pixley stood and grabbed a near empty water pitcher.

"Bring him in, Pa," she said. "I'll set another place at the table."

Slaven was standing at the door by the time Pixley opened it, napkin in hand. "Excuse me, sir. I didn't mean to startle you," he said as Pixley, a petite man in his mid-thirties, took a sudden step backward, dropping his napkin and grabbing instinctively at a shotgun hidden beside an upright piano in the living room. His hands came up empty.

"Mister Pixley?" Slaven said, eyeing the shotgun sitting next to the upright grand.

"Mister Slavin, welcome to my house," he stuttered, picking up the napkin. I'm Myron Pixley, your host."

"Thank you, sir. I'm waiting for Mister Ronin and a couple of other fellows. I wonder if you..."

Pixley interrupted, pointing to the dining room. "We were just talking about you, Slavin. Your friends say you're a Mormon?"

"To be frank sir, I just met those men. If being a Saint is a problem, I'll be happy to wait outside by the barn."

"Relax son, it's cold outside, and I'm just foolin' with you. The Reverend Ronin just said grace. We're about to have something to eat."

He took off his hat and shook his head as he hung his gun belt on some pegs by the door. "Thank you, sir. That's very kind."

"Missus Pixley, I do declare this is the best fried chicken I ever ate," Dustsucker said from the other room.

"Pardon us for laughing at Mattie's story, ma'am. We're not often around children."

"She may be ten years old, Mister Ronin, but I'd hardly count on Mattie Clark being a child."

"Ma'am?"

"Missus Pixley, please don't burden my father's friends with such stories," Mattie said.

"I'm just saying, Mattie. The man who thinks of you as child is going to have another thing coming." She turned and went into the kitchen to draw more water.

"I'm not following, Missus Pixley." Ronin put his hand in front of Mattie, only to have it pushed away. He looked at her sharply. The look was returned. Dustsucker shrugged as Ronin looked his way.

"I'll be back in a moment," she called from the kitchen. "I've got to step out back to get some water."

"I've met a few youngsters," Dustsucker offered, "who were old before their time. Had a sort of wisdom about them, they did. Take Little Wolf, for example, the Washoe boy. He's probably in his early teens. His father, Happy Hands, is as real a medicine man as I've ever seen. It's as if something's rubbed off on the youngster." He took a spoonful of rehydrated corn and put it on his plate. "Truth be told, I'm proud to call *both* of them my friends. I don't care what their ages are."

"A twelve-year-old Indian is equal to any white man I know," Mattie said.

"And you know a twelve-year-old Indian boy?" Ronin asked, laughing, as Slavin came ino the room. "Take it easy, Ian. We're not laughing at you," he said, standing up and gesturing to the empty chair next to him. "Mattie here was just telling us about some Indian boys she knows."

"I was not," Mattie protested.

"Now, now, let's settle down," Pixley said as he took his seat, looking around for his wife. "I want to tell you men what I know about the short little man you're looking for, in the event I don't get up as early as you do tomorrow morning. It's Sunday, you know."

"Yes, sir," Dustsucker said. Kelly and Dustsucker leaned in to listen as Slavin gestured toward the chicken dish and Pixley's wife called from the kitchen, her head inside the outside door.

"Myron?"

"Yes, dear."

"Do you know of any reason why there should be a man sleeping under one of our hay stacks?"

"Dear?"

"A man, under one of our haystacks," she said, returning to the dining room after shutting the door. "An honest day's labor, I said. And you said, 'Don't worry dear. The Shoshone will do exactly what I say and then leave.' And I told you, I don't want him here after dark. 'He won't be here after dark,' you said. But *here* is exactly where you said he wouldn't be — his feet sticking out from underneath one of our hay stacks. Big ugly brown boots sticking through the pile of hay I raked together yesterday."

"Dear, the man left a couple of hours ago. Before Mattie came."

"Well then Myron Pixley, whose legs am I looking at outside my kitchen window?"

Chapter 22
A ONE-EYED NAP CATCHER

Kelly kicked at the boots until the boots shook themselves awake. "What the hell?" someone yelled underneath a pile of dry grass stacked in front of the Pixley's barn.

"You didn't see this?" Kelly asked Slavin.

"I wasn't looking for this," Slavin said, pulling a gun from his belt.

"Put it away," Ronin scolded.

"I just thought …"

"… you're not thinking, Ian. You don't know who that is."

"Indians don't wear boots," Mattie said, "none that I've seen, anyway."

Ronin kicked at the grass stack until a hand appeared. Grabbing it with his right hand, he slid his left hand onto the back of a black man's elbow when Mattie Clark said, "I do believe I know who that is!" And the distraction of a wild-eyed ten-year-old telling a yard full of adults what she knew about the universe and was all too happy to tell was enough for the outlaw Sam Mills to get a leg up and an arm free from a man who just moments before was holding tightly onto a chicken thigh and wondering whether he should take another one off a new friend's serving plate.

Mills plowed into Ronin head first, kicking up yard dirt and stone, pushing him over onto his back. And then standing straight up like a lodge pole pine sprung from the granite dust it was planted in, he drove a dark brown boot into Ronin's crotch, levering him into a sitting position so that he sucked wind like a teenage soprano. "Oh, my god," Mattie breathed.

Kelly reached for his gun, but the badge from Virginia City came up empty when he realized that he had left his gun belt hanging on a hat rack by the front door of Myron Pixley's home. Slavin drew his. "Hold it right there, you son of a bitch," he said, as the one-eyed nap catcher scooped up a pile of grass and leaves and tossed it in Slavin's direction.

Slavin ducked instead of dropping the hammer on the man. Dustsucker grabbed Slavin's gun, shouting, "Clark wants this man alive." He yanked it from Slavin's hands, his finger between the hammer and the back strap, and whipped it toward the house. "Mister, how about you just settle down?" he shouted to the figure he figured had to be Sam Mills. A long scar fell from a dark and dry empty eye socket, scoring a deep line down the man's face from his right eyelid to his upper lip. And he was black, definitely black, not brown like an Indian, or red like a white man who'd spent too much time in the sun. "Nobody wants to hurt you," Dustsucker said, though he knew that to be a lie. Everybody wanted to hurt this sorry son of a bitch, and Dustsucker wouldn't be waiting second in line to cleave a hole into the head of the man who'd just hurt his best friend.

"Fuck you," Sam Mills said.

"No, fuck you," Ronin said, squeezing the words between his lips and as he pivoted and grabbed Sam Mills' left leg from behind. No man was allowed to put his foot on his privates, he'd explained to a good number of men who had either succeeded or tried. The barnyard intruder tumbled forward and landed face down. Ronin grabbed both legs. Dustsucker sat down on the black man's back, as Ronin rolled around to the deputy's right, grabbed the hairs on the back of the man's head like they were reins on a wild horse and handed them to his friend. Sam Mills began howling like an injured yard hound, his head straight up in the air, his belly pressed flat to the ground, his hands hitting the dirt like a buff-bellied field chukar.

"There goes a perfectly good Sunday morning," Pixley said as he pulled a coil of rope off a chair outside the house. "Tie 'em up," he said. "We've still got dinner to finish. And I'm sure as hell not going to have a one-eyed Negro hiding outside my house."

"Mister Pixley," the youngster said.

"Yes, Mattie."

"His being black or white, it doesn't hardly matter, does it?"

"Well, I imagine it doesn't, Mattie."

"Well then, let's not hear any more about people differently colored than you and me, sir," she said. "Red and yellow, black and white. They are precious in His sight," she pronounced as if she were reading the scriptures in the midst of a shit storm.

"That's right Mattie," Missus Pixley said, smiling. "Jesus loves the little children, *all* the children of the world."

The men looked at each other. "Mormon words?" Kelly asked Slavin, who was stooping to retrieve his gun from underneath a Manzanita bush, where it had landed next to the front porch. Slavin shook his head. He'd never heard the words before. They weren't in the *Book of Mormon* or the *Bible* either. He'd read them both. He was pretty sure they weren't anyway.

"Sunday School," Mattie said.

"Yup," Ronin nodded, pulling the man onto his feet and kicking him in the ass so that he began to walk toward the house. "But some of God's children — this man in particular — are less precious than others."

Chapter 23

ALL TIED UP

Ronin pushed Mills into a green Adirondack chair out front Pixley's home. The porch had a nice view of the Ruby Mountains and the porch's posts — plentiful and sturdy — contributed toward a secure enclosure as Kelly and Dustsucker wrapped rope around brackets and balusters so that even a circus monkey couldn't work his way loose.

"Should we finish dinner, Myron?" Ronin asked, stopping to take a breath. "Or would you prefer to put this man on the back of a horse and head for town?" He smiled. "It'd take a hardy son of a bitch, if you ask me, but I imagine someone would be up to it if the only alternative was him staying the night in your home."

"I'm thinking of a couple of chicken legs, Ronin, to be frank, and my wife's delicious peppercorn gravy. Mm-mmm," he said. "I'd rather not be interrupted if you think this man will be safe out here for the time being."

"You let me up and I'll cut you!" Mills said, pulling at the rope's knots.

"You'll do no such thing," Mattie Clark said, surprising everyone who stood there, including the accused, who was trussed up sort of squat-legged, his ankles tethered together underneath a large plant that had been placed onto his lap to help him stay still while he was being tied up. The final picture was that of a man tied to a small tree tied to a large porch. Even if he got loose, he'd have a thorn tree tied to his lap.

"The holly tree looks good on you," Ronin said, "I hope it's not too prickly."

"Fuck you, lawman."

"You're the guest of these men," Mattie continued, "whether you like it or not, Sam Mills. You've already killed your best friend, and you likely feel real bad about that. I imagine you're going to feel that way for a very long time. But if you keep terrorizing folks like you did a moment ago — hiding in people's haystacks, kicking Mister Ronin in the privates and tossing words about like they have no meaning or consequence — you're only going to dig yourself a six-foot hole. My dad wouldn't be at all happy with that, no he would not."

Missus Pixley stood on the porch smiling, by the door in between the porch railing and one of the giant picture windows that looked east toward the Ruby range. *Mattie's mother would be proud, if she could be here to see the way she is addressing this human being, even if he is all bound-up with sin and rope.* "Mattie, you come inside with me, would you?" she said. "I'm sure the men will treat Mister Mills with respect, given that he's only been accused. He hasn't been tried yet," she harped — at least it sounded that way to Mister Pixley, who was looking at Ronin, Kelly and Slade for guidance, unwilling to put his fingers in his ears despite his fingers wanting to crawl in there. The three of them smiled and shrugged.

"I imagine we could get him to Elko," Maverick said.

"John, that might be the best idea," Slade responded. "We can't be going back and forth between Lamoille and Elko tomorrow again. We've got to push on. We've got business ahead."

"That's what I was thinking, Mister Slade," Maverick said. "Myron? How about we have our chicken and then ride all night into Elko with this man in tow? We could take a room at the Depot Hotel to rest up, have a hot bath and then have a nice early supper before heading back."

"You untie me and I'll find you some hot water," Mills said, still seething.

"Now Mills, you keep this up and I'll be the first one to make sure you get what you're asking for. Every one of these men on the porch is your match."

"I don't think so, lawman."

"I'm no lawman," Ronin said. "But I'll serve you up whatever it is you think you need to keep quiet, I surely will, lawman or not."

"Mister Ronin," Pixley said, "how about the rest of us go in and get started. You continue your little chat with our prisoner for a while? I'm thinking John and I can handle a midnight ride into Elko. But I want to get some food first."

"That'll be fine."

The men followed the women into the living room, before Mattie and Missus Pixley called them into the dining room to resume their meal. Ronin looked over at Sam Mills and asked, "What are you looking at?"

"I'm looking at a man whose ass I just kicked."

"Not hardly, Mills. But should you want a second opportunity, I'll be happy to give you one when I get back from Wells."

Chapter 24

HOME BY CHRISTMAS

John Maverick and Myron Pixley were happy to take the credit for finding Jim Finnerty's killer hiding under a haystack, given that the men in search of Toro Latigo feared any sort of public announcement about their involvement would drive Latigo and his companion deeper into hiding. What they wanted, they explained, was an easy catch and a quick return to Carson City, a town Ronin was now calling his "new home," which made the two lawmen smile as they left Lamoille. They understood Ronin's attachment to be to a person, not a place, and that person was Emma Nauman.

Ronin wasn't as religious as he used to be, having left the priesthood so many years ago that he had to make up his prayers rather than recite them from memory. And the experience of hearing him pray at the Pixley's table convinced them that a change in Ronin's life needed to be made. Perhaps it was already coming. The ex-preacher didn't have as much fire in his belly as he used to. Nor was he as focused as they'd known him previously to be.

Not that that was a problem, though both men were concerned that Ronin's new, peaceful persona might not measure up to the situation at hand. Not having Ronin "fully on task" might put the rest of them in danger, Kelly said while pointing the way south toward Hastings Pass.

"Look, I'm confused," Dustsucker said to his friend as they skirted Huntington Valley along the edge of the mountains. "One minute you're playing cowboy with these fellows, and the next minute you're telling people to put their guns away and talk things out."

"There's a problem with that?" Ronin replied, pulling up on Jackson's reins so that the two of them could ride together.

There were three passes over the Ruby Mountains: Secret Pass, which was too far north to be of any use; Harrison Pass, which would still put them north of Shanty Town; and Hastings Pass, which, while out of the way, would drop them south of Ruby Lake. It had taken Ronin a couple of days to convince the others they should head so far south. But Pixley's observations about Latigo offered a choice. The little man and his lady had likely stayed in the ruins of Fort Ruby.

"Guess I'm used to more of a hard-charging man than the hand-holding preacher I saw back at Pixley's," Dustsucker said, hoping they could talk a bit given the distance. There was a spring at the summit which Pixley had said was "drinkable, but barely." He hoped to iron things out before they stopped for lunch.

"I didn't beat the shit out of Mills? Is that the issue?" Ronin asked, looking over at his friend, who wasn't usually so talkative.

"No, that isn't it. You were keeping Clark's confidence that we get Mills back to Elko safely. I understood that. Your friend doesn't think Mills will get a fair shake given his color or criminal history. I don't know. I don't need to know. But if you don't mind me saying, you seem, well, to put it frankly, more settled than previously. And I don't understand it."

"And if I do mind you saying, Dusty?"

"Well, then a good friend might ask anyway. Ronin, listen. I'm concerned for our safety. It's not like we haven't misjudged these miscreants before. Alvira already shot you once. And Toro, the short son of a bitch, has tried to kill us a couple of times. We make any more mistakes and one of us is surely going to wind up dead."

Ronin sighed. Dustsucker was right. What he really wanted to do was head home. The Silver State had called to him pretty deeply while he was sitting at Emma Nauman's place trying to get his wind back. It was the second time he'd recuperated there, of course, so maybe his familiarity with the school was causing him to feel fonder toward it and her than he actually did. He didn't think he'd be settling down so soon. But something was causing him to feel that home might mean the hills and rills of northern Nevada.

Emma Nauman had grown on him, and while he hadn't experienced the sudden feelings he'd felt previously for some women — Bovary for instance, or whatever her real name was. Even Ellie Mae might have stirred him had there been enough time to explore. But his fondness for Emma ran deep, especially after staying there this last time. He imagined Emma making biscuits in the mission kitchen prior to any of the children getting up. He remembered their nights together, where despite the weak protestations each brought to their feather bed, they'd felt and almost acted like husband and wife.

"I'm listening, Dusty. And I'll admit to being somewhat torn ..."

"Torn?" Dustsucker said. "Changed is more like it."

And maybe that was the case. He *had* changed. Why shouldn't people notice? Whatever he hadn't finished with after leaving the Saint John's Episcopal Church in Wichita, whatever he hadn't fully put away, having taken off his priestly vestments and robes, he'd set somewhere at the mission this time. Some closet. Some back room. Some hilltop or sandy bank along the Carson River. He was no longer the same. Something *had* gone out of him.

"I don't know, Dusty. Maybe I am different," he said, as they began to climb a sandy path east toward the mountain's edge. "Maybe some of the fight has gone out of me. Maybe I've been punched too much or shot at too many times ..."

"Or maybe your knees are weak," Dustsucker said, laughing, alluding to the time he'd spent with Emma.

My knees? Real funny. "I don't think my involvement with Emma has anything to do with it, Dusty. Do you?"

Ronin's best friend pulled up on his reins and stopped. "I'm just saying, if you've been with her things are going to be different. Not that I have any recent experience ..."

"No, not that you do," Ronin said, laughing. "And Dusty, being a southern boy, I'll not say where I've been or what I've done. It's just none of your damn business."

"And I'm not asking, Ronin, I'm just raising the point. If you don't have the fight in you to do this because of a woman, then tell us now. Kelly's lost his wife. Slavin, despite his age, is just a kid, and then there's me. The last thing any of us need is to get into a fire fight and have the one man we all count on not be able to perform."

Ronin lifted the short Colt from his holster. It always settled him to touch the gun, a gift from his former congregation. He lifted it into view and opened the loading gate to bring the usual five — allowing for the firing pin to rest safely on an empty cylinder — up to an actionable six. He removed a cartridge from his belt and pushed it into the hole. "I'll be ready, Dusty. Just let me clear my head. Seeing that little girl back there, dropping her off like that with people who might have been her parents if Jim hadn't already been, stirs me to thinking that I want something similar in my life before things get too late. You know what I mean?"

"I do," Dustsucker said.

"Tell the others we'll be fine," he said, placing the pearl handled Colt back into its holster and pulling the longer gun from its keeper sitting cross-wise at his waist. He let it rest on his thigh and opened the gate. "Tell them I'm doing as well as I can, having just had a piece of lung shot out of me and having been whipped at and warned by lesser men, shorter men, less caring men who'll kick my ass or put a bullet in my head if I come back."

"I'm not following," Dustsucker said.

"Tell 'em we're going to even things up sometime in the next few days. We're going to put a little man into a short man's grave and a little woman into a tiny prison cell. Tell 'em they've got nothing to worry about. I'm man enough to do what needs to be done and they are, too."

"Thanks, William."

"You bet, Marcus," Ronin said, smiling — thankful he had a friend who didn't mind speaking the truth to him when truth needed to be spoken. "Now let's ride," he said. "I'm getting older by the minute, and I want to be home before Christmas."

Chapter 25
A TROUSSEAU, A WHIP, AND A BED

"I'm just wanting to be brave, Alvira. I didn't mean anything by it."

He wiped his eyes and remembered the pain of being sent down into what he thought was a well, only to find a cave inside. The whole experience had been frightening. A small boy, a tiny hole, the diminished expectations his family had of him — "They're not less, Antonio, they're just different," his mother had said, though she couldn't quite say it without smiling — had damaged him in ways he hadn't understood until his family was gone. Normal people didn't act that way. Nor were normal people always afraid.

He was fearful also that his relationship with Alvira was cooling.

Alvira, who had never seen a grown man cry before, even if he was a very small grown man, was unprepared for the show of emotion and didn't understand any of what was behind it. Tony hardly understood either, which is often the case with wicked men or bad women, with righteous men and good women, too. "I'm just saying that people can have different views on things," she said. "Everyone's not the same. They don't have to be."

But Tony, who had spent his entire life — all twenty-three years of it — wanting to be the same as everyone else, could only hear his mother's voice speaking. "I'm trying to make you understand," he shouted. "I don't want to go down in the hole," he said, stomping his feet until a light appeared in a ranch house window almost a hundred yards away. "Uh-oh," he said, wiping his eyes. Half a minute later someone appeared at the door with a rifle.

Alvira and Toro knelt down by the back of the wagon, where a large stack of clothing and blankets sat — "my trousseau," she had told him as they'd hurriedly thrown things into the wagon a few months before in Virginia City. "Why do we need a trousseau?" he asked, not understanding that some women have expectations of a relationship that are different than men, not that understanding such would come naturally to a man who had never had an emotionally mature relationship with anyone.

"What do we need with a whip?" she had responded, which was odd given that he was using it at the time, cracking it above the heads of animals he was trying to move, he being so small and they being so much bigger. Occasionally, he'd used it to defend himself. He'd want to use it to defend the two of them, he explained as they rode out of Virginia City toward the Ruby Mountains, which is where they were now, with a fella looking at them with a great big rifle in his arms.

"What's going on out there?" the man shouted. He sounded old. "Who's over there?" the old man shouted before Latigo figured that he could take him, even at this distance, with the 1873 Springfield "Trapdoor" rifle he'd taken off a man in Elko the year before. Generally thought of as simple to operate, a soldier could put eight rounds per minute onto a paper target, or anywhere else for that matter. With practice, Toro had learned to fire as many as a dozen rounds per minute, making the rifle a highly efficient killing machine. He'd wondered about trading the full-length rifle for something smaller, like the carbines used by cavalry soldiers. At 52 inches, the long gun was almost as long as he was tall.

He pulled three brass cartridges from a box in the wagon and stuck them in-between the fingers of his left hand. He pulled the hammer back and listened to it click three times. He smiled, lifting the case-hardened breach block so as to push a .45-70 brass shell into the gun. "Watch this," he said. And Alvira Fae Livestock — who didn't have much use for guns until she met the little man a year ago on a Virginia City porch, watched as he drove a .405 grain piece of lead into the doorway, missing the man but hitting a picture on the wall behind him. The door slammed shut. Latigo pulled the hammer back a second time, and lifting a second cartridge from between his fingers, loaded again. He slammed the breach lock into place and this time hit the man and his lamp as they stared out the window. "There," he said, "lights out."

And Alvira Fae Livestock, who happened to watch the same man kill her sister "accidentally" two months ago, collapsed behind the wagon wheel into the dirt, sobbing.

"Why did you kill him?" she wailed, tears staining her cheeks and jacket. "He wasn't doing anything to us."

"He might have," Latigo said, pulling a third shell from his left hand and loading the trapdoor one more time. "Once a man gets curious about some things, he doesn't stop," he said, walking toward the house. "You coming?"

"Coming where?" she sobbed.

"To the house, of course. I believe I found us a bed to sleep in."

Chapter 26
UNCLE BILLY

It was about midnight when W. W. Ronin got off his horse and walked into one of the cabins. It was all that remained of Fort Ruby. "I was counting on something warmer," he said to Dustsucker and Kelly, who were clearly just as disappointed. Diamonds of light were scattered across a light snow. The moon cast a lengthy shadow through a series of painted log buildings, the chink between the logs long dried out, their roofs blown away in the Nevada sun. "I don't think I've ever seen anything like this," Ronin said, pulling his duster closed, buttoning the front and the back.

"You mean the upright logs?" Dustsucker said, shivering. "It's fairly common in these parts."

Ronin looked through an empty window toward a single horizontal log cabin, the exception to the palisade-style log buildings that predominated at the fort. Poles were stuck deeply into sandy soil, anchored by six years of sturdy service as a military installation and telegraph station. The fort had protected stagecoaches, the pony express and the transcontinental telegraph line — and had helped to control the Goshute and Paiute Indians.

"Hard to believe this is halfway between Salt Lake and Carson City, isn't it Dusty? I'm talking about the juxtaposition," he said. "Dark and light, old and new, here and there, the living and the dead."

"I guess so," Dustsucker responded. He was not particularly given to poetry, though he'd picked up a volume of Emerson's poems one time after a lecture and found them unsatisfying.

"Jimmy said the fort closed when the transcontinental railroad was completed. I just didn't expect it to look so desolate," Ronin said. "In time everything changes, I guess."

"That's for sure," Kelly said, thinking of his own life and looking at what remained of what the Army had come to call "the worst post in the west." Fewer than a dozen buildings laid empty in the nighttime desert. What remained of an officer's residence was piled along the edge of a small pond of water amidst a few trees, stacks of stone and wood and a couple of privies.

"At least we'll have a place to sit," Ronin said.

Dustsucker laughed. "If we get started with some of this wood we could have a fire. I wonder if any of the chimneys still draw?" he said, looking at the soot around one.

"At least there's that," Ian Slavin offered, before getting off of his horse and walking over to the log cabin Ronin had been looking at earlier. "The California Volunteers built this fort," Slavin said, "this one and another one near Salt Lake City. Ever hear of the Goshute War?" he asked.

Ronin shook his head.

"Diggers?" he asked.

Ronin nodded.

"The Goshute have lived here for God only knows how long. They eat lizards, gophers, snakes, pine nuts, whatever there is. And when there isn't, well, they eat insects."

"I'm okay with lizards and gophers," Dustsucker said. "I draw the line at snakes and insects."

"Me too," Ronin said.

"Well, the Goshute were killing the stage business, and there was no way the railroad could be built with all that going on. So the California Volunteers, an Army regiment, built this fort and subdued the Indians until a treaty could be signed allowing every one of the rest of us to pass and build as we pleased. It was a real collision of needs," Slavin said. "The Nevada Volunteers manned the fort after that."

Ronin looked over at Slavin, who was kneeling by the smaller of the cabins. *Collision of needs?* "How do you know all of this?" he asked. "And what's with the kneeling?"

"Uncle Billy used to live here."

"Uncle Billy?" Ronin said, looking at Dustsucker and Kelly, who were tying their horses to the uprights on a larger building next door. They shrugged.

"Well, not my Uncle Billy. I don't have an Uncle Billy," Slavin said before spitting into the dirt. "But "Uncle Billy Rogers, who put the trading post together and acted as an Indian agent, fed a good many of us who traveled through these parts. Hearty meals even. I'll forever be grateful."

"Imagine that had to be hard," Kelly said, kicking at the dust.

"Not really," Slavin said "His wife Catherine, who was at one point married to the Prophet, Joseph Smith ..."

"The Mormon prophet?" Kelly asked.

"Yup," Slavin nodded.

"... along with a good number of other women," Ronin said.

"Whatever," Slavin said, casting a sharp glance at Ronin. "Well, Catherine put in a large garden and an orchard, too. She set an example for everyone in the Ruby Valley, who went on and did the same. Lord, they had a pack of kids."

"How many?"

"Three I think, and then with the five she brought with her from Salt Lake. I guess that's eight."

"Whatever happened to them?" Ronin asked, watching Slavin get up from his knees and put his hat back on.

"Uncle Billy died four or five years back. Aunt Catherine went back to Utah when the fort closed. Billy never joined her.

He kept on ranching these parts. They were good people — true believers."

Kelly bristled. "Ian, I've been a lot of places in my life. And I've met a lot of good people. Presbyterians, Methodists, Catholics, even the Jews. They ain't all been Mormon."

"No, I reckon not," Slavin said, "but it was the Mormons who first settled Nevada, and Uncle Billy was one of them. It would do us all good to remember that. In time, the Mormons made an Eden out of places like this. You'll not find a prettier valley in Nevada than the Ruby Valley."

"It is nice," Dustsucker said.

"The emigrants along the trail called this place, 'Thousand Springs Valley.' Except for its lack of timber — though we've got ourselves a few piles I see — it's perfect."

"Right now," Ronin said, "it's one of the coldest places on earth." He stepped out of the empty building into the middle of what used to be a street. "Dusty, how's that fire coming?"

"I'm getting there."

"Good," he said. "Pull at some of the wood on these buildings if you want. I'm cold. I want a big fire and something warm to eat. And I want to be in Cave Creek by lunchtime tomorrow."

Chapter 27

IAN SLAVIN

Ian Slavin began his legal career having benefited from parents who inquired early and often as to what their young son wanted to do with his life. Unknown to both of them, Ian had decided at an early age not to become a shoemaker.

"It's not that being a cobbler isn't an honorable thing," he told his father, who seemed visibly relieved as the father did not believe his son to be equipped for such a noble and philosophical work. Even a king stoops to the maker of shoes. "I want to do something more with my life," the boy said, averting his eyes so as not to view his father's hurt. "I want to make things happen, father," he said.

The patron saint of shoemakers from ancient times, Saint Crispin, would have been confused by the boy's response, as the making of shoes provided opportunity for shoemakers to do so much more with their lives, teaching the Christian Gospel being Crispin's own life's work. But Slavin's father was not hurt. He smiled, knowing that his son didn't have the talent to be a preacher, or a writer, or a poet or a pope. Still, he was surprised to hear that his son wanted to become an attorney.

"A lawyer?" he said, "How is it you've decided to become a lawyer?" the cobbler asked. He knew that his son had never seen an attorney at work, nor had he ever talked to one so as to understand what an attorney did in his work. "You've never met an attorney," he told his son.

"Everybody knows what a lawyer is, father," Slavin said, barely ten years of age, but gaining in wisdom and stature. "Attorneys are people who make a lot of money from people who despite having too little money still have enough money to share."

Ian's father was satisfied that his boy, though a third-generation cobbler he would never be, had a good head on his shoulders, having stated one of the more profound truths of life. There is money enough for everyone. The trick is knowing where to find it.

Where Ian Slavin strayed no one can say — except that at some point in his life the fever got hold of him, suggesting that he try to better himself one giant step at a time instead of the usual shuffle, one step forward two steps back or two steps forward, one step back. Bad luck had put a giant boot to Ian Slavin's career plans.

The bane of most men in Nevada seeking quick riches on the Comstock, including the gold and silver strikes that came before and after, landed him in an unproductive silver mine in the Ruby Mountains alongside a pack of other hopeless believers intending to get rich by finding one large rock. "It would only take one, gentlemen," he was heard to say to a table full of card players before James Clark put shoe leather between his ass cheeks, launching him onto the street out front the Depot Hotel in Elko where Ronin first found him, their drawn guns greeting each other in the mid-morning sun between breakfast and lunch.

"A lawyer, really? That's all you could think of doing with your life?" Ronin asked, trying not to appear too opinionated about the young man's choices as they rode down the mountain together, knowing that some men seemingly had few choices in their lives and others apparently none. "Your parents were pleased with that?" he chuckled.

"More or less," Slavin said. "They would have preferred I'd been a pastor, I guess, or a shoemaker. But it wasn't in me."

"Me neither," Ronin said, shaking his head, "the former anyway, though I played at it for a while, or rather it played with me." The aging detective, still feeling the hole in his side from Virginia City, genuinely liked the younger man, and thought he could amount to something, though recent turns in the boy's life had suggested otherwise. "Slavin, I wasn't aware that a man could go to school to be so disagreeable."

"Now that's not fair, Mister Ronin. You hardly know me," Ian said, hoping they'd get to Fort Ruby before it began snowing. *It's simply too damn cold.*

"I'm sorry," Ronin said.

"Truth be told, I was hoping to train with an experienced solicitor."

"A solicitor, you say?" Ronin was impressed. He'd heard the word before, though given the abuses in the English legal system and the reticence of many in the colonies to admit that attorneys might be necessary to drive the American dream forward, he'd never heard a person use the word in a positive way.

"Yes, my parents hoped to attract the attention of a California firm that would allow me to practice and study at the same time ..."

"I see," Ronin said, figuring that the training of lawyers was similar to the training of doctors and priests.

"... but they're not many attorneys who will tolerate folks like me, Mister Ronin."

"Like you?"

"Common folk, Mister Ronin. My father was a shoemaker, and the money my father saved to gain someone's attention, well, it simply wasn't enough."

"What did you do?"

"I attended school, until the money ran out. Hastings College, sir," Slavin said enthusiastically, though it'd been a while since he had thought about the University of California and its legal school.

"Never heard of it."

"First law school on the West Coast, Mister Ronin. 'A temple of law and intellect,' the founder says. Perhaps you've heard of Serranus Clinton Hastings?"

"Never heard of him, either." Rich people simply didn't count in Ronin's life. It wasn't often that he spent time thinking about them.

"Really? Well, it doesn't matter. I only took a couple of courses. Despite the man working real hard to keep me there, I simply ran out of money."

"The man?"

"Hastings, sir. A real benefactor, even to the point of building apartments for the poor."

"Is that so? When was this, Ian?"

"Just a couple of years ago."

Ronin was silent. He'd initially been very impressed with the young man. And hearing that the boy had been to school, well that said something, too. But if the man was a quitter — if he let simple things like money, status or connections stand in his way, then he wasn't the man he was hoping him to be. And wasn't the man his friend or Elko needed.

"So Mister Slavin, what is it you're after?"

"I don't understand."

Dustsucker looked over and smiled. He'd heard this conversation before. You could take the ministry out of the man, but resist as he sometimes would, Ronin was still a born nurturer and mentor.

"Everyone comes to Nevada looking for something," the detective said. "What is it you're looking for?"

Kelly pulled ahead, so that he could hear Slavin's response to Ronin's question. If a man didn't know what he was looking for, how would he know if he ever found it?

"Well, that doesn't much matter either," Slavin said.

"I'm sorry?"

"Because my law days are over, Ronin. Hastings would never take me back."

"Am I missing something, Mister Slavin?"

"How do you mean?"

"Well, it seems to me that people start out in a direction for good reason. And while they may veer this way or that, they keep going in that direction even when they don't think they're headed anywhere. It's almost as if life knows what it's doing, you know?"

"You think life knows what it's doing?" Slavin asked.

"Much of the time, though I give you that there are some squirrelly turns now and then." The two men laughed as they came into the valley and the remains of Fort Ruby were coming into sight. "Where do you think your life is heading, Ian?"

Ian Slavin replayed the whole conversation in his head, as he stacked a fire against one wall of the stone-built house, the only one of its kind in the ruins that constituted the former Fort Ruby. The big mistake in his life wasn't dropping out of school, despite what Ronin said. It was believing that school was the whole point of it all, and maybe lawyering, too. The dry-socket which was his mining career — a stupid attempt to regain everything he had lost in one amazing moment — never came to be. And maybe heading back to school wasn't meant to be, either.

He threw an old window frame on to the fire and stood there wondering as the other men began to unpack for the night. Maybe the series of zigs and zags that made up his life wasn't all that bad after all. His life was still heading somewhere. And if Ronin believed in his future, maybe he could believe in his future, too.

Chapter 28

GOODNESS OUGHT TO HAVE AN EDGE

Breakfast wasn't anything to speak of, save Slavin's continued story about law school and silver strikes and the string of bad luck that united the two. "I didn't pull anything out of the ground for sure," he said, "but I did meet some nice people these last couple of years, and I'm hoping to repair things with Mister Clark at the Depot as well."

"That would do you well," Ronin said, pulling a piece of biscuit from the fire. One thing about Dustsucker, he wouldn't eat food if it was dirty or if someone else's mouth had already been on it. "Any plans for the future?"

"You mean, after we catch up to these hoodlums of yours, Mister Ronin?"

"Exactly."

"Well, I wouldn't mind taking a turn at being a deputy," he said, looking at Kelly and Dustsucker, who were washing the previous day's grime from their eyes. "Uncle Billy used to tell me about being sheriff in El Dorado County, some thirty years ago now, I guess. He was commander-in-chief of the Indian war forces ten years before that. I've always had a hankering."

"A hankering?"

"To do some good in the world," Slavin replied.

"Goodness ought to have some edge to it," Ronin and Dustsucker said simultaneously, before breaking into laughter.

"Sorry, Ian. We both have an appreciation for Emerson."

"Emerson?"

"Ralph Waldo…the lecturer and writer," Ronin said. "It gets in the way at times."

"Ah," Slavin said, in the fashion of a man who didn't know what someone else was talking about but wanted to appear as if he did. He took off his hat and nodded toward the northern end of the valley. "It's a bit of a robber's roost ahead," he said, "though not all seventy miles of it, still." He smiled before looking up at everyone's eyes. The lawmen and W. W. Ronin were silent. "They'll not likely be any trouble," he added. It was Ronin who spoke first.

"Thought you were pretty settled out in these parts, Ian?"

"Well sure, Mister Ronin. I mean we haven't had trouble with Indians for years. Ruby Jack used to eat with some of the families out this way."

"Ruby Jack?"

"I'm sorry, I should say Chief Ruby Jack. He used to eat with the Coe family, one of the early stagecoach drivers. Of course Ruby Jack was an old man when I knew him, but he was still well respected."

The three men looked at Slavin. It was Dustsucker who spoke next.

"We're not real used to *angry* Indians," he said. Ronin and Kelly shook their heads in agreement. The name was familiar. "Wasn't Ruby Jack the Indian who had killed a stagecoach driver on Ruby Summit," he asked, "maybe cut out his heart and left it hanging on a bush?"

"Long time ago, Ronin. Anyway, I'm talking about angry white people — robbers, thieves and the like. But as I say, we probably won't run in to many or maybe any of them."

"Good," Ronin said, quietly assessing the possibilities. "It doesn't do anybody any good to stand in the way of a determined man, Ian. That goes for good men and bad men."

"How's that, Mister Ronin?"

"I'm saying, Ian, you set your mind to things you ought to finish them."

"Yes sir," he said. "We're talking about the little man up ahead, right?"

"That's right, the little man up ahead. But I'm also talking about the rest of *your* life, too. A man who has set his mind on something is a difficult man to dissuade." *There's that look again. Is he listening?*

Ronin pulled Jackson from a patch of grass over by some trees and handed Slavin the reins. "Saddle him up, would you?" he said. Slavin was still trying to make sense of Ronin's words, but nodded. Ronin walked over to where Kelly and Dustsucker were standing.

"You hear that?"

"Yeah, I heard that," Dustsucker said. "I'm not looking for any Indian wars, William. Seen enough of that when I was younger. A might embarrassed about some of them now, too."

"What do you make of it?" Kelly asked, tightening a strap around his blanket and pulling his duster off of the back of his saddle.

"I make of it we're going to have some problems — that's what I make of it. There's been a fair amount of freight pulled through this valley over the years: grain, potatoes, fruit, and a good number of pioneers as well. It wouldn't surprise me at all if there were people hanging around who ought not to be there. Either of you remember Albert Hayes?"

"Can't say that I do," Dustsucker said.

"Clark said he used to run criminal enterprises in this valley and the valley we just came through. He had the Indians all worked up with secret signs and passwords, robbing emigrants and the like. 'Not one of your nicer Mormons,' he said. The Elko County sheriff had to get a U.S. marshal out of Utah to help end things. It was a real hell of a mess."

"Well then, let's hope we don't meet up with Mister Hayes," Kelly said.

"Don't need to worry about that," Ronin said. "The son of a bitch took seven bullets before he died and a number of rocks to the head by the deputies who were after him, though he took a few good people with him. I'm just thinking there may be more out there like him."

"Then we'll deal with them, one by one," Dustsucker said. "Let 'em come. We're ready."

"I'll not court that kind of trouble Dusty, not with what we've been through these last few months. But you're right about one thing."

"What's that?"

"We'll deal with them, alright," Ronin said. "One by one, two by two, whatever number they come in, however they want to line up. Then we'll catch up to the two people we care about most."

"Latigo and Livestock?" Kelly said.

"Exactly, Tom." He took a deep and still painful breath. "Mister Slavin?" he called out.

"Yes, Mister Ronin?"

"Let's ride," he shouted. "I'll not be freezing my nuts off out here for no reason."

"Yes sir," Slavin said, dusting the snow off the front of his pants. "I can't think of any good reason to do that."

Chapter 29

MURDER AT CAVE CREEK

"As I understand it, it was Private John W. Purdy of Carson City who was drowned here," Slavin said, pulling at some of the weeds and brush that obscured the entrance to Cave Creek. Ronin and Dustsucker sat on the sand bar by the entrance to the cave, kicking at an empty "Old Commissary" bottle, the contents of which used to be made at the Cave Creek distillery.

"Right here?" Kelly asked, noting the creek to be too shallow to pose any risk, save an extremely inebriated man.

"Inside, sheriff. Some of the ranchers say there's a couple of rooms down there, the usual cavern stalactites and stalagmites, I imagine. I've never been inside. Wanna see?" he said, grinning.

"No, life is already too complex with the kids at home and no family to take care of them," Kelly said. Slavin chuckled. "Any chance they've been here, Ronin?" Dustsucker was kneeling in the stream, examining an upturned rock as the ex-priest looked off toward the horizon.

"Slade seems to think so." Ronin turned to see Dustsucker picking at the sand and river rocks that populated the cool, clear water of Cave Creek.

"I'm just saying," Dustsucker said, "something's disturbed these stones. The pattern isn't like a horse or two, either. You know, scattered about, maybe a couple of deep holes and such. It's more of a line, like a wheel rolling this way and judging by how it's filled in, pretty recently, too."

Ronin looked over toward the remains of a saw mill, distillery, restaurant and bar that was once the town of Cave Creek. Additional buildings, constructed of logs or rock, were piled nearby, mere shadows of what they used to be. Like Fort Ruby, much of what was useful seem to have been burned, broken or scavenged by folks passing through or from nearby ranches. "What's that?" he asked, pointing to a building a couple of hundred yards away.

"Looks like a house, maybe," Dustsucker said, looking up. "Should we stop by?"

"Let's."

Ronin, Kelly and Dustsucker mounted up, with Slavin following a few yards behind. They traveled a few hundred yards north until they came to an empty corral and stopped to hail the home's occupants. Then they noticed the broken window with a lamp burning nearby.

"What the hell?" Ronin said, kicking Jackson into a gallop. Sliding off at the house's front door, he looped Jackson's reins around a post and pulled his long gun from the saddle. He levered a cartridge into the brass receiver and looked to see if Slade and Kelly were behind him before lifting his knee up and kicking at the front door. The cabin's lock shattered.

"Ho, in the cabin!" he yelled, scanning the room until his eyes fell onto an occupant, collapsed over a chair by the shattered front window. "Man down," he said, before entering a second and third room next to a full kitchen. "House is empty," he shouted.

"Jesus," Dustsucker said, kneeling down by the dead man's side. "That's some shell that did this."

"How so?" Kelly asked, looking out the front door to see if Slavin had caught up to them. He was tying his horse to a porch pole.

"Look at the back of his head," Dustsucker said. Brains, bone and hair were splattered across the front room floor and onto a nearby wall. "Ronin, this may be our man."

"Yeah, I wondered."

"Caliber?" Slavin asked.

"Always hard to tell," Kelly said. "It all depends on how close a person is, how fast the bullet is coming and so on. Sometimes you can tell. Sometimes you can't."

Slavin pulled a cartridge from his lever gun and pushed the bullet end against the man's entry wound. "Middle of the fore-head," he said, "and a pretty good match."

"That's what I was thinking," Dustsucker said. "A .45-70."

"Know anybody who uses one of these?" he asked.

"Hell, Ian. Pretty much everybody in these parts. But that includes a short little man named Toro Latigo."

Ronin extinguished the light and looked out the window. "He's nearby," he said. "I can feel him. And he knows I can feel him."

Kelly looked at Dustsucker, who shrugged. "Ronin?" he said.

"Yeah, Tom."

"We're going to kill this son of a bitch, right?"

"Yup. No question about it."

"I mean, we're not going to hang him, right?" Dustsucker looked on, sensitive to due process, but beginning to wonder if it'd be a waste of time.

"Nope," he said. "It'd be a giant waste of a short piece of rope."

Chapter 30
BULLET IN THE HEAD

Alvira Fae Livestock sat quietly in the wagon, musing on how anything so pretty and promising could turn so dismal and dark. She took a cup from the side of the wagon and extended it toward her friend. "Water, Tony?" she asked. He shook his head. She lifted a water bag from beneath the bench seat, and, thinking of taking a drink directly from its spout, decided instead to pour some into her cup. Civilization is something you take with you, she thought, sipping from it while gazing at the fenceless expanse through which they were traveling.

The mountains were lush compared to what she could see east of them. Everything looked so dry. The wagon creaked as her friend drove it north toward Wells. She was parched, and the feeling wasn't fixed by the cool water they'd taken from Cave Creek. The dryness was inside her.

Thirty years prior, members of the Steptoe Survey party named the Ruby Valley after a king's ransom. Not crystals or garnets, but rubies. And maybe it was, she thought putting the cork back into the canvas bag and setting it at her feet. It just didn't feel that way. Dry, except for the rivulets of blood, she imagined. Tony could tell what she was thinking.

"A bullet in the head is better than two in the breast, baby," the small man said, pulling away from the ranch. "It's faster and in a lot of ways it's neater."

Alvira didn't know what to say. It wasn't that she was unprepared to hurt or kill for those she loved. It's just that the old man never saw it coming. She sat silently for a few moments wondering what it was like to die that way — a piece of metal shattering the backside of one's head, leaving memories of one's life splattered all over the place. There was no cleaning the bone and skull fragments from the floor and walls of the house. Flesh and blood were everywhere.

She wondered if folks who died particularly suddenly, even violently, received some special dispensation from God when heaven's gates swung wide to welcome them inside. "I'm sorry," the Divine would say, "we weren't really ready for you here, so take this special mansion we've set aside for people just like you." The thought made her smile. Her sister would have taken one of those rooms, she thought, remembering Jesus' words, "In my house there are many mansions. If it were not so I would have told you."

Ellie May had once remarked that the word for "mansion" in that Bible verse wasn't used that often in the *New Testament*, and that it didn't really mean a physical room or apartment as much as it meant a place in which to live or abide. "We live in Christ," she liked to say. She wondered if the man Tony shot was going to abide in Christ or have to suffer for his sins somewhere else, instead.

"Tony, do you think that man was a good man?"

Tony picked a pine cone up off of the seat and tossed it toward some trees. They'd stop for lunch in a little while, things having gotten out of hand in Shanty Town, which was too bad. While he enjoyed sighting in the rifle at a hundred or so yards — it hit straight on, he had expected the bullet to actually dip at bit — it was a shame that the old man tried to make trouble in the first place. They were only stopping to rest.

"I don't know, Alvira. Why do you ask?"

"I was thinking it was too bad for his life to end that way, so suddenly and all. My sister used to say that the dead really missed the living, that they valued getting in touch with those they loved. I imagine that's true."

"Well then, he'll only have to wait a while, I guess. I mean, it may take a day or two for people to find him there. And that don't mean that the people who do will want to hear anything from him anyway."

"Probably so," she said, wondering who would be waiting to hear from her, should she die in an Indian attack on the way to Wells or by the hands of some robber. Then there was the question whether Tony would grow tired of her as well. "Would you want to hear from me, Tony?"

Toro Latigo scratched the top of his head. *Women say the damnedest things.*

"Sure, dear. I mean if it wasn't too scary."

"I wouldn't scare you, Tony," she said smiling. The gold cap she sometimes wore on a front tooth dangled. She pushed it up into place and waited for Tony to look at her. When he did, she winked and smiled.

"I wish you'd take that damn gold tooth out of your mouth. It spooks me."

"Spooks me, too," she said, remembering that she'd found it along the shore at Lake Tahoe the one and only time she and Ellie were ever at the lake. The day they had spent together at Glenbrook was one of her favorite memories. The tooth was something of a souvenir, despite it having belonged to an Indian man, who had been killed in a moment of cruelty.

"Was it necessary for that man to die?" she finally asked, working up to the point where she wasn't scared to hear his reaction. "I mean, all he did was look out his living room window."

"Honey," Latigo said, "you know what the Good Book says. 'Everyone dies and then comes the judgment.'"

Alvira smiled. She had never heard Tony quote the *Bible* before. It was nice.

Chapter 31
TARGET PRACTICE

Ronin drew down on a discarded can near the house at Cave Creek. Thumbing his first shot and fanning his second, he made the red, rusty piece of tin dance across the courtyard out front of the old man's home.

"Two give you more of a chance?" Slavin asked, leaning his shovel against the south side of the house, where they had just buried "the latest corpse in a string of corpses," Kelly said before offering a prayer. "Dear God," he began, "or whatever justice is left in the universe," he said, before each of the men threw a shovel full of dirt onto the hastily-built box in which the old man lay.

"A bigger hole," Ronin said, while fingering six .45 caliber cartridges into the shorter of his two handguns. "In a gunfight, you don't want to pray and spray, Ian. You want to see the other man praying just before he passes on."

Slavin nodded, wondering if he could ever offer the same sort of retribution Ronin was known for, having dispatched more than a dozen men over the last three years. "They were men who needed to die sooner or later," Ronin had told him on the ride out of Lamoille. Slavin didn't argue the point as he'd narrowly escaped being one of them in Elko only a few hours prior. "Mind if I try?" he said, lifting a Remington from his waist-high holster.

"Don't know that I've seen one of those," Ronin said, pointing to the 7½ inch gun. "Improved Army?" he asked.

"I've heard it called that, though I'm not sure it's true," Slavin replied. The piece was a competitor to Colt's single-action Peacemaker, but had failed to secure a lucrative military contract given a two-year lead by the Colt Armory in Hartford, Connecticut. He offered it to Ronin butt-forward.

"It's heavy," Ronin said, "long, too. You'll not get much speed with this," he said, before returning it. "And your holster's too high. That's why you're breaking your wrist. With a gun that long, you need to wear your belt and holster lower."

"I always heard that speed didn't matter," Slavin said, "accuracy does."

Ronin shrugged. "Look at it this way, Ian. You want to hit what you're aiming at before the other guy hits what he's aiming at."

"So speed matters?"

"Speed kills," he said, tossing a cartridge at Slavin, who caught it with his left hand.

"Good," he said. "You don't want to catch things with your right if that's your dominant hand. It'll be a habit you'll one day wish you didn't have."

"I'm sorry?"

He tossed a second cartridge and drew his shorter gun at the same time. Slaven stood with both fists outstretched, cartridges in each. Ronin smiled. "Keep your right hand your gun hand, so that it will be there when you need it. Okay, you try," he said, returning his Colt to its holster. Slavin handed the cartridges back to Ronin and opened the loading gate on the Remington.

"What are you doing?" Ronin asked.

"Loading my gun."

"Hell, son. There's no reason to carry an unloaded gun, even in church. You're only asking for it." Ronin shook his head as Slavin hung his, his hands at his side.

"I'm not sure I'm ready for this," he said.

"Few men are, Ian. You'll be fine. Now, let me see you shoot."

Ian Slavin — the former law student in San Francisco, who left school when his pockets turned up empty instead of applying himself, getting a job and staying in school — pulled the case-hardened hammer back on a blued Remington Model 1875 and pulled the trigger. Two-hundred and fifty-five grains of lead broke an old blue bottle 25 yards out.

"Hell, son! I thought you couldn't shoot," Ronin said, looking twice to make sure the bottle had actually been hit.

"I never said I couldn't shoot the gun, Mister Ronin, I just don't know how to draw the gun."

"Well, Ian, we can fix that," Ronin replied. "What I can't fix is being too damn stupid to hit the target when you fire at it. Nice job, son. You're going to be just fine."

Chapter 32
SOUND OF ANGELS SINGING

"Did you hear that?" Latigo said, wondering if the coyote's howl a half-mile away was real or imagined.

"I heard a coyote, if that's what you mean," Alvira said, noticing that her man seemed jumpier than usual. They would be celebrating their three-month anniversary in a couple of days, not that they were married or anything, but the relationship was still worth celebrating. She was hoping that life would settle down after the three months they'd spent "seeing the sights," Tony said, though she knew they were really eluding the law in the four counties they'd passed through. "Tony, tell me again where we're going to live," she said, hoping to help him be less fidgety.

Tony pulled his carbine closer to him and placed it across his lap. A .45-70 shell would kill just about anything they would come across, he'd told her when they first started out in Reno. She was nervous then — with the loss of her sister, the sudden change of plans and the hurried flight from Virginia City after shooting Ronin in the chest. He often wondered if the son of a bitch made it. For a preacher, ex or otherwise, he was sure a pain in the ass. Now, all Alvira could do was yammer about the future. He pulled the hammer back two clicks, reserving the last one as something of a safety.

"What are you talking about?" he said, still looking toward the mountains and wondering. He was gazing off into the distance when Alvira touched his leg, making him jump. "God, woman!" he said. Seeing the tears in her eyes, he immediately apologized. "I'm sorry, Alvira. I was just thinking. What is it you were wondering about?"

"If you're not going to listen to me Anthony, I don't know why I'm along on this trip," she said, causing him to wonder the same though he was careful not to show it. She'd been a damsel in distress when he'd first met her, and then standing in the middle of C Street in Virginia City, both of them watching her sister die. Well, it wasn't like he had any choice in the matter. It was up to him to care for her now, though he hadn't had any idea at the time how much work it would mean.

"Of course, dear," he said, still thinking of the coyote's howl. A sprinkling of smaller animals seemed to be answering a hundred yards or less off toward to his right. "Where are we going to live in Wells?" he asked, hoping that he had heard her.

"Or wherever, Tony. I don't necessarily need to live in Wells."

Tony remembered back to the good old days, along the original wagon route in Wells, along the south side of the meadow where an early water tank had offered emigrants rest and relaxation since 1845. "Since 1845," he mused aloud, before realizing that he was stuck between two conversations, the first of which was with the coyotes or whatever was making noise off to his left.

"1845, Tony?"

"Yes, dear. We lived down near Railroad Springs. It wasn't called that, of course, in the early days, and by 'we' I mean my parents. But when Bob Hamill came along, mom said everything began to change."

"Hamill, dear?"

"The station agent, sweetheart. He kept us on our toes, he did, being that he also worked for Wells Fargo. My parents moved out of the canvas shelter they were living in a year or so later, when

the hotel opened and, of course the Bulls Head Bar. Good times."
Another howl off to his right and he pulled the wagon to a stop
and handed Alvira the reins. "When I say 'go,' go honey. Drive
like there's no tomorrow."

He'd raised his Springfield and pulled the hammer back
when two long-haired Indian teens raised their heads a couple
of yards off to the right and began laughing. He shot the brown-
skinned boy closest to him in the chest, pulling the hammer back
three clicks and flipping the trapdoor open before sliding a second cartridge from his right hand and pushing it into the breech.
"Go!" he shouted. With that, a few thousand pounds of horses,
wagon, flour, bacon, coffee, sugar and salt lurched forward, fry
pans and pots shaking like the death rattles of an aging old man.
"Whip 'em!" he yelled as he took aim at a half-dozen other boys
running toward a small ravine west of the wagon. He pulled the
trigger again, and a 400-grain bullet blew out of the barrel at
over 1,300 feet per second, opening another boy's back, killing
him instantly.

"Tony!" Alvira shouted, letting go of the reins and grabbing
his right arm. He shook her hands free and reached for the lines
now trapped underneath his feet, applying steady pressure until
the wagon came to a stop, horses heaving, teens leaving, holding
what was left of their Shoshone friends' lives in harried and un-
steady hands. "Oh Tony," Alvira cried, "they were only playing."

Tony sat motionless for a moment, his hands resting on
his 1873 Springfield, his eyes fixed firmly ahead. He took a deep
breath, and turning toward his beloved, sent a quiet and certain
message as surely as he ever could — like the one he'd sent his
father years before, then his mother and his brother.

Alvira Fae could see the fire in his eyes. It was not a holy
fire, like that which burned in her sister's eyes while preaching or
explaining the way the Lord wanted the dead and the living to
continue growing together, even though the one was so certainly

separated from the other. The fire looked like that in her father's eyes — who'd never really seen her as her sister's equal, and had always hidden the pain of her being different, though she knew. She knew. And Alvira wept inside, like the hapless calf culled from the herd. He knew. He knew like the calf knew that his life was about to end, offered up like an unholy sacrifice for a God who didn't give a damn no matter how much a life would cost or scream. The fire cut into her heart and she knew. She knew that this thing of theirs — this anniversary ride toward a new tomorrow, toward Wells or Salt Lake, it didn't matter — was now over and she was not safe.

A cold spirit crept over her as she fingered the crinkled tin cup in her lap, until a frightened female fist rested within it. And then powerfully — yes, even prayerfully — she punched it into the side of her beloved's head as she listened to the sound of angels, singing.

Chapter 33

FACE DOWN

Antonio Latigo, "Tony" to his late mother and friends and "Toro" to those he is trying to impress or intending harm, fell helplessly from the wagon, spinning like a top. Alvira applied the wagon brake and hopped down in time to see her friend eat a mouthful of gravel. "Leave that alone," she said, before placing her hands on her hips and humming the Christmas tune, "Angels We Have Heard on High, Sweetly Singing ..." Antonio watched her, peering out of a rapidly swelling right eye as she swayed imperceptibly, her eyes closed, her mouth framing each word as it came: "Angels we have heard on high, sweetly singing o'er the plains. And the mountains in reply, echoing their joyous strains. *Glória in excélsis Deo! Glória in excélsis Deo!*"

"Make it stop," he said, hoping that what had just happened hadn't happened, that he was still sitting on the seat of his wagon, and while not necessarily thinking such hostile thoughts was at least poised for a meaningful conversation about the right to self-defense and the history of "Indian uprisings," his mother used to say, in the Ruby Valley and beyond. But the taste of dirt and gravel brought his momentary fancy to an end, as did the look of the woman who had hit him in the side of the head.

"You punched me," he said.

"I slammed you hard, you son of a bitch," she said.

"Why did you hit me?" he asked.

"Why did you shoot those poor Indian boys?" she asked in return. And his good intentions of educating her about the Shoshone, the Goshute and the Paiute tribes, some of whom had made serious trouble for white people a few years back, was lost in the steady hum and beating rhythm which was now his head.

"Oh God," he said, reaching for the left side of his face, which was wetter and stickier than he ever remembered it being. *Blood.* "What did you do to me?" he screamed, before flinching at the shrillness of his own voice. The little man curled up into a ball not more than a couple of feet across. Alvira grabbed her man's collar and belt and lifted him up into the wagon like a fifty-pound feed sack, although a bit heavier and more difficult to lift.

"Now you listen to me, Tony Latigo," she said, taking a deep breath. "There will be no more killing on this trip. No more old men, no more Indians. And if and when the law catches up to us, you'll not load that damn gun of yours another time until I say so. Is that clear?"

"Yes," he mumbled, burrowing underneath a blanket next to a couple of supply barrels and beneath the piles of fancy clothes and valises that formed Alvira's trousseaux.

"I'll not see another man or boy die until we build or buy our own house. And then, if you really need to continue this 'I'll get back at life' attitude of yours, we'll talk about it. Because right now I'm not feeling safe, and the people around us are definitely not safe, and that's no goddamn way to make friends. Do you hear me?"

He mumbled again, but not in a way that suggested clarity, especially for a woman who was seeking so much from so little a man with even less emotional ability or resources to give her — hell, to give anyone what was needed, not that anyone was asking. He had turned into a tiny, hate-filled man. "Do you hear me?" she asked, this time emphasizing the word 'hear' so that there'd be no mistake, absolutely no confusion as to her intent.

So the little man, who so many had ignored or maligned his entire life, enough that any honest person would consent that he was a product of mankind's wickedness and cruelty, spoke quietly the words, "I agree."

She lifted herself up onto the seat, unhinged the brake and took hold of Toro's favorite whip, snapping it across the back of the horses until the wagon began to move forward. "To Wells," she said, "and whatever lies before us." And little Anthony Latigo, now practically asleep, began to dream of his mother and the tiny lead soldiers he'd been given as a Christmas gift one year. He tasted blood. And a smile formed across his lips.

Chapter 34

MATTIE'S
MIDNIGHT RIDE

Ten-year old Mattie Clark didn't think "a woman's place was in the home." Nor did she believe "a child shouldn't speak unless first spoken to." It was her perspective that all of God's children were equal in God's eyes — a conclusion she had probably come to at the Presbyterian Church in Elko. None of God's children were any less important in her mind — be they red, yellow, black or white — particularly the one-eyed black man named Sam Mills who was now in the custody of two older white men riding toward Elko.

Ronin had referred to Mills as a "common criminal" before resuming his dinner at Myron Pixley's house, "now cold," he said "because a black man was found hiding in a haystack outside Myron Pixley's home." John Maverick and William Ronin seemed like reasonable men, she thought. But their hushed comments at supper about Negros, Indians and Chinamen that left her wondering if Mills would ever get the trial her father believed he deserved.

He would want her to do what she was doing, she repeated to herself quietly as she crawled out of her window, saddled her horse and galloped to within sight of the three men heading back to Elko. It was her Christian duty, she said, when the former words rang hollow and she realized just how dark the night was and how dangerous her decision had become. Life was probably like that, she mused when the shivering stopped and the sweating began — one bad decision building upon another.

Maybe Mills had suffered the same slip of attention, she wondered as she rode maybe a half-mile back from the men her father trusted enough to allow her to stay with. Maybe she should ride closer. Maybe Mills hadn't intended to kill his best friend — *I mean, who would choose to do that?* -- she wondered in the chilly December moonlight between Lamoille and Elko, wrapped in the woolen blanket she had pulled from the bed before sliding down the tree outside Pixley's two-story home. She hadn't traveled this way before, making decisions on her own. *But one has to start thinking for oneself at some point*, she figured.

Mattie wondered if Mills had had the same sort of upbringing she had had — a good school, sincere friends, a church family to keep her sins in check and the example of two upright parents who loved her very dearly. They'd be worried if they knew she was riding alone in the moonlight, but maybe she wasn't really alone. *God knows I'm doing this*, she thought, but then wondered how true that could be given that God hadn't kept Mills' friend from being shot, "with a shotgun" someone had said, though she didn't know the difference but had seen a pheasant once blown to bits because it had come too close to a long gun held by one of her father's friends who was hunting at the time. *I'll be okay,* she said out loud when a coyote called from one of the snowy hilltops off to the right, where "the Ruby Mountains watch over all of us," her mother had said the summer previous on their way to the crossroads community of Lamoille. *Good parents, for sure.*

She listened to the silence, and prayed and wondered.

"You know we've got somebody behind us, right?" Maverick asked his friend a couple of miles from the ranch.

"I do," Pixley said, smiling.

"It's bad enough that two farmers have to act like lawmen, Myron, than to have some Indian sneak up on them from behind."

"John, stop it, would you?" Pixley said. "I can't think of a time we've had problems with Indians in what, maybe twenty years?"

"Maybe," Maverick replied, shivering. But with all that talk tonight about angry Indians, Negros and Chinamen, it makes me nervous, Myron. And now we got somebody coming up on our rear. I just don't know what we're doing out here."

Their prisoner looked back over his shoulder, and spying Mattie hunched over her horse to keep warm, smiled. "It's not like a white man to get scared over a little girl," he teased.

"Shut up," Maverick said. "Women don't scare me."

"I didn't say a woman," Mills sneered. "I said 'little girl,' you old wheezer!"

Pixley laughed. "I know who's back there, John. That's Mattie's horse and it looks like Mattie's riding it. She'll catch up in time."

"Mattie? Are you serious? How long have you known? Won't your wife be worried?" The questions came out of Maverick's mouth like an angry Gatling gun, spitting lead at anything that moved.

"I told her that Mattie would probably slide down the tree and join us before we left." He kicked his horse's flank, so as to move closer to his friend. "I've never known that girl to be happier than when she's with her father. There was no way she was going to stay with all of us gone."

"Except your wife," Maverick chided.

"Exactly, John. She's a daddy's girl, and not likely to stay where only women are present. And anyway, Jim will be happy to see her."

"Well, that may be. But I'll not be taking care of this one-eyed murderer *and* a disobedient little girl. That one's on you."

"Hell, John. Mattie's been taking care of herself and everyone around her for years. Probably always will be. You've got nothing to worry about."

The snow's cold white crust crunched underneath the horses and riders for the next couple of miles, until a little girl caught up to them, singing.

Chapter 35
SUNDAY SCHOOL SONGS

"Do you know that song, Mister Mills?" she asked.

"I do not, miss," he said.

"It's called 'This Little Light of Mine,'" she said, smiling. "I'm going to let it shine. This little light of mine," she sang, "I'm going to let it shine, let it shine, let it shine." She sang the whole first verse before looking over at Myron Pixley and smiling. Pixley returned the smile and raised his hands to suggest the obvious question. She nodded and then shrugged.

"Well, I thought I recognized the tune," Sam Mills said, "but I'm not sure I ever heard the words."

"It's a slave song," she said confidently. "I learned it in Sunday School."

"I doubt that, miss."

"You doubt that I learned it in Sunday School or that it's a slave song, Mister Mills?"

"I'm saying it's not anything a dark-complexioned man like me would sing." Mattie looked at Mills, still waiting. "It's no slave song."

"And you would know?" she asked. The tone was so obvious a challenge that Pixley's friend — who had his eyes fixed forward, scanning the dirt road ahead for Indians or signs of Indians despite being told there were none — looked at Mattie and frowned.

"I'm afraid I would, miss," Mills said. "I've been a great many places in my life. And I've been a goodly number of things. Being the child of slave parents, I believe I can say without a doubt that's no song I've ever sung or heard."

"Well, Mister Mills, I had no idea, and I apologize," she said. "It's something I should have asked."

"Where are your parents now, Mister Mills?"

"Well, they're in Atchinson, Kansas, miss. Been there for quite a few years, even before the war ended. Atchinson's been real good to folks like us, more or less."

"Sam Mills, do they know the kind of trouble you're in?"

Maverick and Pixley looked at each other — neither of them had ever met a more precocious child. And there was still the question of what she was doing out on her own at midnight. But Sam Mills laughed. White children seemed little different than colored children, he figured. They were just as independent and just as curious, though, he was guessing, having never had any of his own. "I imagine not, Miss Mattie," he said. "But if they did know, I would tell them the same thing I'm telling you and these other men. I did not intend to hurt my friend."

"Kind of irrelevant, isn't it?" Maverick exploded. "I mean to the family of the man you killed it's all the same, right?"

Mills looked at Maverick. "It says something about my frame of mind, Mister Maverick, not that you'd understand. And I would think it would be very relevant to Jim's family to know that it happened by accident and at the hand of someone who cared for him very deeply."

"Mister Mills," Mattie said, "I believe you. And I'm here to make sure you get home in one piece."

"As if a little girl can add to anything," Maverick continued, looking at Pixley chuckling.

"I'd be careful about that attitude if I were you," Pixley said laughing. "That little girl is the apple of Jim Clark's eye. There's a big part of a big man in that little girl. Push comes to shove, I doubt you'd survive."

"Whatever," Maverick responded, pulling ahead. "I know where I'm not wanted."

"Miss Clark?"

"Yes, Mister Mills."

"I wonder if you'd like to ride by me for a while, I mean if it's okay with your uncle here?"

"He's not my uncle, Mister Mills, but if it's okay with him, I'd be happy to ride next to you. I'd like to hear more about your view of things, and maybe Kansas, too. I've not been out of Elko before, except maybe to Salt Lake, but that doesn't count. There are a good many Mormons in Salt Lake, Mister Mills. It didn't seem at all real."

"Well, now little lady," Mills said, "there are a great many ways of looking at the world. I've learned that over the years there's a Southern way of looking at things and a Yankee way. There's what it means to be white and how you see things if you're black. There's Indian, too, all kinds of Indians — don't be fooled little girl, they don't view the world all the same way. There's Christian like my momma and not so much like my daddy. And I imagine there's Mormon, too. We're all the same, you and me," he said smiling. "How did that song go?"

"The one I was singing?" Mattie asked.

"That one."

"This little light of mine ..." she began to sing.

"No honey, the one you were singing back in Lamoille when Mister Ronin had me tied to the porch posts."

"Oh, that one," she said. "That's my favorite. She began singing like only a child can sing, like the words actually meant something. "They're true, you know, if you want them to be," her Sunday school teacher always said. "It's just a matter of practice."

"Jesus loves the little children, all the children of the world. Red and yellow, black and white, all are precious in his sight. Jesus loves the little children of the world."

Mills wiped a tear from his eyes, taking his wrists off of the saddle horn long enough for the hand cuffs and chains he was wearing to jingle. "Ever hear the words this way?" he asked, before humming the tune and letting his voice resonate with hers. "Fat and skinny, short and tall," he sang slowly, and it was beautiful, truly beautiful. "Jesus loves them one and all ..."

"That's not how it goes," she said.

He looked at her and smiled. "It could go that way, if you wanted it to."

Chapter 36
DRAW

Ronin yanked at Slavin's holster, taking hold of it with his forefinger and pulling it closer to the front of his trousers. "You may be more comfortable on a horse wearing your gun that far back," he said, "but it won't serve you well in a gun fight." He pushed the shorter of his two Colts to the rear to show how much further the gun had to travel if it sat behind his kidneys. "Distance is speed, son. The smaller amount of movement you have to make to bring your iron into play, the faster your shot will be and the more likely it is that you'll survive. Wrap a leather cord or thong around the hammer. It'll stay in your holster just fine when riding."

"You've been in a few gunfights, I'm guessing?"

"You know who I am," Ronin said, "let's not fool one another. Gun play is like communication, son. The faster you get to the point, the happier people are going to be."

"I'm sorry," he said.

"No need to apologize, Ian. Now, let's get back on task," he said, pushing the holster further down on the boy's leg so that the belt trailed along his backside rather than sitting parallel to the top of his pants. He returned the Remington to its holster. "Let's see how this goes." Slavin pulled the 7.5 inch single action revolver from its leather and pushed it out in front of him.

"Well, at least it's level," Ronin said, taking hold of the gun's top strap and pushing it back so that it sat closer to his body.

"I can't see it there," he said.

"You don't need to see it, Ian," he replied. "Oh hell, I guess there's a couple of shots where you'd want to. But even putting the gun barrel in your peripheral vision means you're going to be slower than you might want to be." Ronin pointed to a nearby cottonwood tree. "Twenty-some feet away, sure — it's easy to go one side or the other, particularly if you get excited and begin pulling on the trigger instead of pressing it. But just let the barrel show. Any more than that and you're wasting time."

Slavin nodded. "There's a lot to think of."

"Listen," Ronin continued, catching his eye. "Most gunplay is going to take place well within a dozen feet. You don't want to be poking your piece out at someone, not just because you'll be slower — and trust me, slower you will be if you make it a point to point that thing — but because the man you're shooting at, if close enough, is going to want to grab your gun. Pull it back, don't poke it out, and fire."

"Like this?" he said, lifting the gun up and out of his holster so that it was level.

"No, like this." Ronin kicked his hip up and forward to pull the holster away from his Colt so that the firearm was level. The whole movement took less than a second, maybe less than a half-second, Slavin thought, wondering if he'd ever seen such speed with a firearm before. "What do you think?"

"That's fast."

"Hell son, that's not fast. That's just faster than you. Fast is when you dump it out the back of your holster and shave a piece of leather off the front of your holster as you fire, and the leather piece ends up sitting in the middle of the man's chest." He waited a moment for the picture to settle in. "No extra movement," he said. "Understand?"

"No extra movement." It didn't look like he was getting it.

"Look, let me say it another way. It's not how fast you pull your gun — well it is, but that's not the main thing — it's how simple you pull it. No extra movement, nothing forward that you don't need, nothing backward that you don't want. A friend of mine says it's like a backwards seven."

"Who said that?"

"You might meet him some day. But for right now, listen. The fastest draw, you don't even want to see a seven. You want your leg such, your hand such and your six-gun such that it simply slips out, sits there perfectly level and shoots."

"Wow," he said. "Ronin, how'd you learn all of this?"

He thought for a moment. So much of who he had become began a long time ago: Pulling his hand off of a hot pot, for instance. Who would have guessed that when he was burning himself as a Confederate cook — and not all that good of one — that he was learning hand speed? Or when training in "the sweet science of boxing," as the bishop of Pittsburgh used to say, who would have thought he was learning "economy of motion?" "There's no need to wind up like that," the Irish priest coached. "It's wasted motion. Fist to face, Ronin, keep it simple — fist to face, from wherever your fist already is." Or the gun coach he'd been assigned when touring with the Pinkertons who taught him to shoot to a man's center mass?

It all added up. Life was like that, he figured. He couldn't swear there was purpose to everything that happened to people — not since he'd left the priesthood, anyway and even then — but he sometimes wondered if there was more truth to thinking that way than not.

"How I learned this isn't important, Ian. What's important is that you take what I'm showing you and you do it as fast as you possibly can as often as you possibly can. Want to be dangerous with a gun? Then practice fast and often. Practicing slow is for people who want to meet their clergyman."

"Their clergyman?"

"Yeah," Ronin said, "the one who's going to read words over your grave. Now let's get moving. Dusty?" he called. "Tom?" he said.

"Yeah, Ronin?" Kelly responded.

"We're burning sunlight, brothers. It's time to ride."

"Wait a minute, William," Dustsucker said. "Did you see this?" He was bent over a fire ring off to the right of the cabin. He was stirring the ashes with the forefinger of his right hand because his trigger finger was more sensitive. Ronin smiled.

"What are you looking at, Dusty?" he asked.

"Coals, or what used to be coals anyway. Someone's been cooking here recently." Dustsucker looked up, and pushing on both knees began to stand. "Ronin, I think we're about to help a man meet his maker."

"The man we just buried?" Slavin asked while climbing up on his horse.

Ronin laughed. "Not hardly," he said, untying Jackson's reins from the house, "the man who made the dead man, Ian. If Dusty is right, there's a good chance we'll get to greet the son of a bitch after supper."

Chapter 37
SUPPERTIME

"Sleep well?" Alvira asked, pushing a pan full of bacon off to the side so as to put the coffee pot back on the coals.

"I did," the little man said, rubbing the stars from his eyes. "How long did I sleep?"

"Pretty much all day. I thought you might sleep until morning."

"I don't know what hit me, but I was real tired. I'm hungry," Toro Latigo said, patting his belly. He adjusted his gun belt to allow himself to breathe better, pushing it lower and looping his whip over his revolver. "What did you make?"

"Bacon and biscuits, baby. Want some? Listen, about earlier …"

"Nah, I deserved it. I shouldn't have been looking at you that way. And you have every right to feel differently about my killing people as I guess I have about you killing that preacher back in Virginia City."

"You shot my sister, Tony. I didn't even get to go to her funeral."

"Well, that may be. And her death was tragic to be sure. But I sure wish you hadn't shot that ex-priest. It seemed like all hell broke loose after that."

She stirred the coals with a short stick, pushing the fire out to the side, away from the bacon, biscuits and coffee. Being angry was no reason to ruin things, she figured. Both of them hadn't eaten in a couple of days, not a sit-down meal, anyway. "Tony, you know we don't actually know that Ronin is dead, right?"

"Sure, I guess. I just figure the chest wound you left him with made him as good as dead. Nobody survives that kind of hole in their chest, I mean if you hit them in the lungs and all. I once shot a man in the right side of his chest, and he started shaking. I mean really shaking …"

"Not now, honey. I believe I've had enough killing for one day."

"Well, of course, dear." He pushed a round stone over next to the fire with his right foot and began to sit. "You mind? My head still hurts, I'm so tired."

"Did I brain you that bad?" she asked.

"Nah, it's just that time of year."

Alvira looked around the campsite. It was late afternoon, the second week of December. Very little was blooming, given the morning frosts. She'd seen a dry creek bed a couple of miles off before the mountains began to cast their shadow. She figured that between the cottonwoods and the creek ravine they'd be well hidden should they decide to stay the night. Whatever Tony was feeling had more to do with her hitting him than his rubbing his eyes over the winter sage and rabbit weed. She threw another branch from the tree onto the fire, banked up against some rocks so as to better reflect heat. "Here," she said, offering a wiggly piece of bacon to her man. The drippings caused the fire to sparkle. She leaned in to kiss him. "Tony?"

"Yeah, baby?"

"I'm just wondering, do you think we could be together tonight? It's almost Christmas."

"Well sure, honey. I'm just not very clean. Wanna heat some water? I'll let you wash me after I throw down a couple of pieces of bacon and a biscuit or two. How's that sound?" He smiled.

Alvira Fae smiled back. She never thought she'd get her own man, having had to share men with her sister in Virginia City. And she never much liked the embarrassment she felt with her sister sitting there, or laying there looking, as they did things her father had said to never do to a man, not that he understood. He was too holy, too mixed up in the church. And then one day, all of a sudden Toro Latigo appeared at their front door on D Street. She held a gun on him, the Patterson revolver she still carried in a big brown bag stowed underneath the seat on their wagon next to the tin cup and some jerky. That's what Ellie May said to do. "Point it at him and let him see you when I tell you to. No man likes a gun pointed at his wiener," she said. And of course she was right. It was the first thing tiny Toro Latigo said when he came calling on her the next week. "Be careful where you point that thing," she said, a phrase she often liked to repeat when he was standing in front of her naked. "Be careful," she would say before Tony would leap at her and growl. She didn't care how small he was. They had a good time.

"It sounds good, honey. I'll wash you and then we'll have some fun." She pushed a crispier piece of bacon into her own mouth. "And then we'll sleep until the stars come up, and then we'll get moving," she said, "because I don't know how safe we are out here. I won't feel good until we get to Wells tomorrow evening." She had a sense about these things.

"We don't need to rush, honey. I told you it was a good couple of days' drive," he smiled. When things were going well, he really liked the lady. "If we want to linger any, if you know what I mean ..."

He put the bacon down, a biscuit sitting in his mouth as he bent forward to kiss the woman he would soon ask to be his bride if he didn't get mad again and kill her. "Kiss me, Alvira," he mumbled. And she bent forward from the waist, the coals lighting up her face in a soft and pretty way — the two of them, bending across the flames to touch noses and then lips before saying, "I love you."

"I love you, too," he said, putting the biscuit down by his feet. He wiped his fingers on his pants and then slipped his hand through her hair until he touched her left ear and then held it against the back of her head, pulling. "Kiss me again, dear. I just love how the world feels when you and I make love."

Chapter 38
LOAD ONE, SKIP ONE

The sun was beginning to fall behind the mountains when they began talking about making camp for the night. "It'd be simple enough to stop at one of these ranches," Dustsucker said, "maybe even get a home-cooked meal, though I don't think I know any of these people anymore."

"It's been that long?" Ronin asked.

"It's been a good number of years, William. Elko was a pile of tents last time I was through. And the valley — Fort Ruby on one end and Wells on the other — well, it wasn't anything like this," he said pointing at roads and fences. "Course there's also the railroad. It's sure changed things."

"I guess that it has," Ronin said, thinking of the changes multiple rail lines had brought to Wichita. Elko was no single-line town, either. "A hot-cooked meal would feel real good about now," he said. "Maybe some chicken, some mashed potatoes and some winter peas." It was obvious that despite the dry high desert air, Dustsucker was salivating just listening.

"Maybe an apple pie?" Dustsucker said, before shouting to Slavin, who was riding a little bit ahead. "Ian, do you know anybody out this way?"

Slavin looked up from his saddle where he'd been tapping with his glove, counting the number of months he'd been away from law school, remembering the card games he'd been in hoping to regain his financial footing, and musing on his general lack of success in the valley's silver mines. "It's been a long time, Mister Slade. I've kept mostly to the other side of the mountains since the silver ran out."

"Never was any," Slade said, "at least from what I've read."

"Newspapers don't tell the whole story," he shot back. "They just write what their readers want to read."

"Whatever," Slade said, wondering why Ronin had taken an interest in the young man. They had only packed enough for the three of them, and they'd already eaten the leftovers that the Pixleys had provided two nights before.

"I thought we ate real good last night," Kelly said, laughing quietly. The Carson City deputy was always good for a laugh, he figured, but when he was hungry, well it was plain entertaining. "Didn't you think so, Dusty?"

"The beans were okay," Dustsucker replied, "but there wasn't enough meat ..."

"To go around?" Kelly completed the county deputy's sentence before laughing out loud. "How much chicken did you eat, anyway?" he asked

"Not enough."

"Knock it off," Slavin said. Both men looked over at him, signaling that his tone wasn't welcome. "Sorry," he said, "Mister Ronin, let's just bivouac where we can, get a fire going over by those trees and make some bacon. We can get a fast start on things in the morning. Still think they're close by?" he shouted.

"I don't think they're far," Ronin replied, thinking the young man might want to keep his voice down while pointing Jackson over toward a small stand of pine trees. A dry creek zigzagged nearby, with some cottonwoods on the other side, but no sign of water. "We'll warm up some biscuits and coffee, and figure out what to do then. I could use the break."

W. W. Ronin was not a horseman. He didn't like the care it entailed — the grooming, feeding and such took away from his personal time, and occasionally his business. And he didn't like the ride, either. He was tall and a little too lean to be sitting in a saddle all day. He generally preferred a carriage or a conveyance if there was one, and despite his feelings about the changes the railroads had brought to the West, he'd gotten used to the comfort.

The four men dismounted by some cheat grass and hobbled their horses before grabbing water and biscuits from Kelly's bag. "I could probably fry up a fast gravy," Kelly said, tugging at the flour and salt bags on the other side.

"Nah, I don't want to be sitting here too long," Ronin replied, "unless we're staying the night. I'm thinking there's enough light if we want to keep on going."

"You're set on killing that man, aren't you?" Kelly asked.

"Latigo? Yup. No one puts a hole in my chest and leaves me that way."

"Well, technically it was the woman who shot you, remember?"

Ronin thought for a minute. He remembered every minute sitting against a gravestone in the Virginia City cemetery, his life flashing before him like the chapters of a picture book. He remembered the woman shooting him, the smoke from her rusty revolver, even the bullet, he thought, moving slowly toward him until it punched him in the side and doubled him over. He hadn't forgotten anything. "The midget deserves to die, too. I just haven't figured out what we're going to do with the woman," he said.

"I can tell you what Ash would want," Kelly said, closing the flap on the leather pack.

"Ash isn't here," Ronin said.

"Now, Ronin…"

He shook his head and walked over to the other two. "You getting off that horse or are the two of you getting married?" he asked, staring at Slavin, who was struggling with a leather strap wrapped around his blanket.

"I'm getting off," he said when the Remington got hung up on the strap and fell to the ground, discharging.

Kelly and Dustsucker startled and then winced.

"Seriously?" Ronin yelled from the other side of the horse. "You hurt?"

Slavin patted around his leg and lap. "I'm fine, just a little embarrassed, I guess."

"I mean what the hell, Ian? I thought I told you to wrap a thong around that thing. And why was it loaded?"

"You told me to carry it loaded," he whined.

"Load one, skip one, I said. Five, not six."

Slavin threw his leg off of the horse and jumped down toward the gun, sitting on top of the rock it had struck only moments before. He picked it up. "I guess I was thinking we'd get involved this afternoon. I wanted to be ready."

"Let me see it," Ronin said. He took the revolver and cycled it a couple of times, then pulled out the empty cartridge before resting the hammer on an empty cylinder.

"Ready is good, Ian. Walking the next 30 miles or so because you shot your horse, that's bad. Start a fire, would you? I don't want to be sitting here long."

Chapter 39
SHORT MAN RUNNING

"Did you hear that?"

"Hear what?" the little man said. He was on top of Alvira Fae, grinding away and hoping for an evening of paradise. They could make Wells the next day, he figured, if they got up early and rode late. This would be their last night on the road if nothing happened, and he could be sitting in the Bulls Head Saloon on one of Renshaw and Humphrey's stools begging for a beer by midnight if things went as planned. Assuming the Wells fire hadn't stopped Wells' first bar from pouring some of the best beer in the West — he'd heard the hotel and saloon were fine, given the thickness of the logs and railroad ties — he'd have a few tall ones and then crawl up on top of his brown-haired girl one more time to finish things before deciding when and if to get married.

"The gun shot," she said.

Latigo groaned and rolled off of his travel mate. "A gun shot?" he said, leaning against the wagon and fumbling with the buttons on his pants. "I didn't hear no gun shot."

"That's because you were humming, Tony. I have to say again, that's just weird."

"My not hearing the noise or my humming?"

"Your humming."

Latigo made a mental note not to rush to judgment on the marital thing — "better to live on the corner of a roof than with a contentious woman," the Bible said — and if Alvira was going to be anything like his mother, well then there'd be hell to pay at some point. "What direction?" he asked.

"Over by the pine trees, a couple hundred yards that way. Remember?"

"I remember," he grumbled. Jesus, he hated the back and forth. He grabbed his hat and rifle and began to creep along the creek bed. "No noise!" he whispered. Alvira nodded.

Sure enough, not more than two hundred yards away, W. W. Ronin, Marcus Slade, Tom Kelly and a man he didn't recognize were kneeling down in the sand trying to start a fire. Latigo pushed himself up against a rocky shadow and tugged at some sage. *No sudden movements*, he thought before deciding to crawl back to camp, where Alvira had already begun to quietly hitch up the wagon.

"You were right, I guess."

"About what?" she whispered, pulling her coat closed.

"Well, two things. Ronin is still very much alive, as are the three pals he's brought with him. And it's quite possible that one of them discharged his gun, as they've got him a little ways away from the fire tending to some horses. It doesn't appear as if they're at all happy with him."

"What are you going to do?"

"I don't know. I'm afraid they'll hear us if we start moving."

"And if we don't?"

"I'm afraid we'll have to deal with things in the morning just like we're dealing with them tonight."

"Well, Tony, we're not dealing with anything right now. But if you ask me, action is always better than reaction. All the morning will get us is sunlight."

Latigo smiled. *I sure love this woman.* "Well then, I expect I should shoot someone. Maybe I should shoot two someones."

Alvira nodded.

"Here's a thought. Give me, say, fifteen minutes to get into position. Then you begin moving slowly, quietly if you can up the road a bit. I'll hit as many as I can and then catch up to you, running."

She nodded. They hugged. He grabbed his gun belt and rifle and began walking up the ravine. Somebody was going to die tonight and he didn't care who.

About six-hundred feet up the gully he found the men again, arguing.

"Are you telling me that I've got to sit with these horses while you eat just because I dropped my gun?" the man said, attempting to tie the horses to one of the trees. The man was stomping his feet, either because he was cold or angry. "I'll just not do it." *Okay, he's angry.*

"You'll do whatever we say you're going to do," Dustsucker said, picking up a couple of limbs and walking back toward the fire.

Ronin shook his head. "It'll be too hot and too easy to see."

"Hell, there isn't anybody out here to look at us," Slavin yelled, tired of the bullshit they were feeding him about "getting ready" and "being quiet," like he was some sort of child. He was twenty-some years old and had seen the elephant. *Okay, not the elephant, but I've been in a few fights. I can handle myself,* he mused before sitting down on a rock to keep the horses company.

"Look, Ian. We don't need the noise. And we don't need to lose the horses just because you're hungry and some Indian is looking for horse flesh. Just keep your eyes open and you'll get your chance by the fire. You're first watch, champ. It'll only be a few minutes. We're not staying the night."

"You don't want to sleep and get a fresh start in the morning?" Kelly asked.

"No. Too much has happened. I'm thinking we'll find him tonight, if we get a hurry on."

"Have it your way," Kelly said, pulling a couple of pieces of bacon from the bag and laying them on a rock by the fire. "You want some, Ronin?"

"Yeah, cut me some. I'm going to take a walk to see what I can see. I'll eat when I get back."

The three men nodded. Ronin took a few steps south when he heard the crack of a large caliber rifle to his left. Slavin fell backwards, crumpled into a ball and began screaming, "I'm hit! I'm hit!" Dustsucker and Kelly dropped to the dirt and began crawling away from the fire when a second shot rang out, kicking up sand by Ronin's boot. He fell to a crouch and rolled forward — "hand, forearm, shoulder, foot," the Frenchman used to say, a decent combat roll — until he stopped next to a tall cottonwood tree and sucked himself up against it.

"Slavin, you okay?"

Slavin squeaked "yes" but was holding his shoulder. Dustsucker and Kelly were nowhere to be seen.

"Who's out there?" Ronin yelled, half expecting someone to answer, when he heard the sound of a short man running.

Chapter 40

THE BULLS HEAD SALOON

The future of Wells never looked brighter than in February 1869 when the little water stop on the Emigrant Trail saw the arrival of the Central Pacific Railroad. A post office came first — not that it mattered as it closed a year later — then a passenger and freight depot in the form of a discarded railroad boxcar, then finally the Bulls Head Saloon. The Bulls Head Saloon! Surely, other hotels, bars and stores would follow as the CPRR began to move freight from the little towns north, south, east and west.

Nevada pioneers H. R. Renshaw and William Humphries were among the first to see the commercial potential of a city set in the middle of a desert surrounded by lush green meadows — by Nevada standards, anyway — in the shadow of some of the most beautiful peaks in the West, the Ruby Mountains. Using logs and recycled railroad ties to build a one story structure, they imagined a time when the town's temporary teamsters, railroad men, miners and cowboys would give way to permanent families wanting to live their lives on America's frontier.

But the dream never really amounted to much more than a crossroads where thousands of people and cattle, and railroads in every direction, crisscrossed their way in and around the hoped-for metropolis. By 1880, the town had dropped from 300 people — not counting a sizeable population of Chinamen who helped to build the railroad — to 244 persons. The difference wasn't much, but the trend was set. It took real faith to believe that things would ever change. Not that any of that mattered to the barkeep, who was simply happy to have a job listening to out-of-work miners and end-of-trail cowboys wondering if this was how it would always be.

Occasionally, Bobby McKee wished to see the kind of days he'd seen when the place first opened — where men tested their metal against imported whiskeys and beer, and measured their manhood in wide-open fist and gunfights. But the rail connections that brought meat to the hungry and mining metals from the Clover and Starr Valleys were too little to grow a significant city. And the town — where hastily erected storefronts burnt easily, like crispy bacon on a barbecue fire — never gave birth to anything more permanent than a boom and bust economy. The increasingly empty tables and bars of the Bulls Head Saloon were proof of it.

Big Bobby believed in the future, though the future wouldn't have anything to do with him. A bright and robust man in his fifties, he'd seen the best that Wells had to offer: frontier street honky-tonks and too-many-to-count freight wagons and stagecoaches bound for regional mines that would never really amount to much except for broken dreams and the human fodder that foolishly pursued them, even when the luck had leaked out. Wells was a railroad and a cow town at best, and try as Bobby could to bring a little bit of class to an otherwise dusty piles of tar pitch and logs on Front Street, the future would be what it would be. A shining city set on a Humboldt hill would not be a part of it.

He picked up a glass and headed toward a washtub, but halfway there pushed a dish rag into it instead, setting it down on the bar for the next cowboy or railroad man who would ask for a single malt scotch as a better breakfast or dinner. He kicked at a newspaper someone had left on the floor until it grasped hold of his right hand like a minister on the make. "What the hell?" he said, pushing his bad leg out in front of him and setting himself down next to an empty table like the general he sometimes pretended he was. "Bring me my sword, you son of a bitch," he murmured as everyone had gone for the night, not that anyone would have listened. The Bulls Head Saloon was closed for its once-a-year cleaning, whether it needed it or not, and Bobby McKee had a few things he needed to do before he turned down the lights.

He shook the paper, smoothing out a wrinkle so that he could better see the article he was looking at. "J. B. Fitch, goddamn it," he yelled. The newspaper piece suggested that Fitch, the county's first sheriff — a mason by trade, the contractor who'd built Elko's Masonic hall, the W. T. Smith residence and the Reinhart Store in Elko — was asking for monies due him from the State of Nevada for his part in constructing the University of Nevada in Elko. And that maybe he was done with being a four-term sheriff with time off to soak the good citizens of Nevada for construction projects he had proffered here and there. And that maybe he was looking for something different, an inn for instance or a bar he could turn into an inn, capitalizing on all those relationships he'd built over the years in the building trades and law enforcement. And maybe he was looking at Wells as a possibility, not that his wife didn't like it in Elko, it said. She was getting up there in years and he was too so probably it was time to do something different.

"Goddamn it!" yelled McKee, an old Gaelic name which meant "fire," not that he tried to hide it. He couldn't hide it, he said when asked — "It's my core. It's my fundamental," he argued, not that anyone understood what he was talking about except that they didn't want to hear that he was upset and didn't like to see him wistful and wondering what would become of his efforts, his getting up there in years and all. Not that he owned anything to speak of and not that he wanted to own anything, save his reputation as the caring man and hopeful man he hoped to be even if

Wells wasn't going to become the caring and hopeful place he had wanted *it* to be.

"I'll not see this building torn down by some knucklehead sheriff," he said, "who wants to build a livery out back and a hotel up top. I'll not have it," he said, crumpling the paper up into a ball of who gives a shit and throwing it at the mirror behind the bar. "It's not going to happen," he said, lifting himself up onto his good leg and step-dragging his way across the floor to the back door, where a couple of Indians stood hoping for handout or a hand up, it didn't matter as long as they got something to eat, goddamn it.

"Listen, my friends," he said, though they weren't really his friends. He handed them a bag of peanuts and watched their expectant faces turn to disappointment. "You got rifles?" he asked. The tall and the short men nodded, both Shoshones he figured, though he couldn't tell, one Indian was the same as another. Red and yellow, black and white, Indians were someone with whom he didn't want to spend the night. "I've got work for you," he said, grabbing the shorter Indian by the arms and looking into the eyes of the taller one, imploring them to follow him back into the saloon. "Come 'ere," he commanded, "I've got more food for you, too," he said, having just put away an early pre-Christmas spread of free peanut butter and jelly, the poor man's answer to just about everything that's bothering him — "Your claim going to hell? Have a sandwich. Your wife leave you because you don't have any money? Who gives a shit! Have a sandwich."

"Boys," he said, "I need you to do some shooting."

"Shooting?" the big Indian asked, though he wasn't the equal of the General's height and girth. Bobby could press a horse to the ceiling if he needed to, and he could pretty much do it twice after a good night's sleep, which didn't occur much anymore given his worries about Wells and his curiosity about why no one in his family ever came to see him in Wells, which was "just plain out of the way," his son said. "Too far," his daughter reasoned before taking trips back east to see his family, "my grandparents, you understand. They're getting older," she explained.

"No megalomaniac like Fitch is going to want to buy this business if he realizes this town is shit under water," McKee said to no one who was listening, not even the Indians in the doorway who were eating his peanuts like there was no tomorrow, and maybe there wasn't. He didn't know. Not that it mattered.

The Indians smiled as all they really wanted was supper. They understood all white men to be a little bit crazy, driving wagons across the desert to goddamn nowhere, places just like here or there, wherever they came from. But being outcasts — fence builders, house painters, horse feeders, "who gives a shit as long as there is money involved" sort of men — killing a couple of crazy white folks really didn't matter. "You want us to shoot some people?" the tall one asked. The smaller man raised his eyebrows and smiled.

"I do," Big Bobby McKee said. "Anyone, actually. Tall or small, it really doesn't matter."

"Then you cook us a big steak tonight," the Indians said, still standing in the doorway between the street and the saloon, a crossroads of sort between one kind of crazy and another. "And you cook us a big steak tomorrow night until we bring you some white men's heads," they said.

"I don't need to see their heads," Bobby replied, having always wondered what it was that made some brown people so much like white people: cruel and careless and nutty in a wanton kind of way. "I just want a couple of bodies laying outside of town, my good friends. You can just tell me when you've done it," he replied. "I'll go see for myself."

The Indian boys nodded, at least that's what the General remembered them doing as he laid down in the back of the saloon for the night, preferring to live and sleep in the midst of things

that he understood than to miss anything else on its way to somewhere else. And the coyotes howled, a little more often that night
along the Humboldt River than they usually do — where men
and women had dreamed dreams for as long as any white man
could remember, which was only about 40 years, and a brown
man couldn't imagine what his future looked like with so many
crazy white men running around.

Chapter 41
CLEAN AS CAN BE

Ronin pulled the yellow kerchief from around his neck and ran toward Slavin, who was rolling around in the dark like a child who'd been stepped on, except that he hadn't been stepped on, he'd been shot. The loud rapport suggested a large caliber rifle, like the .45-70 that Latigo had used in Virginia City. The echo of those first shots from Mount Davidson into their third-story window at the International Hotel was still echoing in Ronin's ears as he knelt beside his new friend.

"Tell me you're fine," he said, pulling at his shirt and jacket until he could see the entry wound, a relatively small hole to the left of Slavin's humerus with very little blood. *Good, no artery was hit.* He pulled a clean white handkerchief from his pocket — one of a dozen or so he used to carry when he was a priest to use at a baptism or to hand to a crying family member at a funeral — and pushed it against the wound, about six inches higher than Slavin's nipple, just under his collarbone. "Lean forward," he said, hoping to see a single exit wound. *Confirmed.* He wiped the sweat from his forehead with the sleeve of his right hand and did the same just under his nose. "You're a lucky man, Ian. The bullet went clear through."

"Clear through?" he screamed. "What the hell does that mean?"

"It means it didn't tumble. It means it didn't hit a bone or a good piece of muscle. Small muscled girly-man that you are, my friend, it means that you're going to be okay." Slavin winced under the name calling but got the point.

"Sorry," he said.

"Don't worry about it," Ronin replied, pulling his friend's jacket back in place and handing him the silk yellow kerchief Emma Nauman had given him prior to stepping onto the train. "Hold this against the handkerchief," he said, and keep it knotted up real good. I want to see pressure on that wound so that you don't bleed too badly." He looked around. "Where are the others?"

"Over here," Dustsucker answered, standing next to a cottonwood tree and looking out toward the darkness. Kelly was walking toward him, having pursued the shooter north along the wagon road until it was clear he couldn't catch him.

"Single man, Ronin," he gasped. "Short little guy from what I could see. Expect it's Latigo by the silly gait of his legs. I heard a wagon and some horses as well, though I couldn't see more than a couple of hundred yards ahead. I imagine that's Miss Livestock, reining herd."

"Well, that confirms it then. A .45-70 slug through Slavin here, likely the Trapdoor he's been using ... Put that back on, Ian, you don't need to be looking at that! ... and a wagon and driver heading north. I'm figuring it's the two of them, and if not we'll catch those sons of bitches, too."

"Do you think they're headed for Wells?" Dustsucker asked, peeling the handkerchief away from Slavin's shoulder wound and making a face. "Ewww," he said. "That looks bad."

"Jesus, Dusty. Didn't you just hear me tell him to leave that alone? It's clean. Not a whole lot of fibers, either. And it's just one single hole on the backside," he said before kneeling down to pick up his rifle. "I can't think of anywhere else out this way other than Wells, save maybe a ranch or two. Ian?"

The boy nodded.

"They're going to want some distance between us, Ronin."

"You're right, Tom. Let's get this boy stable and then we'll follow the wagon tracks. I don't want Jim and Mattie Clark's favorite person dying from blood loss out here in the middle of nowhere."

"This is hardly nowhere, Ronin," Slavin said, wincing from the pain but determined to keep his mouth shut.

"Ian, let's not make those your last words. We're going to heat some water and clean it up before we get moving. You have anything clean in your saddle bags?"

The boy paused for a moment, a lifetime of memories streaming across his mind's eye: his parents, their church family in Salt Lake, the stories he'd heard from some of the senior church men and women of faith who'd journeyed there from Cathage, Illinois and parts east before that. He looked up, tentatively. "I've got some holy underwear," he said, "that I was saving for my wedding night. I don't imagine it wouldn't be too wrong for you rip it up and use that."

Dustsucker started laughing. "Holy underwear?"

"Yeah."

"What the hell is that?" he asked.

Ronin raised his hands. "Let's talk religion later. Get some water heated and begin cleaning that wound. We can talk all about the secret Mormon stuff later."

Dustsucker put his arm under Slavin's left arm and grabbed hold of the right side of his pants. "That hurt?" he asked.

"Not as much as you tearing up my underwear, Dusty."

"Don't call me Dusty, son. You haven't known me long enough."

"Sorry sir, I didn't think that would be much of an issue given that you're about to destroy something I value more than life itself."

"A union suit?"

"More or less."

"Son," he continued, "if you care more about your underwear than the life you're living, there's something seriously wrong with your religion."

Chapter 42
EMMA'S PRAYER

Emma Nauman didn't have any real connection to these incidents: the pursuit of Antonio Latigo, the capture of Sam Mills, the death of the old man, the two Indian boys or the shooting of Ian Slavin, whom she had never met but would greet a couple of months later when Ian would come to Carson City to visit his new friends. But she did have a sense, in prayer, that something was terribly wrong with Ronin's mission in eastern Nevada.

Sitting in her regular chair by the front window of her Carson Valley home, meditating on the Christian principles that had brought her to Carson City and encouraged her to build a mission to the Washoe, Paiute and Shoshone people, she felt "a stitch" in her spirit when thinking about her beloved. The momentary feeling or concern interrupted her prayer and caused her to wonder if Ronin was safe. As she had no way to find out, she spent the next few hours in fervent prayer discerning what God would have her feel or do.

William Washington Ronin was never quite present, she thought — his being a man and all, the men in her life having been more inclined toward thinking about their lives than feeling the feelings of their lives — and he was never fully gone, she mused, she being a woman and valuing the emotions that rolled so regularly and turbidly through her life. So when the feelings came that her intended was in danger, that the people with whom he had surrounded himself weren't entirely safe and were perhaps even at great risk, she sat even more deeply into the old rocking chair that had become her soulful friend. Clasping her hands even more firmly and moving her lips even more fervently, she brought her requests to the Holy One who had never failed her. Discounting the disappointments she had experienced with her husband Henry and his abandonment — of their Christian mission and their Christian marriage when he fled without warning to parts unknown — she could still count on God to keep her man safe. And if she couldn't — those other issues now regularly ignored and occasionally forgotten — how was her life worth living?

It was Emma's early morning spiritual practice "to gaze" on the Lord Jesus Christ in such matters and to simply "glimpse" at the issues before her, the habit bringing a certain balance to her inner life, insuring that no one thing was more important than the Lord of Everything. But this morning's prayers felt forced — she sweated and ached and agonized — and when she was finished there was no noticeable peace.

When Ronin boarded the train on Telegraph Street a few weeks before, she had tied a yellow scarf around his neck, a promise of sorts that she was with him, she said, "and God, too," she reminded him, though she knew it was a reach given Ronin's unbelieving ways.

"It's not that I don't believe," the ex-priest had told her many times before — by the Carson River where they sometimes picnicked or outside the Methodist Church where they occasionally worshipped. "It's not that I don't think there's some intelligence to the universe," he said, "some Over-Soul that holds all things together and lends reason and justice where order doesn't seem to be apparent. It's just that I don't practice these things anymore," he said in the fashion of a man who could no longer speak of his family without crying or too easily remember his middle name. "Too long, too little," he sometimes stuttered, though she didn't know what he meant and he never would say anything more. It was simply too sad.

"I don't know where my man is," she prayed, "I don't know what he's doing," she said to the One in whom she trusted the outcome of all things. "I just want him well," she said. "I just want him returned to me safely," she said, hoping that that God in heaven would be more present than she ever was, or that she could ever hope to be.

The morning went quickly. By lunch time, a cold cup of coffee sat by her prayer chair in the living room just a couple of feet from the large windows that looked out on the Sierra Nevada range a few miles away. She opened the Bible sitting on her lap and turned to the *Psalms*, a constant source of encouragement and prayer when things seemed dark or she was discouraged. She turned to the 121st chapter and began to read: "I will lift up mine eyes unto the hills," she said, "from whence cometh my help. My help cometh from the Lord," she read, "who made heaven and hearth. He will not suffer thy foot to be moved — he that keepeth thee will not slumber. Behold!" she said, "he that keepeth Israel shall neither slumber nor sleep. The Lord is my keeper. The Lord is my shade upon my right hand. The sun shall not smite me by day," she read, "nor the moon by night. The Lord shall preserve me from all evil. He will preserve my soul, my going out and my coming in, from this time forth and even for evermore."

And you know what? Emma Nauman felt better, she really did. And even though she couldn't be with the man she loved, even though she couldn't experience what *he* was experiencing or go through what *he* was going through — even though she wasn't absolutely certain that things would turn out well for the one she hoped someday to marry — she was of this one thing: God was with him. And that, she said, would be enough.

Chapter 43
JUSTICE

This wasn't Sheriff Tom Kelly's first rodeo. Sure, it was dark out and he hadn't actually gotten a good look at the man as he sprinted into the night toward the waiting wagon a couple of hundred yards away. But he knew, and he knew that Latigo knew, that he was as good as caught now that they'd seen him. Sooner or later, the four of them would catch up to the man and give him what he deserved. "Ronin, look, this is your deal," he said, "and I'm happy to be along for the ride. But if you don't mind me saying, it seems to me that the two of you can care for Slavin here and cut me loose to get a head start on that wagon. There are a lot of ways to Wells, my friend. Let's not lose your son of a bitch now."

Ronin looked up from the fire, where he was boiling a piece of Mormon underwear with a backwards "L" on it to use as a bandage. "It's a square," Slavin had said when Ronin took a pair of shears to the crotchless cotton undergarment and smiled.

"It's bandage now," he'd replied, moments later apologizing for making light of the young man's endowment ceremony as a Mormon elder and priest.

"Tom, just be careful," he said. "And if you start to veer off the main road, make sure you leave us something to follow, okay?"

"You bet," he said.

"I don't need to tell you he's mine, right?"

"You don't," Kelly replied, though the Virginia City lawman was never comfortable with vigilance committees or those who took the law into their own hands. "We'll argue what to do with the man after we catch him. Fair enough?"

"Fair enough," Ronin said, before watching Kelly take a run at his horse and, slapping its back end with both hands, leap up into his saddle. The horse was quickly at a gallop, spitting dust and gravel everywhere. Ronin shook his head.

"I don't think I'll ever get used to that," he said, looking at Slavin, who looked to be in some pain. "Listen, Ian, it's not my intent to make fun. I imagine it all means something to someone. It's just that we need the cloth." He thought of his own initiation as an Episcopal priest. It wasn't all that different.

Slavin nodded and swallowed hard.

"Take this and rub at the edge of the wound, would you? I want all that blood off of there."

He nodded. "They're sacred symbols," he said, "if you're interested."

"I am."

"Well, they're not something to be spoken about, certainly lightly. I've heard about your interest in the Masons. Do you recognize the two symbols?"

"Is that a square and a compass?" Ronin asked. The backward "L" was embroidered on the right side of the garment so that it sat over the heart. A compass-like shape was sewn onto the left side of what looked like an unbleached cotton union suit, except for the open crotch and collar.

"More or less," Ian said as he dabbed gingerly at the sides of the wound just underneath his collarbone. "The square represents justice. It's God's promise that we'll get everything that is coming to us."

"Most of us do," Ronin said, "whether we deserve it or not. And the compass?"

"An undeviating course, at least that's what my bishop says. It's a reminder to keep the commandments. Do you believe in the commandments, Mister Ronin?"

"You mean 'you shall not murder, you shall not commit adultery, you shall not steal, you shall not bear false witness?' That sort of thing?"

"Yeah," Ian said wincing, as Ronin took the hot cloth out of his hands and began vigorously brushing against the blood, which was already beginning to dry.

"More or less," he replied, smiling. He threw the smudged wet cloth into the fire and grabbed a second clean cloth from the pot. "I figure the commandments are a sort of guideline," he said. "They're what separate us from men like Mister Latigo." He rested his arms on his knees. "When we kill indiscriminately, when we take what isn't ours, it causes pain." He began to rub at the edge of the wound again. "Somebody has to pay."

"And you?"

"Well, Ian. I'm the guy who makes people pay," he said, throwing the second cloth into the fire. "Ian, you're a thoughtful person. Except for your drinking and gambling, you're apparently a religious person, too. So let me ask you a question."

Ian smiled. "Shoot."

"What makes a man go bad?" he asked. "I mean Latigo had a mother and a father, just like you. And he probably had a good church home. Hell, he may even be Mormon ..."

"I doubt that," the boy interrupted.

"Don't be so sure. But look, I'm asking. Don't laugh at me, but there was a time in my life when I used to think it was all about baptism."

"Really?"

"Sure. Wash away the old and then the good comes in. You know, the grace of God which keeps us from ... you know the drill."

"I don't know," Slavin said. "I just figure some people do better than others. And a lot of us do pretty bad."

Ronin smiled and gestured toward Dustsucker, who was trying not to listen but found the moment between two otherwise angry men interesting, if not tender. "What do you need?" he asked.

"Put your finger on this," Ronin responded, holding the clean, boiled cloth to Slavin's chest. "Don't press too hard. Ian, raise your hands over your head." He began to wrap the boy in a long piece of boiled underwear cloth. "I don't imagine you ever thought you'd wear your temple garment this way." Slavin grinned. "Here's how I see it, Ian." Ronin paused to make the turn under Slavin's right arm. "Every one of us has choices in life. Some of us choose more wisely than others. I don't punish people because they choose poorly. I punish them Ian, which is to say I hurt them, when they become a danger to others."

"And that isn't murder?" Slavin asked.

"As in the commandments?" Ronin asked.

"Yeah."

"No. Murder is what happens before I get to a man. It what he's done to his mother, his father, his sister or friend. I'm what comes next."

"And what is that?" Ian asked as Dustsucker looked up.

"Justice, Ian. I'm what you call justice."

Chapter 44
BOWS AND ARROWS

It had become the habit of the two men to do what they did with bows and arrows, not handguns or rifles like a crazy white man would. Stick an arrow into a hapless freighter or railroad engineer and folks automatically think "an Indian did this." But put a bullet into the man's hat or handkerchief everyone assumes otherwise. Many a red man had been blamed for a white man's murder in earlier times. The men who had stood earlier in the backroom of the Bulls Head Saloon knew that, which is why the two out-of-work townies from Deeth didn't mind dressing as Indians when work was available.

"Mike," the shorter one said to the taller one, who was pulling a saddle off of a brown mustang a few miles out of town, "this is going to be fun, don't you think?"

"How so, Eddie?" the former piano player known as "Shoeless Mike" replied.

"Well for one, I enjoy being useful. It's a hard life if you ask me, and there are too few opportunities for a man like me to get a reputation. You know what I mean?"

For the record, Shoeless Mike didn't give a damn about reputations, though he enjoyed being known as a tall fellow who could tickle the ivories from time to time, and he did just that in some Montana mining towns until a city marshal broke his finger for "poking it in all the wrong places" he said, so he didn't enjoy playing the piano as much anymore. And he didn't particularly like having his questions answered with other questions, though he hadn't braced his friend Eddie about the annoying habit, not yet anyway though he was sure that the day was coming. "Eddie, you don't need a reputation. What you need is a job," Shoeless Mike said.

"I have a job," Eddie said. "I work with you."

"That you do," he said, wondering what the two of them would do if they weren't doing this job for the man at the Bulls Head Saloon.

"So what I'm thinking," Eddie continued, "is that we'll find a water tower or something out this way and hunker down until some-one comes by for a drink and then stick a few arrows in him. Don't you think?" Eddie, who wasn't the brightest of planets and Shoeless Mike, who was the sun around which Eddie liked to revolve, thought all nowheres had a water tower, because their town — the railroad town of Deeth had a population of 30 more or less, mostly less — was such a fixture along with a post office and a saloon and a ware-house. It wasn't much, of course, though it did mean that Deeth could sometimes do business, which of course it did for the nearby Starr and Ruby valleys, which needed a shipping and supply point on the Central Pacific Railroad.

It wasn't as if they didn't have alternative means of doing violence. Eddie had once used a 4-inch knife on a mule deer that was injured, killing it after a half-hour's worth of back and forth and in and out, none of it being very convincing for someone who wanted to make a reputation on being part of Nevada's rough and tumble. And Eddie once, when playing the piano, had beaned a man with a pair of boots after he'd made his poor opinion known of the piano player in question. The boots ran off with the man who was beaned by them, thus the moniker for an otherwise com-petent piano player, 'Shoeless Mike.' Not wearing boots gave Mike a better sense of the music's timing and dynamics he had since discovered, but getting a broken finger only increased the number of clinkers made while playing. It wasn't a month or so later that someone slammed the keyboard cover down on all of his fingers in the middle of a song because of the mistakes, but by then he'd already gotten his nickname and he was thinking of quitting the instrument anyway.

Mike had a nice Winchester, though with his trigger finger a little shorter it seemed to pull to the left more often than not and with his other fingers being painfully broken by the keyboard cover it was sometimes difficult to hold. And Eddie still had the knife he had used to butcher and kill the mule deer. But both men had, on the suggestion of a Shoshone friend, gotten hold of a couple of bows and arrows. It was with those tools they made their livings. "Eddie, there's no water towers out here. You find water towers where there are railroads," he said.

"Well, that may be. But I bet there are water towers elsewhere as well, you know?"

There was that question again.

"So maybe there are water towers near mountain streams, Eddie. And maybe there are water towers where there's a lot of rain and so on," Mike patiently said. "But I don't think we're going to find any water towers out here where there's nothing but nowhere and nowhere is everywhere, if you know what I mean."

Eddie nodded. "So what are we going to do?"

Mike, who had finally finished pulling the saddle off of his horse and stowing it under a pile of weeds so that he honestly looked like an Indian, pointed to a pile of rocks by the roadside. "We can sit there and if a wagon comes along we can ask for a ride." So they did, on a pile of rocks that marked the grave of an early emigrant cast aside because of disease or hunger, Mike didn't know though he was certain the cause of death was much more likely than Indian attack, though that was pretty much what they were going to do if they could get a wagon or a rider to stop.

Eddie, who was certain they could find a water tower or a warehouse or a saloon or post office they could sit in while waiting for a passerby, decided to trust his friend and take a seat, too.

"These rocks?" he said, already sitting down, but holding the reins of his horse in the event that his friend Mike had pointed to some other pile instead. There were a few others nearby. Mike nodded.

"You going to take your saddle off, Eddie? That's what Indians do. They ride bareback, you know."

"Nah, I'm going to keep it on," he said. "Well, I'll be," he continued. "You look down the road a piece, Mike, and I believe you'll see our first customer coming: a woman and a couple of horses driving our way."

Shoeless Mike squinted, shielding his eyes with his hands. "You're right. Maybe you'll have a chance at building that reputation today, Eddie," he said, smiling. "And maybe we can start calling you 'Ready Eddie' or 'Steady Eddie,' or maybe even 'Eddie Spaghetti,'" he laughed, thinking the whole point of getting a nickname was stupid but it was neat that his friend liked that sort of thing. But a man might just as easily might be called 'Sally' if he wasn't careful.

"Maybe you'll just call me Eddie the Murdering Savage!" Eddie said, pulling himself up sideways on the far side of a sunbeaten saddle so that his silhouette was hidden as he hung from the horn. And the two of them waited, by the stone-covered grave of a nameless emigrant, a few miles south of Wells — a solitary Indian (or so it seemed) and his two horses.

Chapter 45

ATTEMPTED ROBBERY

Something seemed odd. Maybe it was the fact that one of the horses had a saddle or that the man was holding two bows and a couple of quivers. Whatever the case, Alvira Fae reached into the wagon and shook her tiny lover awake. "Tony," she whispered, "there's something strange ahead."

Toro Latigo peeked over the front seat. It was nighttime, but with the cover up and a December moon there might be some chance he could be seen. What he saw made him wonder. In the middle of the road stood a tall white man dressed like an Indian holding onto two horses. Everything about him suggested there was someone else hiding somewhere.

"Ho, on the road," Alvira shouted, stopping the wagon a hundred feet from the man.

"Ho, in the wagon," the man shouted back before the horse with the saddle pulled free from his hand and began trotting their way.

"Control your horse, sir. I'll not have it come any closer without my raising my gun," she said, reaching under the seat for the big brown sack that contained her Paterson revolver. She half-cocked the hammer and looked to make sure a percussion cap was in place. A .36 caliber ball would cripple the horse and anyone clinging to it. Though it was dark, she wanted to be certain before she killed a perfectly good animal. She pulled the hammer all the way back and put her finger on the revolver's trigger. She let it sit comfortably in her lap. "Toro?"

Nothing.

She looked over her shoulder as she saw her man drop off the back of their wagon onto the road and sneak off into the darkness. The Paterson had a 12-inch rifled barrel. It was a big gun for a little woman. But with a blade sight in the front and a notch in the gun's backside, it would hit whatever it was aimed at. Still, she wanted to be sure. "Mister, you need get hold of that horse. Just keep your hands where I can see 'em ..." she started to say, when the horse bolted and a rider — hanging off the far side of the saddle, a hand on the horn, the other grasping a large rusty knife — came into view. She pulled the trigger. The man and the horse fell onto the road, leaving a little man underneath the horse, screaming.

The tall Indian-looking man dropped the reins of the horse he was holding onto and in one motion pulled an arrow out of the sack on his waist, fitted the nock of the arrow to the bow string and began to draw back. Then she saw her lover flying through the air like an angry sage rat, grabbing the tall man's head and violently twisting it so that the man lost his balance and let an arrow fly in the opposite direction he had intended.

Tony landed on top of him and began punching him with the butt end of his rifle. It all happened so quickly Alvira didn't have a chance to cock the Paterson a second time. "Stop," she yelled. And the little man on top of the tall man, her lover, paused with his right fist still up in the air. The taller man, now bleeding in the sand, stopped trying to unseat her lover, and the smaller man painfully stuck under the dead horse shut his mouth and waited. "Misters," she yelled, "what the hell were you all trying to do?"

"Doesn't matter," Tony said, picking up a rock and slamming it against the skull of poor old Shoeless Mike, who despite saying he didn't care about nicknames, knew his name — gained by playing the piano in his socks with no shoes after a man had made fun of him — and regarded it as something to be proud of. Someday, he believed, he'd find his way out of the desert into a real town where piano players were even more appreciated and a man didn't need to make his living by killing another man or by stealing his poke. But sure as the night was black, Shoeless Mike looked like he was laying there dead.

Alvira Livestock pulled the hammer back again on the Paterson revolver. "Since I can't ask him," she said, "maybe I should ask you," she said, turning her attention to Mike's friend Eddie, who was also of the town of Deeth and who was remembering it there — a seasonal campsite for the Shoshone as far back as anyone could recall and all the emigrants who began passing it on the trail in the 1840s, and the railroad and store, the livery and the saloon which were among the most pleasant places he had ever seen on earth. He was sure now that he too was about to die like his friend Shoeless Mike, who had the absolutely best nickname and maybe he would have a name like that someday.

Alvira Fae had hopped down off the wagon and was straddling what was free of the poor man caught underneath a dead horse in the weeds just outside the railroad town of Wells. "Stop mumbling," she said, her legs fully exposed all the way up to her waist if he was to look up, which he wouldn't because his mother had told him not to do those kinds of things a very long time ago, but not long enough.

"Please ma'am," he said, "I meant you no harm."

"Well, I think that's obviously not true, mister …"

"Eddie, ma'am. Call me Eddie."

"… Mister Eddie. So tell me a few things that are true," she said, putting her shoe on his shoulder, which was so clearly out of whack that he screamed. "Broken, is it?" she asked. "Just like my heart, Mister Eddie," she intoned. Toro began laughing. *Good times.*

"Talk to her, you stupid polecat," he said.

"Clever, Tony. You mind?" Tony stepped back and nodded.

"I'm sorry, Eddie. My crazy suitor here wanted to mix it up with you, but I'm not going to let him, assuming you tell me what I need to know. You see, we're headed to Wells, which I'm guessing is where you're from, and it would be fun to know a few people there before we arrive, wouldn't it honey?" Tony nodded. "So I'm wondering, what are you doing out here?"

Eddie swallowed. He looked at the woman's suitor. Really? He was probably the smallest man he'd ever seen. Maybe he had a nickname? Maybe it was 'Short Hat?' Or 'Tom Thumb?' Nah, it couldn't be 'Tom Thumb,' as there was already a midget by that name in the circus. Maybe it could be 'Tiny Tim?' Yeah, that's what he'd call him if they became friends. He looked into the man's eyes. No, they would never be friends. The man's eyes were dark and deep. They were going to kill him for sure, no matter what he said.

"Ma'am, I'm working on my own," he replied, "I really am. I apologize that I've interrupted your evening. I had no idea others were thieving out this way," he said. "I'll be happy to go and leave you to your work, if you like." He looked up her skirt. How could he avoid it? And that was maybe the big mistake. He saw her extend an old rusty revolver toward his head. A Paterson, he thought, from Paterson, New Jersey. And that's all he saw, except for maybe the flash and the little round ball that caved into his head and put his lights out, permanently.

"Wow," Toro exclaimed. "That was amazing!" He cracked his whip at the man's hand that held a small 4-inch blade that had seen better days if the edge was to be believed. The hand didn't move. He picked up the blade and handed it to his woman friend.

"I thought it was bigger," Alvira said. "It looked bigger," she mused, taking it from Toro's hand and pushing it into the cotton belt at the waist of her dress.

"Scary things often do," Latigo said. "It was big enough to stick you, dear. You did good," he said in a measured way so as to signal pride and to evoke happy feelings between the two of them.

"You did too," she said, in the same fashion, suggesting that she'd noticed. "I love you."

"I love you, too," he said, jumping down off the rock he was standing on and running over to see if Eddie or Mike had good shoes.

Chapter 46
DEETH, NEVADA

Tom Kelly, who'd made every effort to stay out of sight as he caught up to the two people wanted by law enforcement in Virginia City, felt sure he'd been spotted when Alvira yelled "stop" into the weeds off to the left of the wagon she and Latigo were apparently riding in. But she was yelling to her man, he later figured out, given that Latigo paused mid-stream in his beating of a large Indian-looking man only to pick up a rock and finish things off.

And when the woman pointed the Buntline or whatever the hell it was at the poor man stuck underneath the dead horse, he thought for sure he'd been seen, given the damned thing's muzzle flash then Latigo pulling out his whip and all. But when the two of them got back up into their wagon like nothing had happened and continued on — leaving a tall man lying in the middle of the road with his neck broken he imagined, and a small man with a bullet in his brain he guessed, not to mention the horse they'd killed as well — well to be frank, he relaxed some. And then when they were finally long out of sight heading toward the town of Wells, he stood up to visit whatever was left of the two men he'd seen murdered before his very eyes.

"Tell me you're actually still breathing," he exclaimed to the taller of the two men lying in the middle of the road. He was genuinely surprised.

"Barely," the man wheezed. "What the hell was that about?"

"You tell me, partner. You all seemed pretty happy to try and stop them."

"You saw that, then?"

"I did."

"Well, I guess we didn't expect to be on the shit end of the outhouse, that's all I can say." He offered his hand hoping to be pulled up. "I'm Shoeless Mike. You?"

"Sheriff Tom Kelly, Virginia City."

"Figures," he said withdrawing his hand. "And I was lying here thinking it couldn't get any worse. Listen sheriff, any chance I'm going to be able to get back on my horse and go find a doctor?"

Kelly laughed. It wasn't as if all the miscreants he'd met knew they were doing wrong. He'd long given up on the church's teaching that God had placed in every man and woman a silent witness to the moral good inside of them. Some men in his experience just never seemed to have anything like that in them. Still, he was always surprised at the brazen gall of some folks — murderers, thieves, it really didn't matter — who when caught red-handed, their hands in the till or on the gun or unfastening a strange woman's brassiere, still hoped there might be some grace in him or some technicality in the law that would enable them to get away.

"Mike, is it?" Kelly said.

"Yes, sir."

"Unfortunately Mike, despite your being a dirt bag and all, and I use that term respectfully, I don't see any way to hold you. There's no proof of your attempting to rob these people. That is what you were hoping to do, isn't it, son?"

"Um ..."

"That's what I thought. And given that the woman just shot your friend, I'm sure the judge in Wells, assuming there is one, is going to see your drawing a bead on them with your bow and arrow here as self-defense."

"Exactly, sir, which of course it was."

"I thought so," Kelly said. "And given that there's no crime in your dressing up like a six-foot Indian. Really Mike, an Indian? A six-foot tall Indian? And since you've got this horse here that's going to take you to wherever it is that you call home, well I figure as long as I don't see you again or hear of you again, maybe there's no problem in letting you get the hell up on your horse and ride out of here."

"And my friend?"

"Your friend is dead, son."

"Oh, my God."

"Yeah, really."

"Then, that's it?"

"That's it, son. But hold on a minute, Mike. I don't suppose that you would want to give an old lawman like me a hand up given the favor I'm doing you?"

"Sir?"

"Where am I going to find these other two?" he asked.

"Them, sir? There's really only one place in Wells where people like that go, sir. I mean assuming they're not riding on to Salt Lake."

"And that is?"

"The Bulls Head Saloon, sir."

"Thank you, son. And you, Mike, where are you headed?"

"Well, if it's nothing to you sir, I'm going back to Deeth, where I was born. I should have stayed there from the very beginning."

Chapter 47
A NEW TOMORROW

Bobby McKee had the back table cleaned off and the scraps put away as soon as the Indians stumbled out of the place. "The sons of bitches," he murmured as he pushed the broom into the far corner of the room and stood it up next to an old iron bucket and mop. A steak a day wasn't much, he figured, if you could get a couple of brown-skinned Indians to do what no white man would do. And doing something about a potential bid by Ben Fitch to buy the place was the only way the Bulls Head Saloon was going "to stay the way it was," he'd told a few customers who stood by the doorway watching him wash the place, insisting that if the Elko County sheriff bought the Bulls Head Saloon it would become a pretentious Baltimore brownstone, goddamnit.

McKee kicked at a large brass spittoon until it splattered back into place underneath the main bar alongside a very nice brass rail, if you asked him. There were few like it in eastern Nevada and finding just the right person to keep it shiny was always a tribulation, he said as if someone was there to listen and that the trouble of finding a suitable someone had been mentioned in the Old Testament *Book of Job*. He was locking the back door, hoping to catch a little sleep when a wagon came to a stop by the saloon's back door. "Excuse me!" he heard a woman calling. "You in there, excuse me!" she said, pointing right at him.

What was Big Bobby McKee to do, given that he rarely ignored a woman's plaintive cry or plea and that the woman in question seemed so attractive, though you could never tell after midnight. A man needed to have a woman stay until morning so that a closer examination could take place to be sure. "Yes ma'am?" he said, as a strong-looking brunette woman in her mid-to-late twenties stepped down from the front of the wagon and walked up to the windows. Except for the gold tooth in the middle of her happy-to-meet-you smile, she was a vision of everything a single man hoped to be dreaming about as soon as his head hit the pillow. She walked over to the door. She was in fact quite shapely.

"Is there any way you could spare a glass of wine for a couple of tired travelers?" she asked through the door, now locked but soon to be unlocked if his unexpectedly happy hands had anything to do with it. He looked through the window pane, but spied no additional party. *Perhaps she has a child? Perhaps she's speaking of a pet?*

"Ma'am, I'm closed," he said, "but give me a moment." He dried his hands on the apron he had been wearing all day, and seeing that it was dirty suddenly cast it off and reached for another before taking a lanyard of keys down from a nearby shelf. "Are you traveling alone, ma'am?" he asked in his best Irish brogue, a tongue he didn't speak, an accent he didn't have. She smiled, and as soon as he opened the door he realized he had looked *out* but not *down*. There in front of him stood the smallest man he had ever seen. "Your son?" he asked anxiously.

"Funny," Latigo said as he pushed his way into the saloon. "What kind of bar shuts down in the middle of the night?" he barked. And McKee, who was twice the width of the man and twice the height and easily four times as strong, couldn't believe what he was hearing. His enchantment with the woman called out the better in him.

"One moment," he said before turning to face the little man standing in the middle of the room. "It's our once-a-year cleaning day, sir. As our customers like to say, 'whether it needs it or not.'" He shook his head dramatically as if to summarize the silliness of the effort. A saloon constructed with used railroad ties could clean up only so much. No mother would ever serve her child off of this floor.

"Yeah, well it's still got a way to go," the tiny man said, looking up at the ceiling. *That's two,* McKee counted silently. *I can't imagine a better day for a beating.* He smiled, before turning back to the woman who had first gotten his attention.

"A glass of wine ma'am? And perhaps a job for your little friend?"

Latigo put his hands on his hips, his whip sitting on top of his six-gun, which trailed to his knees. But Wells would be his home, he reminded himself. He was not going to shit in his own backyard. "Interesting that you'd mention that, sir," Latigo said. "We're new to town, my wife and I." McKee did a double take and noticed that the woman didn't nod before looking back at the man now sitting on a chair at one of his tables. "I'll need employment as will she. Do you have anything?" he asked.

And in that moment a smile sang its way across Bobby McKee's heart. Bagpipes played, fireworks went off and a handsome man inside of him began dancing. Wouldn't it be funny, he thought, if he met a woman after all these years, in a business where he loved to work? And wouldn't it be wonderful he imagined, if that woman might someday become his wife? And wasn't this the perfect answer he thought, to the perfect storm heading his way: an attractive woman, an entertaining midget, and a

whole new tomorrow for the Bulls Head Saloon? If circus owner
P. T. Barnum could employ one of their kind — a tiny-framed,
opinionated piss ant of a man, he'd heard — he could find a place
for a singing, dancing, joke-telling midget, and maybe the little
man wouldn't mind polishing the brass rail occasionally, too.

Chapter 48
CHURCH TALK

"Look, Ian. You don't need to agree with my take on things," Ronin said as they passed the freshly-dug grave alongside the road just outside of Wells. "But this is how I see it. All of us are seeking something, whether we're religious not. It's as if we're propelled by the things we seek. They have power over us."

"Maybe we're drawn to them," Slavin said, thinking of a Bible scripture his Bishop had handed him when he left California. "But thanks be to God," the text in Paul's *Second Letter to the Corinthians* said, "who always leads us to triumph in Christ." The Bishop had been certain that it was what he needed to hear at the time, having run out of money at Hastings College, "the temple of law and intellect," the college brochure said.

"Exactly. You wanting to be an attorney, for instance. What was that about? Or your coming to Elko County, Nevada to work in a silver mine? Who travels from San Francisco to settle in Cornucopia, Cherry Creek or Elko? Nobody does, unless something draws them there."

"So you think the man in that grave back there had it coming?" Slavin asked. "Like his fate had been chosen for him?" He looked over his shoulder and caught Dustsucker looking that way, too. There was something about a new grave that was different than the headstones and crypts of people who had been dead for a while.

"Hell if I know, Ian. I could give you the textbook answers, but that wouldn't make them true or honest. I'm just struck by the 'here I am agains' I bump into along my way. It's as if something was pushing at me, or tugging at me as you say, to put me in a particular place at a particular time. Like tonight, on our way to Wells." Slavin looked up into the sky. There'd been rare moments in his life where he'd seen as many stars. There had been no moments where he'd seen more.

"Ronin," Dustsucker called out. Ronin tugged briefly at Jackson's reins until Slade caught up.

"Yeah, Dusty?"

"I don't mean to be interrupting all this spiritual talk," he said, "but Tom left us a message by that poor son-of-a-bitch's grave. Did you see it?"

"I did."

"I didn't see it," Slavin said.

"The cairn," Dustsucker said, "the little rocks piled on top of each other. It's Tom's way of saying 'up ahead,' or 'keep on coming.' What do you think we're going to find in Wells, Ronin?" Dustsucker asked, kicking the flanks of his horse so that he was riding in between the two men.

"Damned if I know. I just hope Tom doesn't attempt to corral the two of them all by himself. He's likely to get himself hurt if he does."

"They're that tough?" Slavin asked.

"That unpredictable, Ian. Antonio Latigo is a criminal with a long trail of murders and misdeeds behind his name. Thus the name 'Toro,' the bull."

Slavin nodded. "And the woman?"

"He doesn't know what to make of the woman," Dustsucker said, laughing, "despite the fact she left a .36 caliber ball in his chest. We almost lost him then."

"Ronin?"

"Exactly," he continued. "The woman is crazy, from what I can tell. Given the death of her sister, she's carrying around a lot of anger nowadays."

"Dusty, you don't know that," Ronin interrupted.

"Did you see the hole in that man's forehead?"

"I did not."

"Well, I dug around a bit while you and the Mormon here were off praying together. I'm no doctor of course, but that was no buffalo gun that shot him. It was close up, judging by the powder burns, and a much smaller ball or bullet."

"We weren't praying together, Dustsucker."

"I told you not to call me that, son, and I don't really care. Ronin?" he said.

"Yeah, Dusty."

"You need to get to the point that you're willing to put a bullet in that woman's head. No hesitation, you hear me? You do anything less than that and there's a good chance you'll get another 'happy to meet you' ball in your lung or heart this time. And that would be the end of you."

"I imagine it would be," Ronin replied, smiling at Slavin, who appeared to be grappling with the back-and-forth between him and Slade.

"Dusty?"

Dustsucker growled. "Yes, Mister Slavin?"

"Why is it you don't like me?"

"It's not that I don't like you, Mister Slavin. It's that I don't think you belong on this trip. Wounded or not — and it seems to me Wells would be a good place to leave you — these two desperadoes are serious business. Hotheads need not apply."

Slavin hung his head and appeared to be thinking when Ronin interrupted. "Dusty, is that Wells up ahead?"

"It sure is. Black as midnight."

"Except for a lamp in that saloon over there," Slavin said.

"Well then, let's head over there and get us a drink. We'll figure out what we're going to do after we get a couple of drinks and a meal under our belts."

"I don't drink, Mister Ronin."

"Ian, everybody drinks. Some people drink more than others. And incidentally, it seems to me I've seen you on the inebriated side of sober and heard some stories as well."

"That may be," Slavin said. "But I'm a new man now that I got shot. And I won't be drinking ever again."

Dustsucker and Ronin smiled at each other. There wasn't anyone so untrustworthy, so unstable, so dangerous or painful to be with than a person who thinks himself perfect when everyone else is happy to simply try.

Chapter 49
NO WAITING NECESSARY

It didn't take Tom Kelly long to find the wagon or the two people who had ridden in it. Fresh tracks along the frozen ground outside Wells led right to a pile of railroad ties known as the Bulls Head Saloon on the commercial row. Looking through the windows of the saloon from the railroad depot across the street, Kelly witnessed the evolving conversation between his suspects and the saloon's proprietor. He noticed the tension in the room as well.

He had met the female suspect before, when he'd visited the Livestock sisters during a private investigation instigated by the owner of a local Virginia City saloon. Alvira Fae Livestock was the less comely of the two women, the difference accounted for more by the woman's attitude than her appearance as the sisters were twins. They hadn't spoken, but Alvira had made a lasting impression on him as she was carrying an old Paterson revolver concealed in a shoulder sack. The short man he had never met, but the little man's appearance — as much as he could determine given the lighting — confirmed that he was looking at a full-fledged dwarf and not simply a shorter person. Both individuals matched the descriptions given him by witnesses along the way, were well animated and caused him to think more quickly than he had intended as to how to prevent their escape.

For all the hoopla regarding the Bulls Head Saloon — it being the first business building in Wells and having "a full shelf of quality beers, wines and liquors" — the edifice had more the appearance of a hastily erected railroad shack than a commercial watering hole to be proud of. He wouldn't spend any more time than was necessary in Wells before hog-tying his suspects, meeting up with Ronin, Dustsucker and Slavin, and heading out of town.

Tom and his wife, or rather late wife Winifred, had grown up in New Brunswick, Canada, traveling over 3,000 miles to be part of the California gold rush. When the yellow was well panned and fortunes turned elsewhere, Tom found a position as a miner in the Gould and Curry Mine in Virginia City. Later, as a police chief and city sheriff, he'd continued to work the mines, even their lower levels where the pay was better and cash was needed to support his large family and A Street house. Bars like the Bulls Head Saloon were no place to leave one's time and money, and he generally had no part of it even in the trendier establishments in Virginia City. With Winifred gone, there was every reason to hurry back. He'd not dally any more than necessary.

Crossing the street with his Winchester in hand, he peered into the window of the saloon just in time to see the owner, judging by the man's clean appearance, pick up the little man, twirl him overhead and toss him into a table by the saloon's front entrance. The midget, however — apparently unnerved and uninjured by the experience — quickly stood back up and brushed the splinters off. The woman was immediately out of her chair and began shouting.

As he couldn't make out what was being said, he placed his ear against the window when he was surprised by a sudden knocking against the window. "Can I help you?" the little man asked. Tom was startled enough that he replied.

"No," he said, before he panicked and answered again. "Yes," he said, thinking there was nothing he could do now but to introduce himself and bring the matter to a swift conclusion. "Would you have the owner open the door?" he asked.

Tony Latigo smiled, looked over at Bobby McKee, whom he had grown to like despite the large man's preference for tossing small persons willy-nilly and without warning across a barroom. "Bob?" he asked.

"Yes, Mister Latigo?"

"The man outside the window is asking if you'd let him in. Shall we?"

McKee, never an individual to not think about money, looked at his new friends — a surprisingly strong and resilient little man he no longer needed to offend and his angry but pretty soon-to-be ex-wife. "Why not?" he said, and with that he practically skated across the floor swirling so as to unlatch the front door. "Can I help you?" McKee asked, as Tom Kelly pushed past him and entered the saloon.

It being a small room, the barkeep being so large and Latigo standing only a dozen feet away from him — Miss Livestock perhaps an equal amount of feet in another direction — Kelly didn't know what to do or say. *So much for planning*, he thought to himself before blurting out a complete untruth. "I'm Tom Dickenharry," he said before realizing how funny the words sounded when leaving his lips.

"Dick and Harry?" the little man replied, "That's totally funny," the little man said before bearing down on Kelly with his eyes as if to insist that he give his real name. And he was about to, Tom was, the whole scene being so strange and unnerving, when he heard the midget say, "And exceptionally creative, too!" McKee smiled, but there was no telling what was running through Alvira Livestock's mind as she didn't seem to be listening. "Aliases don't need to be serious," Latigo continued. "Why shouldn't they be entertaining, too?" The little man began laughing. *Why shouldn't they, indeed?* "None of us are using our real names here," Latigo said, "especially my new friend, the saloon manager. Mister Dickenharry, meet Mister McKee," he said. And it was all so unreal, so very unreal.

Alvira sat back down in her chair after the brief intermission of having another stranger enter the room. *I mean, if Tony's not upset being tossed like a round of cheese why should I be?* She raised a finger to Bob McKee, who was stuttering an easygoing explanation that he wasn't the owner of the saloon but would be glad to buy it if something could be arranged that would better fit his station in life, and none too soon he wanted to point out, given that the Elko sheriff — a man who's had his entire life handed to him on a silver platter, what with a brick machine just outside of Elko turning out 35,000 bricks a day under steam or 25,000 a day only using horses, and being owed all kinds of money by the state of Nevada for the erection of their new college — was thinking of buying this little place, "which I call home and turning it into a hotel and eatery, which would be just awful," he thought of saying before taking the woman's order of a glass of wine and maybe a biscuit. Kelly, surprised and off guard and now disturbed by the utter craziness of it all, stood watching the three people who were talking all at once before shouting, "I'm the Storey County sheriff and I'm here to arrest you. Well, not you," he said, pointing at the saloon owner, who was starting to mumble about not being the owner but liking a chance to do something with his "hard-earned efforts other than pour another glass of wine for a wonderfully attractive woman." But with that admission, every eye turned suddenly his way.

"Arrest me?" Latigo said, grabbing at his whip and slamming the whip's pommel end Kelly's way, hitting him in the stomach and causing him to drop not only his rifle but handgun as well. The twin had hold of Tom's hair before he knew it, pulling his unprotected face toward a table. And that's all he remembered, until he woke up with a giant headache and overheard the midget saying to McKee and his companion, "What are we going to do with this guy?"

"This is not my problem," McKee said, always careful to keep a secret as sort of an unspoken rule that the profferer of secrets would keep the listener's secrets as well. "It's your issue," he said, "assuming what he says is true. I don't want any part of it." Alvira nodded. There was no reason to involve the handsome man.

"You don't need to be any part of it," she said.

"I won't be the only person to decide," the small man interrupted, stamping his feet.

"You sure as hell will," Alvira said in a scolding tone. She looked over at Big Bobby McKee, who was reclining against the bar, his big broad chest sticking out like a rooster on Easter morning, crowing and growing all sort of handsome on her. He was looking at her fondly and smiling. "You got us into this mess," Alvira said, smiling back. "And you'll sure as hell get us out."

Chapter 50
EARLY A.M., RONIN

It was the middle of the morning, the early morning, when W. W. Ronin and his crew entered the town of Wells along the tracks running parallel to Front Street. Commercial row was practically empty — a couple of hurdy-gurdy girls stood guard, leaning up against empty saloons hoping for an additional dime or dollar before turning in for the night, and a noisy group of Indians appeared to be huddled on the train platform tossing cards into an empty hat. The moon was bright and there wasn't anything on the street that didn't move without a shadow.

"Find a doctor," Ronin said.

"I'll be fine for another hour or two," Slavin replied. He pulled a clean handkerchief from underneath his shirt, sniffed it and then said, "See, I'm not bleeding. God is taking care of me as I told you he would."

"Whatever," Ronin replied. "Get your ass up the street, find a sign that says 'doctor' or 'surgeon' or something like that and slam your hand against his door until someone answers. I'll not have you laying in the middle of the road distracting me when I can have you lying down in a veterinarian's office."

"You want me to see a horse doctor?"

"Ian, I don't care who you see. I just want you taken care of. Now get moving."

Slavin jumped off his horse and tied it to a post out front of the first building he came to and began walking west toward the railroad station. He crossed his arms in a sort of Mormon or Masonic prayer posture — right hand over his heart, left hand holding his elbow, submissive as could be because that's what his mother had taught him — and began peering in each of the doors and windows he passed. He seemed to be mumbling under his breath or perhaps praying.

"I don't get him," Dustsucker said as they continued riding toward the train platform. "I mean, the guy took a bullet to his shoulder. Why wouldn't he want to see a doctor?"

"Why don't you like going to the barber? I don't know. Asking why isn't going to help us," Ronin replied, eyeing the Indians who were eyeballing them when they tied up to a concrete post on the train side of the platform.

"You don't have to jump at me," Dustsucker said. "I'm just saying I don't understand him, and what my dislike of barbers has to do with anything, I don't know."

"I'm sorry, Dusty. I don't understand him either. I want to be a lawyer; I don't want to be a lawyer. I want to dig for gold ..."

"Silver."

"Whatever. I don't want to dig for gold. I want to be a sheriff, but I've never done anything about that, either. Some men are boys their whole lives, it seems."

"And it bothers the hell out of the rest of us."

"It does that. Say, you think our horses are going to be safe here?" Ronin looked at the three Indians who were tossing cards. They were arguing over a card that had rested briefly on the brim of a well-worn and discarded top hat before being knocked inside of the hat by another player's card.

"Seem to be well fed," Dustsucker replied, laughing.

"As in nobody is going to eat my horse tonight?" Ronin asked.

"Exactly."

"Hey, is that the Bulls Head Saloon across the street? I believe it is," Ronin answered himself before pulling his 1866 Yellow Boy from a leather sleeve hanging from the saddle. The brass sparkled underneath a railroad station lamp, its yellow gleam reminding Ronin why he liked the Henry and the 1866 design that followed it. It was simply prettier than anything that came along afterward. "Let's take a walk," he said, walking to the east side of the platform and standing in the shadows.

"Ronin, the place is dark--I mean closed. I rather doubt there's anyone there at this point. Why don't we hit one of the other saloons and wet our whistles? Sunup shouldn't be too long."

Ronin gazed up at the stars, as if their position would tell him the time. Looking at the moon, he said, "Alright, but let's tie up across the street. I'm not real fond of Jackson here, but I've had him a long time. Besides that, I've got stuff in the bags."

"We both do."

"Sure enough. Let's move."

They untied their horses from the platform and began leading them across the street when Slavin called out. "You guys going to get something to drink?"

"We are."

"How about I tag along?" And it was just about that point in the conversation that a little man opened the door of the Bulls Head Saloon and peered outside.

Chapter 51
EARLY A.M., NAUMAN

It was the middle of the night, the very early morning sometime around two or three o'clock, when Emma opened her eyes and knew she should be praying. Right then, right now she thought, her lips beginning to tremble as the Spirit poured forth speech she couldn't hear or understand. They shook for a while, dried from the five hours she had laid in bed, "dead to the world but alive in the spirit" she liked to say, sometimes hoping for dreams like the ancients Hebrews had. Abraham, Jacob, Joseph, one of the pharaohs she thought, Samuel, Daniel, Joseph the father of Jesus, Pilot's wife — they'd all had dreams where God was speaking to them or where an angel delivered a message and a mortal listened as if their life depended on what the Holy One had to say. If only she could sleep like that.

"In the last days it shall be, God declares," the scriptures said, "that I will pour out my Spirit on all flesh. Your sons and daughters shall prophesy. Your young men shall see visions and your old men shall dream dreams." In sons and daughters, there was hope, she thought, that someday she'd be the clean conduit of God's best intentions and mercies.

So when the Lord woke her with a start — and there was no other explanation for it, she figured listening to the sounds outside, which seemed undisturbed and no mention of her name being spoken within the house — she tumbled awake like a drunken sailor on his way back to a boat after a night of carousing, which of course she never did though she was sure she was just as much a sinner, her private intentions being what they were. Not that she acted on them, hardly ever anyway. She immediately began thinking of her man, even as the words sprang from her lips, words she didn't understand though they sounded like another language or perhaps a heavenly language now that she was no longer whispering and the Spirit was bringing forth speech she could listen to and interpret.

The Apostle Paul demanded that an interpreter be present in more public conditions when speaking in heavenly tongues like the angels, she thought, or the first missionaries to the islands or the Orient. But she wasn't speaking publicly, so of course Paul's words in *First Corinthians* didn't apply. Still, she wished she could understand what the Spirit was saying to her, or saying to God. It was so confusing. And then the thought came. "It's about my man," she said out loud, achieving a sort of union between soul and flesh. "You want me praying about my man," she said, thinking she should slip down off of her bed and onto her knees, her head against her hands against the mattress. "You want me praying about William," she said, throwing the covers off and sliding out of bed. She put her slippers on and her robe as she had begun sleeping naked with her man — not that they ever did anything, not much anyway — and it didn't seem at all appropriate to be praying that way.

"Dearest Jesus," she said as she began to sob, a prayer away even though they were separated by at least 300 miles of towns and track, "there may be trouble," she said getting up from her knees and looking around for a dress or a skirt, the ache inside her hounding her awake, her prayers only making the craziness worse. "What am I to do?" she said, pacing the room, a dress on, a slip too and slippers, though she'd never go outside without shoes. Maybe she should find her shoes.

"Miss Emma?" a voice called from the front room. It was one of the men staying at the ranch.

"Parker?" she said, hoping he hadn't seen or heard her, but then why would he be there calling her name if he hadn't?

"Yes, ma'am."

"Are you okay?" she asked, knowing that she didn't need to check on him. It was him who was checking on her.

"Are *you*, ma'am?" he replied, not wanting to come back into her room. It was bad enough that he had opened the house door and entered, she being the only woman at home and he being the only man, a hired man at that.

"I am, Parker. Please go back to bed."

"I will, ma'am. And you?"

"I will. I was awakened and probably called out. Please do not worry."

"I will not, Miss Emma. Have a good night," he said as he closed the door to the house and wondered about what Miss Emma had said. She had not called out, not in that middle of the night dreaming sense when a person is awakened with a start and groans or shouts. She had been praying. He recognized that. He often prayed at night, too.

The hired man walked back to the barn, where he had gone to check on an appaloosa who had injured herself the day before. God smiled on those who were kind to animals, he thought, though he really didn't know the church's teachings on such things, his priest never speaking about animals and such, simply what men should do and sometimes women, too. But he was certain, if there was a God in heaven who cared about men and women, and children too, that that same God loved animals. Horses for sure, maybe not coyotes, but certainly dogs, though he wasn't sure about cats. And praying at night was sometimes the only way he could voice these things as his wife thought him sometimes looney, moving his lips in such a way as to form words she didn't understand. He didn't understand them, either. But some-times, when the Spirit came over him, he was certain that God was saying something important even if he couldn't understand it. And he knew the message he needed to pay attention to wasn't always in the speaking. It was sometimes in the hearing. And so he wanted to be ready.

"You're going to be fine," he said to the appaloosa, who was already lying back down to go to sleep. "Everything is going to be just fine," he said. "God is telling me so, *mi caballita*."

Chapter 52

EARLY A.M., LATIGO

It was the early hours of the morning, between midnight and six o'clock, when Toro Latigo didn't usually speak or stir, "or do shit" he said as he opened the door of the Bulls Head Saloon and jumped onto the boards shaking his head and hoping that a little air would clear the raging thoughts he was having when Alvira began pointing her finger his way. It wasn't like he didn't notice with all the negativity she was expressing. It was hard to miss all the smiles and grins she was showing Bobby McKee, a man she didn't even know except for a few moments looking through a window glass and some empty promises that there might be jobs headed their way if she wouldn't mind waiting on tables and he wouldn't mind mopping some of the stalls out back. He'd looked out back and the thought that he should be picking up after pigs made him physically sick, not that he showed it to the man he knew someday he'd have to kill, his being so big and all.

So when Alvira began pointing at him and saying it was all up to him — that this thing with the sheriff was *his* problem when all he had done was help her with her deal with a tall man named W. W. Ronin and his fat friend, who were closing in on the girls' entrepreneurial enterprises in Virginia City — well, it just blew the cork out of the bottle, he thought while sitting down on the edge of the boardwalk and staring down into the dirt. Who needed this kind of grief, he wondered, remembering times past when he'd been frustrated by similarly mean expressions and inordinate demands. He put an end to them, he surely did — dumping one man into an Elko hot spring, not that anyone was looking for him, and weren't there hot springs in Wells? There had to be, goddamn it.

Toro Latigo picked up the whip he'd used a few months earlier to scold Ronin into an unconscious submission and wound it into a tiny circle before fitting it over the butt of his gun. He looked around the boards for his Springfield. *Where did I leave that? It must still be in back of the wagon.*

Not one for school — he'd been a troubled child from the beginning and had beat up at least one teacher who had tried to get him to do his arithmetic — Toro Latigo began to count the days since he left Virginia City with the constabularies trailing so closely behind him.

In Reno, there'd been a little trouble with a night watchman that had to be addressed. The man ended up upside down in a trash bin behind the First Methodist Church because he'd asked too many questions. "You'd think a midget would be welcome in a Methodist church," he said before punching the guy in the balls and watching him crumble like a man about to ask a woman to get married except that he didn't get up and there was no woman with him. Alvira had given him all kinds of hell for that, saying if he couldn't respect a church how could he ever respect a woman since a woman gave birth to the church and was the Mother of the Church, she said. But only a Catholic idiot would understand what that meant he said before being punched in the face.

Then there was the rancher in Lovelock who insisted they were driving their wagon across his land though he had been there a million times—probably not that many but certainly more times than the man had men in his bunk house. He'd invited the cattleman to step down from his saddle, he being so small and all, and the man complied. So when he had his back turned he'd panned him — the iron fry pan right upside his head. It probably served him right for Alvira to drive a tin cup into his noggin some weeks later though he thought the two incidents shouldn't be thought of together and imagined the fist-whooping he'd given the cow man once he had fallen was justice enough for being so ignorant.

Now he was having to watch his woman make eyes at some twit twice as tall and maybe twice as stupid, though there was a chance that "Big Bobby" McKee, as Alvira had taken to calling him — at his request of course — might be smart enough to win his woman away from him. And then what would he be left with? A couple of horses and an old wagon he'd been sleeping in ever since his parents died, though to be horribly honest he'd been sleeping in it long before then, maybe as long as he could remember.

He took a step toward the alley thinking he'd reclaim his Trapdoor from the wagon — a gun bigger than him, or at least it felt like it some days, though he'd battered the man who'd first owned it and would batter the man who thought it was too tall for him, just try. But when he turned, he noticed a hunched-over cowboy just a block or two south of the train station rubbing on his shoulder and heading his way.

"You guys going to get something to drink?" he heard him call out.

"We are," someone said from the shadows over by the train depot across the street.

"How about I tag along?" the crippled man said, though it wasn't clear that he was crippled — he was just walking that way.

And it was just about that point in the conversation between the two men that he heard Alvira Fae say from behind him,

"Toro? Is that Ronin standing over there on the platform? Oh my god," she said — the smiles suddenly fading and the giddiness quickly gone, and Big Bobby McKee standing there like the fool he was, not knowing whether to grab the girl or rescue the bottle of wine she'd been drinking from.

That's when he heard the words from across the way: "Son of a bitch!"

Chapter 53
EARLY A.M., SLAVIN

It was the early morning, when good Mormons are usually fast asleep though more than a few sometimes stumble in the darkness that separates the Gentiles from the Saints. Ian Slavin hopped up onto the sidewalk and noticed a little man who looked remarkably like the wanted man the others had described. He was sitting on the end of the boardwalk with his head in his hands and it appeared as if he was crying.

Being a religious man, at least recently, Slavin initially imagined that he'd come up alongside the troubled man and ask if there was anything he could do to help. Life was hard enough. No one should face things alone. He remembered the story of the Good Samaritan. The Samaritan took care of the man, his mother had said many years ago, without asking if he was a robber on the Jericho road or if he was wealthy enough to pay his way. And Christ didn't give any thought to his own safety, she had said in their family meeting. Christ was always at risk, she said, especially when sharing unpopular and radical ideas.

But then he remembered the other stories — that Anthony Latigo had murdered his parents in Elko County many years previously, and countless others between the temple in Salt Lake to the courthouse in Carson City over the years. So he hesitated. He didn't make an effort to do "the right thing," "the Christian thing," the very thing his mother had counseled he ought to do if the situation ever presented itself.

So when it became clear that Ronin and Dustsucker were headed to a saloon instead of taking care of their business — not that he'd been told what they were about to do — he forgot that he was thinking about serving kindness and compassion to the little man sitting on the edge of the boards, pulling his hair and looking from side to side. He didn't recall that he was in search of a commercial row physician who might take care of his shoulder. And in his distraction, he overlooked the little man sitting on the sidewalk who was now angrily turning his way. It was three-o'clock in the frickin' morning, he figured, and he was so very tired.

"You guys going to get something to drink?" he called to his friends across the street, completely oblivious to what was unfolding in front of him. He heard Ronin's response — it sounded distant, so very far away that he could barely hear it for the buzz and the bother of everything racing through his mind — so he asked again. "Can I tag along?" And that's when he heard the first shot.

He dove to the boards, scraping his right palm against an old nail that had worked its way out, and made himself as small as he could possibly be. And he saw the little man's gun pointed his way. Right at him, a .45 or a .44, not that it mattered. Either caliber would blow a big hole through his body which was already doing so poorly that when the other men weren't looking he was walking hunched over, like an old man on his way to an outhouse.

He saw the little man spin around as if surprised that someone was shooting at him, and someone sure was! A board fixed to the saloon doorway suddenly swung free as if hit with a hammer, and windows on both sides of the entryway shattered, dropping large shards of glass onto the boardwalk and into the street where the little man was still twirling, trying to make sense of things. A fourth shot landed right between his legs. Everything happened so fast he wouldn't have noticed it if it wasn't for the patch of dirt that kicked up into the little man's eyes, causing him to fall backward into the saloon.

"Goddamn," he said before feeling guilty that he'd taken the Lord's name in vain. "Holy shit," he said before thinking the lesser words weren't a whole lot different and there went his attempts at being holy. He would now surely have a beer or two if he made his way out of this without feeling another bullet hit his body like the shoulder shot did. It hurt so much.

Slavin looked over toward the boys standing on the train platform and it was clear who was doing the shooting. Dustsucker was leaning over. It looked like he was grabbing Ronin's Yellow Boy leaning against the wall of the train station. A couple of Indians had taken off running down the tracks headed toward Elko, which was fifty miles away or more. It would take them ten hours or so to make it there if they continued on their feet. But Ronin — Jesus Hallelujah! — was smooth and confident and shooting like there was no tomorrow: his right leg outstretched, his gun hand a good ten inches away from his holster firing the first shot, the subsequent shots — maybe four of them, he couldn't count them they were so fast — inching out from his torso until his Colt stood a scant 12 inches or so from his belt. God, he was fast.

When the little man fell into the doorway, Ian Slavin assumed the gun fight was over and rolled over onto his back, looking up into the early morning sky. A handful of stars peeked out between clouds, but the moon, the glorious moon, was illuminating everything in the street. Then he heard Ronin whispering to him and realized that what he was saying wasn't at all what he wanted his bishop to hear or his mother to know about.

"Holy shit," he was saying over and over again, until Ronin yelled at him and told him to shut up.

"He doesn't need to know where you are," he said. *No kidding.*

Chapter 54
RAM FANNING

Ronin drove his right foot forward and dumped his 4-inch Colt out of its holster so that it sat parallel to the platform a couple of inches behind his holster. He thumbed the first shot as the gun was coming out, in maybe less than three-tenths of a second. Then he ram-fanned another three, pushing the Colt forward into his outstretched finger. Fanning with the hand, he'd learned, would break the gun. The lightest touch was the fastest touch, and his whole purpose was to do his best to keep the little man from moving back into the saloon.

But Latigo stumbled backward through the doorway into the open arms of Alvira Fae, who was standing there with her mouth open saying something — he couldn't hear what, but her look indicated surprise and disbelief. A couple of feet behind her was a large man he couldn't identify, who had hold of a bottle of wine and was hurrying to the other side of the saloon.

Ronin took to the street, dumping his empties and one live cartridge in order to load six more. He kept his eye on the door and made a quick check for his friend. Dustsucker had picked up his rifle and pulled his 10-gauge shotgun from its scabbard. Tom Kelly, who had left them a good couple of hours ago, was nowhere to be seen. *He should have been here by now.* Slavin was lying prone on the boards by Richardson's Barbershop.

"Holy shit," he was saying over and over again.

Ronin counseled him with quiet gestures to keep it down. "Shut up," he whispered. "He doesn't need to know where you are." The street was suddenly silent, having erupted into an early morning gunfight when good people would normally be in bed, and in fact most were except for Ronin and his friends, who were now certain they had located their man though they had driven him back into hiding.

"Here!" Dustsucker said, tossing the Yellow Boy Ronin's way before taking up position on the front left side of the saloon. "Where do you want me?" Ronin motioned toward the back and mimicked the blast of the shotgun so that Dustsucker understood. Whatever came out the back door should be met by the blast of Dusty's street cleaner. A shot into the dirt by the doorway would put more rocks and dirt into the doorway than most people could tolerate. Ronin took cover by a rain barrel a couple of feet away from the door.

"Toro. Come out with your hands up. You too, Miss Livestock. It's time to face the music." And then the damnedest thing took place. From inside the saloon an unforgettably shrill voice began to sing, "Just Before the Battle, Mother," a song popular among Union troops during the Civil War. "Just before the battle, mother, I am thinking most of you. While upon the field we're watching with the enemy in view." The goddamned dwarf was singing! What the hell?

Ronin looked over at Slavin, who had pried himself up from the boardwalk and was sitting against the exterior wall of Hamill and Meigs Department Store. "Comrades brave are 'round me lying, filled with thoughts of home and God. For well they know that on the morrow, some will sleep beneath the sod."

"Jesus, God," Ronin said loudly before remembering that it was his criticism of the little man's singing talents a few months before that caused Latigo to come after him. "Farewell, mother, you may never press me to your heart again. But, oh, you'll not forget me, mother, if I'm numbered with the slain," the singing continued. "Really?" Ronin yelled, gesturing to Slavin to move up the boardwalk to be closer to the saloon's front door. "Are we really going to have a concert, you piece of shit?"

"Don't be talking to my man that way," Alvira said from just behind one of the holes where windows previously had been. "I'll not tolerate it, Mister Ronin, and he will not either."

"Whatever," Ronin snorted, gesturing that Slavin should draw his gun and cover the doorway. Slavin nodded. He lifted the Remington from his holster and opened the gate to load an extra shell. He smiled.

"What's with the singing?" Slavin whispered.

"Long story," Ronin whispered back. "Man fashions himself something of an entertainer. Have song — will travel. Crazy, right?"

"Very," Slavin hissed. He pushed his back up against the pitch that painted the outside of the saloon. "You know, a little bit of cedar and this place wouldn't look so bad," he said when he heard another voice from within.

"You think this place looks bad?" Bobby McKee yelled from behind the bar. "Wait until you see it when Ben Fitch gets hold of it. It will be a real shit hole, I'm telling you!"

"Who's that?" Slavin whispered.

"Hell, if I know," Ronin said. "But if he doesn't find a bigger place to hide than the inside of that bar, he's going to be eating an awful lot of lead."

Chapter 55
INSIDE THE SALOON

"I thought you said he was dead."

"Alvira, I didn't say that. I said he was *probably* dead."

"Well, we're in a fine fix now," she said, watching Bobby McKee finger the lip of an open wine bottle as if wondering if he should take a sip or top it off and put it back on the shelf as new. "What do you think, Bob?" she asked.

The manager of the Bulls Head Saloon looked over and shrugged. "I don't imagine they're going to come in here shooting anytime soon, though when they do there won't be a safe place anywhere."

"What are you saying?" the little man said with a sneer on his face. *The bigger they are the faster they fall.*

"I'm saying the obvious Mister Latigo. You stay in here and you're going to end up Swiss cheese. Good news is you can't shoot through these walls. So unless they come in, you all seem pretty safe to me. Never met a bullet a railroad tie wouldn't stop."

"That's true." Latigo picked himself up from the saloon floor and propped a chair against the front doors. "We got some time, I guess." He paused for a moment before looking at the two of them. "You and Alvira, you going to do it?"

"Excuse me?" McKee said.

"I see how you look at each other."

McKee smiled. Miss Livestock did not. "Mister Latigo, I understand you're upset. You're a tiny man and I imagine life has its challenges. And I get that things aren't exactly going your way right now. You've got a couple of marshals outside who you apparently have history with. But listen, every day is a new day. And what I'm hoping to do or not hoping to do with your wife here isn't really any of your business."

"What?!" Latigo's head leaned forward. He clenched his fists into tiny balls.

"Relax, my friend. I'm simply saying whatever it is you're afraid of isn't on today's menu. Good enough?"

Latigo, who'd rarely been spoken to that way, had a sort of religious respect for the present moment. And while he was making notes about what tomorrow might bring — a dead girlfriend perhaps and a very dead boyfriend if McKee kept it up — had come to a place in his life where he appreciated the thought that most days had enough challenges than to be distracted by yesterday or tomorrow's troubles. Thinking like that kept the craziness at bay. "Mister Kelly, what do you think?" He pulled the wadded up kerchief out of the Virginia City sheriff's mouth.

"I think you're a dead man, Tony," Kelly mumbled. "And whether or not Big Bobby here screws your girlfriend or wife is really unimportant. You're a dead man and you just don't know it." Kelly strained against the ropes wound tightly around his legs, hands and chest. The barroom chair to which he was tied strained at the effort. Latigo pushed the kerchief back into his mouth.

"Thank you gentlemen, I think that's good advice. Miss Livestock, I'll have a beer please." He pulled a second chair over to the doorway and faced the saloon. "And some crackers, also." She stood in the center of the room staring at him.

"You want milk and crackers?" she asked in disbelief.

"Beer and crackers, baby. Or I shoot your boyfriend. I don't care." McKee put the bottle on the shelf behind him and fingered a double barreled shotgun underneath the bar. Pulling the hammer back would make too much noise. But at least he knew where it was.

"Mister Latigo, that's my job. Let me give you what you need." Alvira looked suddenly in McKee's direction. *There will be no more killing.* McKee smiled and turned his back. He grabbed a brown bottle from the shelf. "Glass?"

"Bottle's fine," he said, pulling another chair to him with the toe of his boot. "My apologies, Mister McKee. It's nothing personal, you understand."

"My taking a liking to your wife?"

"No, I wouldn't have it any other way," he said, smiling at Alvira, who was not smiling back. She appeared nervous. "My shooting you," he said.

"Ah," McKee said, walking out from behind the bar so as to stand in front of the door. He handed the bottle to Latigo and began to turn.

"McKee?"

"Yeah." He turned around.

"You like my singing?"

"Music's a good thing, Tony. I admire the fact that when the elephant is looking your way, you don't mind singing a tune."

"I don't just not mind it, Bobby. I like it. I've often thought if I had my life to live differently it would have been nice to have been in show business. You?"

Big Bobby McKee, the manager of the Bulls Head Saloon in Wells, Nevada — not the owner, but the barkeep and he was hoping to keep things that way — thought for a moment as to what he might say. He'd often imagined himself in sales, maybe for Montgomery Ward, or for a carriage company, or some big company back East where lots of money changed hands. He'd have been good at it he figured, but the opportunity had never come up. It was too late now. If the saloon would have him, he'd

stay as long as he could even if Ben Fitch bought the place goddamnit. He looked up. "Tony, may I call you that?"

"I don't see why not."

"Here's how I see it. We're all in show business, Tony. The
only question is whether anyone is looking our way."

Chapter 56
WHERE A WINDOW USED TO BE

Marcus T. Slade was watching all of this from the outside front corner of the saloon, where a window used to be before Ronin sprayed the place with lead. The Ormsby County deputy sheriff sometimes wondered if the ex-priest could hit the broad side of a barn, but then the midget was almost 100 feet away from where Ronin stood when he began shooting and the draw was a quick one. Even Bill Hickock would have had to take aim at that distance.

Then there was the question as to why anyone would be so stupid to barricade the front doors of a saloon when windows twice as broad as the front doors were wide open. He shook his head and smiled.

"What?"

"I just can't believe people are so dumb."

"Yeah," Ronin whispered. Slavin had taken up a position at the back of the saloon, instead of staying out front, so that Dustsucker and Ronin could enter by the front.

Dusty fingered his badge. "You ready?" he asked quietly.

Ronin shook his head. "Give me a minute. I don't often pray, but I'm thinking I want to."

"Good idea," Dustsucker said, beginning to mouth the words of the bedtime prayer, "Now I lay me down to sleep," before realizing there were likely better prayers than those that ended with "and if I die before I wake, I pray the Lord my soul to take." The whole thing about praying was strange, as far as he was concerned. *What is about to happen is entirely up to me.* He opened his eyes as Ronin began to signal that he was going to kick at the front door and that he should put his shotgun on anything that moved away from it. Ronin would take the window on the other side of the door should the door not spring open. Dustsucker nodded.

Though armed entries were uncomfortable for him, Ronin had spent years perfecting his hand-to-hand skills. What he hadn't picked up in the war he later begged from an Episcopal bishop in Pittsburgh who taught him how to box. They met at the Locust Grove Seminary in Lawrenceville at the time. Classmates John Schoenberger, Felix Brunot, Charles Knap and Thomas Howe all had an interest when they weren't dealing with war orphans, or the aged and infirm. The local bishop, a fiery Irishman with a talent of putting fist to face and other parts of people's bodies showed them the ropes, so to speak. "Take a good pair of gloves with you when you head west," the bishop had advised before he left for Wichita, and he'd been right. Once settled, he'd found a similarly talented Frenchman who showed him how to use his feet and legs.

He took a deep breath and loaded his left leg by bringing his right knee to his chest. He repeated it a couple of times to make sure his form was correct, his fists grasping his rifle in front of his face, then let his leg fly toward a mark just above the door knob. The doors of the Bulls Head Saloon literally exploded.

Toro Latigo went flying toward the back wall, legs all askew and screaming, followed by pieces of two table chairs that shattered against the floor and walls. To his surprise, Alvira Livestock was standing unmoved in the center of the room with her hands on her waist, her eyes wide and mouth agape as if seeing a ghost. A man he didn't recognize, Big Bobby McKee was reaching underneath the bar until he saw Ronin in the doorway, left leg still forward, his Yellow Boy leveled at Latigo, who was momentarily plastered face-forward to the back wall of the saloon. Dustsucker stuck his head through the hole that used to be a window, giving both Livestook and McKee a silent warning that any movement — any movement at all, it didn't matter — would result in their taking up residence in a local cemetery or mausoleum until the blessed day when Christ returned to judge the living and the dead. McKee slowly raised his hands.

"Tom!" Ronin shouted, kicking a third chair out of the way as he entered the saloon. He strode purposefully into the room, keeping clear of its occupants but allowing his rifle and vision to scan at the high ready. He looked over at Dustsucker. "Got it?"

"Got it."

He lowered his lowered his rifle and grabbing hold of his knife made swift work of the ropes that trapped his friend. He pulled the kerchief from Kelly's mouth. "You okay?" he asked, while looking at Miss Livestock and the large man with his hands up behind the bar.

"A little embarrassed," Kelly said, coughing. "I won't be heading to church I suspect until I make a good confession."

Ronin laughed. He was thinking some pretty harsh thoughts himself, fully expecting to kill the men within. He looked over at Dustsucker as if to ask a question. Dustsucker shrugged. "Well, then have at it my friend," Ronin said, pulling the gun out of Latigo's holster and spinning the little man around until he faced the wall, sobbing. "The son of a bitch is all yours."

"Not my style," the lawman said, taking the gun from Ronin's hands and tucking it into his pants. "To be truthful though, I wouldn't mind a beer."

It had gone too smoothly, Ronin thought as he lowered his rifle, put his hand on Kelly's shoulder and walked over to the bar. McKee lowered his hands to the front of his apron as Dustsucker climbed in the window and pushed the woman to the wall with the front end of his shotgun. "Ma'am," he said.

"Deputy," she returned.

"You too, Toro. Walk slowly this way," he said.

Latigo took a couple of steps and then stopped. "How do we know you won't kill us?"

"You don't," Dustsucker replied, Ronin turning to say the same. The two men laughed. "You sure as hell don't," Dustsucker continued, "not that you deserve any better. Get down on the floor." The two complied, Alvira Fae Livestock, strangely quiet but submissive and Anthony Latigo, his gun gone, his whip lying on the floor like a dead garden snake. Once face down, they reached out toward each other so that their hands were touching. "Friends to the end, I guess," Dustsucker said.

Ronin turned to the man behind the bar. "Barkeep," he said…

"McKee," the man said, quietly.

"…we'll have those beers now." And that's when the trouble started.

Latigo was on his feet before anyone noticed, their attention having turned toward McKee at the bar. The tiny man leveled a kick to the deputy's shins, having learned at an early age that even the tallest man could be chopped down to size if you kicked at his groin or feet. Dustsucker flinched, discharging a barrel of dimes and rock at one of the mirrors, before bending completely over and grabbing his left leg.

"Damn!" McKee yelled, seizing his own shogun from beneath the bar and then wondering what to do with it now that he was holding it above the counter. The big man had no intention of running afoul of the law. Until recently, he'd not thought of hurting anyone, save maybe hoisting a few men toward the ceiling and throwing them out the front door when situations within the saloon demanded it. Well, there was a spindly man a while back who broke his neck in one of those circumstances, but it wasn't McKee's fault, Ben Fitch had said, the son of a bitch. "Small-necked men shouldn't be acting like big shots when there are bigger men around," McKee had articulated and Fitch actually believed his explanation. And then there were the two Indians, not that anybody knew about them or the bodies he'd recently asked them to produce outside the city of Wells as a message to the same son of a bitch who now wanted to buy the saloon and change things, I mean really change things.

So McKee was standing there thinking about all of these things, oblivious to what was going on around him when he heard the little man say, "Are you going to shoot them or am I?" And there Latigo stood, the deputy all doubled up and lying on the floor holding his leg and Ronin and Kelly with their hands pointed toward the ceiling, their guns still in hand. The midget was holding the deputy's shotgun, waving it back and forth like it was a flag at an Independence Day parade, while waiting to decide which of the three men he was going to shoot. McKee groaned.

"Well then," Latigo said, "I guess it's going to be me." He leveled the shotgun so that it pointed belly-level across the room at Ronin and Kelly who appeared nervous as hell and no wonder. The little man levered the second hammer back, the first having already been discharged, when Alvira Livestock — the lesser of the two twins from Iowa, sent west by a father and a mother who hoped their daughters would find God and whatever God had for them, who McKee hoped to sleep with someday, if not today then maybe the next day or the day after that — reached up from the floor and grabbed Tony's testicles, "two low-hanging fruit" she later said, situated approximately two feet from the saloon floor.

"You mean-spirited, God forsaken, son of a bitch, goddamnit," she said as Tony winced, the shotgun now pointing toward the floor. "I told you no more killing." And with the little man looking all frightened and in excruciating pain, the bigger man — who was twice the width of the little man, twice the height and easily four times as strong — dropped his double-barreled shotgun onto the bar, picked up an iron pan from the shelf behind him and slammed it onto the top of the little man's head. Toro Latigo crumpled to the floor.

"There," he said. "I couldn't stand that man from the first time I met him."

Ronin lowered his hands and laughed. "Neither could I." The two men smiled at each. "Miss Livestock," he said, "back onto the floor. Mister Kelly, help our friend up. And Mister ..." he paused.

"McKee. Bobby McKee."

"Mister McKee, how about those beers?"

Chapter 57
HAND AND
LEG IRONS

It didn't take long to wrap up what went on in Wells. And no one argued when Ronin suggested that the five of them take the train back to Elko. The prisoners, Toro Latigo and Alvira Livestock, sat quietly in hand and leg irons amidst businessmen and families journeying the greater distance, from Salt Lake to San Francisco. Ronin and Dustsucker sat opposite each other on the other side of the aisle from Slavin, who was enjoying his temporary position as a U.S. deputy marshal. Having borrowed Dustsucker's badge, he was periodically prodding them to keep their conversation to a minimum. "There's no reason for two prisoners to be talking to each other," he said while pinning on the badge.

"Other than romance," Ronin said, laughing.

"Isn't going to be any romance where they're headed," Slavin said.

Ronin and Dustsucker looked at each other. "No, I guess not," Dustsucker said, thinking of the prison in Carson City where stranger things had happened, though he'd never heard of a baby being born.

"What do you make of these two?" Ronin asked, looking at his friend.

"It's a funny way for things to end," Dusty said, "I mean with everything they've been through. Her losing her sister ..."

"... him killing her sister you mean."

"She stepped in front of the bullet," the little man said before being slapped in the back of the head.

"I'm not telling you again, Mister Latigo. Keep it down. Mister Ronin isn't talking to you."

"Mister Ronin isn't talking to you," the little man mimicked. Alvira smiled.

"What are you asking, Ronin?" Dustsucker continued.

"I'm just saying, with all the killing, all the suffering in-between, all the hope and plans that they'd get away and start a new life together, I'm frankly surprised that we found them."

Dustsucker nodded, pulling his hat down over his eyes. Nothing surprised him anymore. People hurting each other, good people sometimes, sometimes bad people getting away — none of it seemed right, and the differences between the good and the bad? It was so hard to tell who should be arrested and who should be thanked and elected to be the next mayor. *I just do my job.* He started to drift off.

"Dusty?"

"Yeah?"

"What do you make of any of this?" He was thinking of the woman he'd nearly fallen in love with in Virginia City, Alvira's sister, and the woman he surely loved who was waiting for him back in Carson City at a Christian mission that made simply no sense to him given that its only purpose, or so it seemed anyway, was to make Indians into something other than what they are. "I mean, is it worth it to you?"

Dustsucker opened his eyes and pushed the brim up on his hat. He'd heard this before from his friend, who had a habit of spending so much time looking inside himself that he sometimes missed what was happening around him. Emma Nauman for instance. How long had it taken him to catch on to the fact that there was a good woman there hidden under all that Bible stuff?

"I don't know what to tell you, William. I don't know if any of this is worth it," he said, "but I don't know what else there is." He leaned forward so as to speak more intimately. "Look at those two, for instance. They're just like you and me. They do what they do hoping to become something different, or to have something different — a new home, a better place to live, maybe the chance to have children, who knows? And yet they sit there in chains because they deserve to sit there in chains. They've done wrong, my friend." He leaned back. "That's why they deserve it."

"And that makes sense to you?" Ronin asked.

"Yeah," Dustsucker replied, "and it's worth it."

The train rocked a bit as it began to slow down coming into the Elko station. The Depot Hotel sat to their right where a nice dining room and a hot bath awaited them. Ronin looked for the Elko sheriff and then noticed his friend, Jimmy Clark, standing on the platform next to his daughter Mattie. He smiled. He'd be in Carson City soon. Yeah, it was worth it.

Chapter 58
ELKO JUSTICE

"Mister Ronin, how nice to see you again," the hotel owner called out. Clark appeared rested and happy, his daughter Mattie satisfied. The look was uncharacteristic for both of them.

"Mister Clark, how goes it?" Ronin asked. Clark straightened his tie, smiled and offered his hand. "It goes well, William, thanks to you."

"How so, Jim?" He stepped down onto the platform in Elko across from the Depot Hotel, his canvas duster billowing behind him. It was still a week or so before Christmas and the weather had turned exceptionally cold. He left one hand on the railing to help other passengers disembark, and he greeted Clark with the other.

"Well, you got us our criminal. Mills arrived here a few days ago in the custody of Myron Pixley and John Maverick. They said you found him in a haystack."

"Not me," Ronin said while looking at Mattie, who smiled. "But I was happy to drag him *out* of the haystack." Both men laughed. Dustsucker appeared in the doorway and touched his hat to say hello. Livestock and Latigo followed with Tom Kelly and Ian Slavin close behind. Slavin had hold of the handcuffs that locked the little man's wrists behind him. "How's Mills doing, Jim?" He offered his hand to Alvira Livestock, who looked at it and rejected it.

"Well, I have to say it is crazy what a black man will go through for justice in these parts. A jury just found him guilty this morning and Judge Flack sentenced him to death. But we're hoping the state court will overturn on our appeal."

"Wow. That was quick," the ex-preacher said. "It's as if they were waiting for him."

"Well, no man has ever been hanged in Elko County," Clark said. "I'd hate for him to be the first."

"Any *women* been hanged?" Alvira asked, sarcastically. Her attitude was thick enough that it hung in the air. Had it been any sweeter — real or otherwise — you could have cut it with a knife and served it as cake.

"Not yet ma'am," Clark said, laughing. "But there's always a first."

The prisoner turned abruptly away. Clark faced his friend. "There's talk about a half-burned body being discovered over in Carlin, Ronin," he whispered. "Naturally the wife is a suspect, so we may see a woman hanged sooner than later. I hope not, but that's how it's looking."

Ronin nodded. Clark was a closet liberal, if there was such a thing. His faith taught him to forgive, his scriptures said that judgment belonged only to God. While he didn't have a problem with hog-tying an evildoer or beating a man caught while committing a crime, life seemed too precious to be ended hanging on the end of a rope. And Elko County was too new to be caught up in such things. "As I've said before," he continued, "justice is swift in eastern Nevada, gentlemen — a lot faster than it is where you live given the pundits and politicians, and everyone's hands being in everyone else's pockets. It turns out, Mister Ronin, that Sam Mills is something of a fortune-teller."

"Seriously?"

"Yup. He's been throwing cards for some of the guards and deputies. Fact is, he's pretty entertaining, so they've let him go on with it. He tosses cards nearly every night at the jailhouse. I'd book him here if it was okay with Ben Fitch."

"Funny, I don't imagine that Mills foresaw any of this," Ronin said.

"Hard to say, William. Maybe that's why he hid in a Lamoille haystack. Running away just seemed too lame."

Ronin smiled, turning to check on his friends. They looked tired. "Listen Jim, any chance of our getting a private room for lunch?"

"Absolutely. I happen to know the owner," he said laughing. "Want to stay the night? I owe you at least that ..." Clark pulled at the front of his vest and straightened his tie.

"I don't think so," Ronin replied. "I want to get back, and I don't yet know where the marshal wants to lodge these two. Dusty, do you know?"

"Well, Justice Flack's court is as good as any I suppose, he might try them here. Though I suspect Ash would much prefer our bringing them to him rather than his having to travel out this way. My vote would be to take him to Carson City. Tom, are you okay with that?"

"Having seen your jail, Dusty, they'd be more comfortable in Virginia City. But that'd be a longer trip. Either one is okay by me. There isn't any reason to leave them here if they're going to end up in the capital city prison."

"Carson City it is, then. So, just lunch then, Jim. Something secure if you don't mind."

"Secure?"

"As in hard to jump or run from," Ronin said, smiling.

"I get it."

The eight of them started up the hotel steps when Mattie Clark came over to Ronin. She smiled. "Good to see you, Mattie."

"Good to be seen, Mister Ronin. Listen, I just want to apologize for misbehaving back there in Lamoille. I could have got myself in a lot of trouble. You kept me out of trouble and I'm most appreciative."

"That's what friends do, Mattie — they care for each other. I noticed you nodding in agreement when we were talking about Sam Mills. Are you still pulling for him?"

"I am," she said brightly.

"How come, Mattie? You know he killed a man, right?"

"I do," she said. "He killed his best friend."

"You know too that Judge Flack's verdicts are rarely overturned."

"That may be true, Mister Ronin, but I'm a believer all the same."

"How's that?" Ronin stopped on the steps, his hands on a railing so as to give the ten year-old his full attention. Wiser words had come out of mouths a good deal younger.

"It all comes down to what you just said, Mister Ronin. I'm the only friend Sam Mills has, me and my dad anyway. So I want to be a good one."

Chapter 59
PUT A SOCK IN IT

As it turned out, they stayed anyway. One story led to another. A bottle of beer and a glass of wine led to more serious drinking, and when the stories turned more thoughtful, Clark shooed his ten-year old daughter off to bed.

"Listen, Jim, while you say good night, I'm going to check on our prisoners," Ronin said, pushing back from the table and heading into a small room opening only to their dining room.

Ronin crossed the private dining room and entered a 10-by-10 space used to store tables. "Miss Livestock," he said as he came into the room, "are you getting what you need?" Alvira stopped mid-chew, holding a piece of chicken between her lips. A hand and leg were cuffed to two different table legs at two different tables. Latigo was similarly fixed, but had a spoon in Alvira's potatoes. "Aw," Ronin said, "nice to see the two of you helping each other." Latigo put the spoon down.

"Fuck you."

"Don't imagine you'd like to get us something to drink, would you?" he snarled. Ronin grinned. "Actually, I'm feeling pretty good about all of this. I thought I might buy the two of you a couple of beers."

"Really?" Alvira put the chicken leg down and grabbed a napkin. She dabbed at the middle of her mouth and then at both corners. Their plates were nearly empty.

"How about some ice cream, too?" Ronin asked.

"Seriously?" Alvira said, turning her head to her side. It hadn't ever been her experience for a man to offer her anything without wanting something in return.

"Nah," Ronin said as he pulled the plates away, pausing long enough for her to reach for the remainder of her chicken. "But to be frank, I'm feeling pretty chipper about things," he continued. "The two of you are mean sons of bitches to be sure. My apologies ma'am," he said before continuing.

"Not needed," she replied.

"You're going to get what you deserve for shooting me, for killing your parents" — he looked at Latigo — "and for God knows how many other people you've bilked, whipped, shot, dropped a stone on, beat-up or insulted during this life of yours. But there's no reason I can't be kind in the meantime," he said, smiling. "I'd like to think I'm turning a new leaf."

Latigo laughed. "I doubt it."

"You in particular will bear the full weight of justice, I'm sure. It will be awful heavy for a little man," he said grinning. Latigo tugged at the table. Neither his ankle nor wrist chains would give. "But meanwhile," Ronin continued, "I'm inclined to get you what you need. Incidentally," he said, "we're staying the night."

"Really?" Latigo asked, his eyebrows raised.

"The two of you mind sleeping together?" Ronin smiled.

"Not at all," Latigo said. "You're a better man than I imagined."

"Maybe."

Ronin sat down and waited. A few moments passed by quietly, with no one saying anything. Then Sheriff Tom Kelly entered the room with a couple of beers.

"You serious about this?" Kelly asked.

"Absolutely. I'll stay right here while they drink them."

"It's up to you. But I wouldn't give them shit after everything they've done."

"I know."

Kelly left the room, closing the door behind him as Ronin slid the bottles closer to the two prisoners. "Listen," he said, "tell me something before I give you these."

"I knew there had to be a catch," Alvira whined, looking over at her friend who couldn't take his eyes off of her waist and breasts. "You're disgusting," she said.

"It's no big deal," he responded. "I like women."

"Well you don't have to stare."

Ronin interrupted. "Look, I want to ask both of you something. What happened that you went down this road? You too, Toro. I mean if you had it to do all over again, would you live your lives this way?"

"Seriously?" Tony asked.

"Serious as a couple of beers," Ronin said. "Think of me as a student curious about why people make the choices they make."

"And you were a minister," Alvira said.

"That was a long time ago, ma'am. There's been a lot of water over the damn since then."

"Well, I'll tell you what I think," Latigo said, sitting up. He'd likely killed more men than Ronin had ever befriended, not that he was counting. Good friends were hard to find, and the ones he'd made, he ended up killing anyway. Likely it was the same with Ronin, not that it mattered, not that he cared.

"Go ahead," Ronin said.

"If I had it to do over again?" He licked his lips. "Hindsight being what it is ..." He was thirsty and didn't give a damn what anyone thought at this point. "Truth be told, I'd rather have grown up like my brother. I don't believe he ever did anything wrong."

"Mormon?"

"Yup. The whole family, except me I guess."

"True believer then?"

"Aren't we all, in one way or another? But then, I never did half of what people think I did," Toro said, smiling. "I'm as pure as the Salt Lake sands."

"I'll bet you are," Ronin replied. He pushed a beer Latigo's way.

The little man grabbed it, put his lips to the bottle and took a long sip before putting it down and smiling. "Ahhh, that's tasty!"

"And you, Miss Livestock? Your sister was a beautiful lady, inside and out from what I could see. I miss her. What made you so different?"

"Really? You think so?" she said, smiling. "She was more of a bad girl than you choose to remember, Mister Ronin. But then aren't we all? I don't imagine your parents are all that proud ..."

"I expect not," Ronin said. "So what happened to you?" It didn't matter what his parents thought, or Alvira Livestock either. He'd long ago decided that the only person he needed to please was himself.

"I just did more of what you didn't do, Mister Ronin. And to be frank, I'm not sure I wouldn't do it all over again. Some people need to suffer. They need to lose their money, or their wives, or their businesses, maybe even their lives to come to that place where they discover what life is really all about."

"Which is, Miss Livestock?"

"Living, Mister Ronin, "that's it, pure and simple," she said, looking him in the eyes. "I'd do exactly what I did before, knowing that I had few choices in the matter being a woman, the second of two twins, not as beautiful and not as smart."

"Huh," Ronin said, pushing the beer her way.

"You haven't seen the end of me," she said, sitting there holding the bottle in her hand before lifting it and putting both lips over the bottle's edge. When she put it down, half of the beer was gone. Even her boyfriend looked over in surprise. "I'll be back. You just wait and see."

"Maybe so," Ronin said, getting up from the table. He took a pair of cuffs from the back of his belt and placed one cuff on Latigo's left wrist. "You both ready to go to bed?"

"You bet!" the little man said, grinning. Livestock eyed Ronin warily. Grabbing her right wrist he cuffed them together. He undid Alvira's left wrist and cuffed it to Latigo's right wrist so that they faced away from each other, their backs up against each other, their bottoms touching. He then did the same with their legs before tossing a blanket onto the floor and helping them lay down. *Looks uncomfortable.*

"I'll get you some pillows," he said.

"What's this?" the little man shouted. "You said we could sleep together," he said, spitting and growling and making all sort of manly noises.

"Stop that," she said. Toro immediately complied. "Mister Ronin?"

"Yes, Miss Livestock."

"Do me one more favor, would you?"

"What is it?"

"Put a sock in Tony's mouth, I believe I want to get me some sleep."

The ex-priest smiled. He was going to collect the same amount of money, whether they were quiet or noisy. He much preferred quiet. "Gladly," he replied, and pulling the sock off of Toro's right foot, did just that.

Chapter 60
CARSON CITY

"That's pretty much how it happened, Emma."

Emma slid closer to Ronin, the two of them sitting on the sofa in the front room of her house at the American Gospel Mission just south of Carson City. It felt like months since she had seen him, though it had only been a week or so. Still, when Ronin wasn't at home she could feel a hollow place within her.

"Will you be staying?" she asked.

"I don't know. I know I shouldn't, you being the mistress of the mission and all, and it being clear that I don't need the convalescent care anymore." He grinned. She smiled.

Emma patted his knee before getting up and turning his way. "How about I make you a nice cup of tea?" she said — the exact words his mother used to say, even though his mother knew he didn't drink tea and that the answer would always be, "Thank you, but I'm not thirsty." The words were an invitation to deeper intimacy he figured out sometime after her death. "Stay a while. Talk to me." Would that she had said that, but maybe he wouldn't have heard them anyway.

"Sure," he replied, giving her his hand and pulling himself up. They walked arm in arm into the large kitchen where children at the mission dined twice a day. Lunch was often shared in the fields, or in the shop or sewing room. Breakfast and dinner was a community affair. "You've been busy?" he asked, knowing that he should ask something about her life but not knowing what it was that he should say. Intimacy didn't always come easy to the ex-priest, though he wanted it to.

"Sure," she said, smiling. She put a tea kettle on the stove and opened a vent to fan the flames. "There was the Christmas program on Wednesday night, of course — lots of church people, and a few from the capital as well. You should have seen it, William. The children were wonderful! And I've done a few things for Henry's family in Ohio and sent them that way, though I don't know the packages will make it by Christmas. I'm sorta looking forward to the time alone. Unless …" she paused.

"Unless?" he asked.

"Unless you're coming over," she said. "I can't imagine that you want to be staying at the Ormsby House over the holidays. Christmas is coming up, you know. You should be with somebody. With family or friends," she added. She blushed.

"That's true."

"How 'bout you stay here for a little while?" she whispered.

Ronin stuck a spoon into his cup and moved it around a bit, not that there was any liquid in it or that he had anything to stir. "I don't know, Emma. I want to do right by you."

"I know you do, William."

He thought about the question he knew he should ask. It wasn't as if they hadn't been together, the first time he cuddled her. There were more intimate times after that. Even the words he swore he'd never say were on his lips practically every day when he was with her. There'd been a few times he didn't hold back and told her, "I love you."

"Emma?"

"Yes, William?"

He stuttered, thinking it was time but not wanting to rush things. He wanted to be sure. And there were always the differences between them — she being so religious, his being not so much, her being a person of some prominence in the community, his being something of a saddle tramp until the job was done or a wound meant that he needed to be cared for. And then there was the fact that they were both so damned independent.

"I'm thinking … how about we move toward a date, dear?"

"A date?" she said, knowing exactly what he was saying but believing that he should spell it out. It would be good for both of them if they were certain what each other was saying and what each other meant by what they were saying.

"How about we set a date to get married, Emma? I mean …"

She jumped from the stove into his chair, straddling both of his legs so as to sit there. She wound her arms around him and hugged him tightly. "I would *love* that," she said, pausing so that each word stood alone as if she would never be alone from that day on and that only the words would forever stand that way. "I would *love* that!" she reiterated so that he would know how much she loved him — foibles, frailties, faithlessness, all of it. None of it mattered except that he was her man and she had known it from the very first day she met him. Tears formed in her eyes despite her smile.

"Emma?" Ronin asked.

"Yes, William," she said, not letting go. Not even an inch, ever.

"There's a lot that we have to do before we can be together."

"I know, dear. And we'll do all of it," she said before pushing back on his strong, broad shoulders so that she could look at him, right in the eyes, and smile. "There's so much between us, my love. I'm so happy." She pushed her face up against his, soft against scratchy.

"I am, too," he said, thinking of the divorce that she still needed — Henry Nauman hadn't been heard from for a year or more, and there was common ground that needed to be explored and turned farm-like, his plans, her plans, the mission's plans and so on. But he didn't say any of it. Nary a word, because he knew the silence was too holy.

"We'll do it all," she said after a moment. "But let's not begin tonight, my love. Let's start tomorrow or maybe tomorrow night," she said before planting her lips fully on his and saying with her mouth what she had already said with her heart. "I love you."

Chapter 61

THE END OF
SAM MILLS

The next morning came early. The chickens seemed to be making as much noise as the roosters and Ronin stayed out of sight until the mission children were absent the kitchen. Emma appeared in the bedroom doorway with a cup of coffee.

He laughed. "Dear, something you're going to have to get used to, I'm afraid. I don't drink coffee in the morning, but I have no hesitation over taking you back to bed." Emma beamed. She never thought she'd be with a man like this. She'd felt no embarrassment the night before, no inhibition, though they'd given some care "to save something for the wedding night," he'd said, laughing.

"Not that it matters," she'd returned.

"I had no idea, my love. What do you drink?" she asked, a twinkle in her eye.

"Water's good," he said, "or whatever." He walked toward her as she raised a sheet of paper toward the level of his eyes.

"You might want to see this first," she said, "a telegram from James Clark in Elko." Toro and Alvira were sitting in the Ormsby County jail. *Maybe it's about Mattie.* He took the unbleached paper from her hands and held it up by the window so as to be able to read it.

"Western Union Telegraph Company, Norvin Green, President. This company transmits and delivers messages only on conditions limiting its liability, which have been assented to by the sender of the following message. Errors can be guarded against only be repeating a message back to the sending station for comparison, and the company will not hold itself liable for errors or delays in transmission or delivery of unrepeated messages, beyond the amount of tolls paid thereon, nor in any case where the claim is not presented in writing within sixty days after sending the message. This is an unrepeated message, and is delivered by request of the sender, under the conditions named above. Received at ... dated ... to ... blah, blah, blah," he said quietly before reading aloud.

"Sam Mills executed. Conviction upheld. Hung eight minutes, neck not broken. First person legally hanged in Elko County. Last words: 'If I had money and a good lawyer I would have got clear.' Sincere regards, James Clark, Elko."

Ronin's weight buckled beneath him. He sat back on the bed.

"What is it, dear?"

"You remember that I told you about Sam Mills?"

"The man who killed his best friend?"

"Yes," he said, struggling. "Well, they hung him — a poor black man with no friends and no money, save what the Clarks offered him. He maintained his innocence to the end."

Emma sat down on the bed and put her arms around her man. "I know it's hard, William. The good suffer, the bad prosper and you try to do so much to make things right." The big man nodded, strangely upset.

"I didn't know him."

"I know," she said.

"How is it that I'm so emotional?"

"I don't know," she said. "But this I do know, God is with us. I'm with you. And sometimes that has to be enough."

THE END

POSTSCRIPT —
A HYMN TO SAM
MILLS

Sam Mills died after being dropped six feet through a trap door with a rope around his neck. Because he was a small man, his neck was not broken. Contemporary accounts indicate that his body and legs convulsed for at least three minutes. Attending physicians noted that the heart ceased to beat eight minutes later. A half hour passed before his body was taken down.

Mills was the first person legally hanged in Elko County. He maintained his innocence until the end. It is remembered that Mills kept busy in jail with fortune telling cards and by singing his mother's favorite hymn.

1. "Come to Jesus, come to Jesus,
    Come to Jesus just now,
    Just now come to Jesus,
    Come to Jesus just now.
2. "He will save you, etc.
3. "He is able, etc.
4. "He is willing, etc.
5. "He is waiting, etc.
6. "He will hear you, etc.
7. "He will cleanse you, etc.

8. "He'll renew you, etc.
9. "He'll forgive you, etc.
10. "If you trust Him, etc.
11. "He will save you, etc."

How many verses he was able to finish before he died is not recorded. Sam Mills was 28 years old.

AUTHOR'S NOTES

The former mayor of Napa, California, was my friend. I got to know him when he answered the call of the Nevada Presbytery to become interim pastor and head of staff at the St. John's Presbyterian Church in Reno, Nevada. Ralph Bolin went on from there to become the installed pastor of a church in Elko where he unexpectedly died a few years later. Ralph was an extraordinarily talented man, serving the people of Napa with creativity and vision. His service to the Covenant Presbyterian Church in Napa, to the St. John's Church in Reno and to the First Presbyterian Church in Elko was notable and true. Simply said, he had a heart of gold.

While many stories might be told of Ralph, I'll tell only one. Once, having traveled with the Reverend Bolin on church business in Las Vegas, he asked if I wanted to visit a local strip club. I stumbled about, telling him that I didn't want that sort of thing in my head — it says something that I didn't give any thought to either of us losing our jobs, given that a Baptist clergyman had just done so during their national convention there — when he uttered the words "I need someone to go with. I haven't seen my daughter in a good many years. I believe she works there." I think it was in that moment that I understood everyone has a story, and that some of those stories — whether they belong to the ordinary or the ordained — are painful at best.

I relished the opportunities I had to visit with Ralph in Elko, and have often thought that he and I — had we been released from the constraints of distance and time, not to speak of the inordinately heavy ministerial mantle or persona with which we both struggled — would have become best friends. Ralph, I miss you. This book is in some ways the result of your introducing me to the complex beauty and history of eastern Nevada.

Readers of this series of Westerns are due a brief explanation of what is factual and what is not-so-much in this book. Once again, I've done my best to use and relate Nevada history in the 1880s as I understand it. This book, the fourth in a series of W. W. Ronin Westerns, focuses on eastern Nevada, particularly the towns of Elko and Wells and the places in-between. Previous and future efforts — *East Jesus, Nevada, Lady of the Lake, The Pinkerton Years* and the next-to-be-published *Home Means Nevada* — primarily relate fiction and non-fiction stories, people and places in western Nevada, particularly Carson City, Reno, Virginia City, Glenbrook and Genoa. Careful readers will note where I've excursed, so to speak, from the real details of Nevada history-telling for the sake of a good story.

For example, in this fourth book, James Clark, the Depot Hotel, his daughter Mattie (though I've altered her age), Elko sheriff and entrepreneur Ben Fitch, the criminal Sam Mills and his Lamoille neighbors who pulled him from a haystack, the Bulls Head Saloon and Fort Ruby are all real. I've dug a bit — say in the case of Fort Ruby, where very little evidence of the fort or settlement around it still exists — so some of what you'll read about these people and places is real, too. Similarly, though I have no evidence that U. S. Marshal Augustus Ash or Virginia City Sheriff and former Police Chief Tom Kelly ever pursued criminals as far east as Wells, it's been fun to remember their efforts and to honor them by including them in this book.

Interested readers will appreciate the following should they want to read more deeply. For a quick and dirty review of eastern Nevada, see Shawn Hall's books, *Connecting the West: Historic Railroad Stops and Stage Stations in Elko County, Nevada* (Reno, NV:

University of Nevada Press, 2002) and *Old Heart of Nevada: Ghost Towns and Mining Camps of Elko, Nevada* (Reno, NV: University of Nevada Press, 1998). The pictures alone make the purchase worth it. Similarly, Howard Hickson's brief treatment entitled *Elko Nevada: One of the Last Frontiers of the American West* (Elko, NV: Northeastern Nevada Museum and Northeastern Nevada Historical Society, 2002) was helpful and is enthusiastically recommended.

More serious interests will be served by reading the following, now out of print: *Nevada's Northeast Frontier*, by Edna Patterson, Louisa Ulph and my late friend Victor Goodwin (Reno, NV: University of Nevada Press and the Northeastern Nevada Historical Society, 1991, originally published in 1969), *Fearful Crossing: The Central Overland Trail Through Nevada* by Harold Curran (Las Vegas, NV: Nevada Publications, 1982), Greg MacGregor's wonderful coffee table book, *Overland: The California Emigrant Trail of 1841-1870* (Albuquerque, NM: University of New Mexico Press, 1996) and Robert Ellison's remarkable work *Territorial Lawmen of Nevada*, Volume 1 (Minden, NV: Hotsprings Mountain Press, 1999). I wouldn't have been able to write this piece of historical fiction without the guidance of these authors and books. I'm grateful for their more serious efforts.

My deep appreciation to my "beta-readers," for their careful review of the story and manuscript — Bill Kreb and Cathy Parr, who volunteer every Monday at Tuality Community Hospital in Hillsboro and wait patiently for the week's efforts. And to Dave McNeill, a resident of Minden, Nevada, a wise and true man, martial artist and innovator who occasionally keeps me out of trouble in my writing and otherwise. And Carley Friesen — dreamer, barista, community connector, pastor, wonderer — who was co-pastor of two Presbyterian Churches in Wells and Wendover during the late 1980s. Carley pointed out that "living in the shadow-side of the Ruby Mountains" was a big part of her understanding the Wells community. That insight helped to provide the tension between two of my characters: Ben Fitch and fictional character but real-life fast draw friend Bob McKee.

Finally, the case of Sam Mills. I didn't have the heart to ask the Elko County clerk's office to find the court transcripts for a 137-year old court case. Still, the extraordinary story of William James Finnerty's death at Halleck Station and the subsequent hanging of his best friend Sam Mills leaves one wondering how the case might have been treated in more contemporary times. It's remembered that Mills missed his friend "more than anyone did" and continued to argue his innocence even after climbing the steps of the scaffold constructed for his execution.

On December 21, 1877, a depressed 5-foot-eight Sam Mills shook hands with his jailers and was hanged, telling the gathered crowd (men only) that he did not have a fair trial but if this was justice he was prepared to meet his maker. Mills' family in Atchinson, Kansas, was too poor to help him or to attend.

His mother's favorite hymn, talked about in a number of sources, is difficult to document. Patterson, Ulph and my late friend Victor Goodwin write that the words of the hymn read:

"Come to Jesus
Come to Jesus
Come to Jesus
Just now here on my heart
A burden lies
I must pronounce thee just and wise
If my poor soul is spent in hell
The righteous Lord approves it well."

All I can say is perhaps. The rule in Biblical criticism — my only experience in constructing an accurate and historical narrative — is that the more detailed the account, the more likely the story is a variation on the original and has likely has been tampered with. For instance, the latter section of the hymn is found, in part, in one of the *Psalms*. It is repeated as a whole in a sermon by the then popular very preacher, Charles Spurgeon (1834-1892). The first part is similar to a number of early African American hymns in Southern hymnals of that period. While the meter of the words is tempting, suggesting that the two stanzas *might* have in fact been sung together — I've gone with a related hymn from the same period for the sake of the story.

Additionally, *This Little Light of Mine*, though not a period piece as represented, has some universal appeal and is included to remind the reader that all of us — even those who say they do not — live as true believers of one sort or another. Given that we all believe in something, as one 20th century theological writer suggested, let me disclose that one of the main precepts of this book — and I apologize if it sounds too preachy — is that you and I may want to live our lives more wisely.

This book is dedicated to my children, Rachel and Joshua and to my late son, Jared — who lives with us always — and to Nancy's children as well, Lindsey, Kelly and Tim. All of whom busy themselves living successful lives. Dear ones, it's taken *me* too long to realize that not all that is green is money.

ABOUT THE AUTHOR

Gregg Edwards Townsley is a reflective, free-thinking ex-pastor, martial artist, writer and western fast draw enthusiast living in St. Helens, Oregon. No stranger to the places his characters inhabit — Reno, Carson City, Virginia City and Lake Tahoe — he raised his children in northern Nevada, from 1984 through 1993, as pastor and head of staff of the First Presbyterian Church in Carson City. Gregg enjoys hearing from his readers, posting updates and background to his work on his website and blog at www.greggtownsley.com. You can find him on Facebook: www.facebook.com/GreggEdwardsTownsley, or subscribe to his Twitter updates at http://twittter.com/greggtownsley. The author encourages your review of this book and his others at www.amazon.com.

48287397R00164

Made in the USA
Charleston, SC
28 October 2015